TALKING SMACK

HONEST CONVERSATIONS ABOUT DRUGS

ANDREW McMILLEN

First published in 2014 by University of Queensland Press
PO Box 6042, St Lucia, Queensland 4067 Australia

www.uqp.com.au
www.andrewmcmillen.com
www.talkingsmack.com.au

Cataloguing-in-Publication entry is available from the
National Library of Australia
http://catalogue.nla.gov.au/

ISBN (pbk) 978 0 7022 53232
ISBN (ePdf) 978 0 7022 53058
ISBN (ePUB) 978 0 7022 53065
ISBN (kindle) 978 0 7022 53072

Typeset in 12/17 Bembo by Post Pre-press Group, Brisbane
Author photograph by David Ball
Printed in Australia by McPherson's Printing Group

Permission to quote from David Nichol's book *The Go-Betweens* (Allen & Unwin, 1997) kindly granted by Allen & Unwin Australia; permission to quote from Paul Kelly's book *How to Make Gravy* (Hamish Hamilton, 2010) kindly granted by Penguin Books Australia.

Every effort has been made to contact copyright licensees for permission to reproduce material. Please contact the publisher if material for which you hold the rights has been reprinted here.

University of Queensland Press uses papers that are natural, renewable and recyclable products made from wood grown in sustainable forests. The logging and manufacturing processes conform to the environmental regulations of the country of origin.

Contents

Forethoughts

'See, I think drugs have done some good things for us, I really do. And if you don't believe drugs have done good things for us, do me a favour: go home tonight, take all your albums, all your tapes, and all your CDs and burn 'em. 'Cause you know what? The musicians who've made all that great music that's enhanced your lives throughout the years? *Real* fuckin' high on drugs.'

This gag, by American stand-up comedian Bill Hicks, is sampled at the beginning of a song by Californian alternative metal band Tool. Immediately after the punchline, the audience knowingly laughs as one.

I would've been around twelve years old when I heard it for the first time. I didn't understand the joke's concept or context. I just laughed because the audience did, and because my new favourite band had obviously thought highly enough of this funny guy to quote him – three times – on their second album. (Pancreatic cancer had killed Hicks two years prior to its release, at age thirty-two.)

Years later, I realised that the lyrics to this particular Tool song – 'Third Eye', the final track on the 1996 album *Ænima* – are about expanding one's consciousness by opening up the proverbial 'third eye', which allows perception beyond ordinary sight. The subtext is that illicit drug use is a short cut to achieving that end.

While that idea is fertile ground for a compelling lyrical narrative set to the violent clash of drums, distorted guitar and bass, it took a long time for me to confront this in reality. One reason for this, I believe, is that the conversation surrounding drug use in modern Australia is a black-and-white battleground bisected by stark pathways: the straight-and-narrow of alcohol, caffeine, nicotine and prescription medication, and the dark-and-crooked of cannabis, cocaine, ecstasy, heroin and methamphetamine.

The message that's been cooked up and reinforced for decades by powerful societal figures – police, politicians, public-health officials and much of the media – is that you're a fine, upstanding citizen if you stick to the former path by purchasing these government-approved mood-altering substances. Conversely, if you seek out and consume anything in the latter category, you're a criminal, a loser, and a bad person.

Through my adolescence, I trod the straight-and-narrow line uncritically. As far as I'd come to understand, illicit activity was associated with antisocial behaviour, drug trafficking, violence and crime. It was rare to hear any alternatives to these overpowering, fear-based messages; films and TV shows – usually made in the United States – provided the only compelling contradictory visual evidence. But these were fictionalised versions of reality. At an intellectual level, I could not entertain the possibility that illegal drugs had the potential to be fun, safe, life-affirming, non-habit-forming – or all of the above. These sorts of stories are rarely told in our society.

Like many Australian teenagers, I abused alcohol – a socially acceptable form of intoxication – on a consistent basis. A hangover is often greeted by your peers with a wink and a playful shake of the head – physical evidence of an apparently memorable night.

In 2007, at age nineteen, I extended one foot across to the dark-and-crooked by smoking cannabis for the first time. I still upheld the old dichotomy in my mind, but now I was a student at a residential college attached to the University of Queensland and was feeling 'experimental' – living proof of a classic quote from an early *South Park* episode centred upon drug education: 'There's a time and a place for everything, and it's called college.'

Smoking pot became an occasional, illicit thrill. It felt different from those years of boozing; it felt naughty. It made the mind somersault in strange and interesting ways. It attuned the ears to different frequencies, which made music even more attractive than usual – quite an achievement, as I've obsessed over music for as long as I can remember. For the first time in my life, I found myself 'dabbling with drugs', and enjoying the company of the outsider types attracted to such behaviours.

I drew the line at weed, though. It took another five years for me to work up the courage to cross it by trying anything 'harder' than smoking a joint. In hindsight, this distinction feels absurdly abstract. What is the difference between smoking pot and swallowing MDMA powder, the psychoactive ingredient in ecstasy? One drug grows from the earth and the other is the product of chemical synthesis, sure. But both are illegal in the eyes of the law. Both are frowned upon by large sectors of the community. The mental leap required to use both substances appears so small as to be insignificant.

Yet, for me, the chasm between the two was vast. I had learnt through the media that any public figure who admits to enjoying illegal drugs can expect to have their character assassinated by moralising commentators who claim to speak on behalf of concerned parents and citizens. A textbook example of this type of demonisation is the story of rugby league player Andrew Johns, who admitted that he enjoyed ecstasy after being 'caught out' with an E in his pocket in London in 2007. Cue sensationalist reporting and a remarkably heavy-handed interview on *The Footy Show*, where he was essentially forced to atone for his supposed sin. In retrospect, the entire episode smacks of hypocrisy; Johns was grilled over his occasional and apparently harmless use of a stimulant, despite the fact that the excessive consumption of alcohol – a substance whose harms are well known – has long been a conventional way for both players and fans to celebrate sporting wins and losses alike.

There are very few industries in which the use of illicit drugs is permissible, if not tacitly encouraged. Music is one such profession. It's not the only one, but it's certainly the most visible and instantly identifiable. Who besides the archetypal 'rock star' can get away with wanton hedonism on any kind of regular basis?

'Sex, drugs and rock and roll' may be a cliché – or even, in 2014, something of a myth – but the phrase perfectly encapsulates what our society tends to expect from those who sling guitars, lean on microphone stands and bash drum-skins. Smart rock stars adopt a larger-than-life pose; crowds feed off the life we imagine that they're living. It doesn't matter whether that life is in reality tame, tedious or even intolerable. So long as the image is consistent, the sunglasses are worn indoors and the act is well rehearsed, we are sated.

It helps, too, that we tend to perceive creative people – musicians, painters, actors, writers and the like – as living 'on the edge', outside of the social norms and expectations that come with nine-to-five, salaried jobs. It's on the edge, we're led to believe, that 'the magic happens': that by pushing the boundaries of the human mind and body, great work is created.

Drug use is a natural fit with that ideal. Who wants to hear about a musician who treats the creative process like a job, with the regimented hours and routines familiar to so many of the rest of us? That's mundane. We'd much rather hear about how a hit song was written at the tail-end of a five-day bender in Ibiza, its creators torn and frayed after a non-stop cocaine- and booze-fest.

Whether or not this type of debauchery ever happens is irrelevant: it's the *idea* that's potent. Most of us couldn't live that way, even if we wanted to, so we live vicariously through the myth. 'Sex, drugs and rock and roll' is shorthand for 'someone else's job is more fun than mine'. It's our nature to covet that which dangles beyond our grasp, and, for many, the imagined life of the popular musician is one such carrot.

In late 2012, after five years of freelance journalism, I was invited to submit a book proposal on a topic of my choice. Before too long, I was struck by the thought of combining two of my interests, music and drug use, by investigating the thread that linked them.

The seed had been subconsciously planted some twelve years earlier, as my developing brain took in the appealing sounds of Tool and their appreciation of Bill Hicks' dark humour. I was not naive enough to take his comedy at face value; it is simplistic to assume that all musicians were *real* fuckin' high on drugs when creating the songs that enhanced our lives. But it's an assumption worth investigating, in order to separate fact from fiction.

As a journalist, I hunt for stories. The purpose of *Talking Smack* is to seek out and record real stories about drug use in Australia across the last four decades, from the 1970s onwards, by speaking with some of the nation's prominent musicians, singers and songwriters. The goal from the beginning has been to capture the truth about a fraught topic that is rarely discussed with candour, or without judgement.

Talking Smack is not a reductive text with easily digestible conclusions, as there is nothing simple about the nuanced matter of drug use. Nor is it a scientific analysis of the effects of certain substances. I'm not interested in statistics; instead, I have endeavoured to uncover true stories about the realities of this tricky topic and present them without prejudice.

When approaching artists for these interviews, I outlined my request for an honest conversation about drugs. To borrow a cliché, I wanted the truth, the whole truth and nothing but the truth. I have no reason to believe that anyone I interviewed failed to meet this request.

Keep in mind, though, that what follows is the individual's interpretation of events. This is not about finger-pointing, blame-shifting, or naming other parties who may or may not have been involved in certain activities. (Handily, this should keep my publisher's lawyers from exerting themselves too strenuously.) Instead, each chapter is the story of one musician's life, viewed through a lens focused on their experiences with drugs. In some cases, those experiences are incidental, or even non-existent; in others, they are significant and consuming.

It is worth pointing out, too, that my interviewees are as fallible to the inconsistencies of human memory as you or I. At one point during his 2008 memoir *The Night of the Gun*, the *New York Times* journalist David Carr — a former alcoholic and crack-cocaine addict — paused the narrative. 'But was it really all thus?' he wrote. 'When memory is called to answer, it often answers back with deception. How is it that almost every warm bar stool contains a hero, a star of his own epic, who is the sum of his amazing stories?'

In that book, Carr decided to report on his own past, spending two years pulling documents and interviewing people he hadn't seen in two decades. 'By turns, it became a kind of journalistic ghost dancing,' he wrote. 'Trying to conjure spirits past, including mine. It felt less like journalism than archaeology, a job that required shovels and axes, hacking my way into dark, little-used passages and feeling my way around.'

Talking Smack is not that kind of book. Wherever possible, I have fact-checked matters relating to time and space. But most of what you'll read in each chapter is an individual's retrospective interpretation of how things were, and how they came to be, based on a single face-to-face interview. I am not concerned with multiple points of view. Just monologues.

Steve Jobs said in a famous 2005 commencement speech that it's impossible to connect the dots looking forward; his point, I believe, is that we can only make sense of our behaviours by looking backward. Oftentimes, objects in the rear-view mirror appear clearer than what we see through the windscreen.

My fourteen interviewees have my timeless admiration and sincere thanks for being involved with what any rational human would describe as a thorny project. None of them had much – if anything – to gain by entrusting these stories to a journalist. I suppose it has been ever thus, given the purely transactional nature of most entertainment interviews. But, in this case, they never even had a product to sell – neither new music nor forthcoming tour to promote.

Perhaps 'street cred', or a desire to build or uphold a certain reputation – the aforementioned rock-star myth – could have been a motivating force. But I found no such vanities while working on this book. Instead, many of my interviewees agreed to talk to me because of the two simple words that follow.

Drugs exist.

To pretend otherwise is foolish. Some have been developed by pharmaceutical companies to treat human ailments. Others occur naturally. Still more were created for innocuous purposes and later discovered to have psychoactive properties (as with MDMA, which was first synthesised with the goal of stopping abnormal bleeding). These differing substances attract different people for different reasons. For some, it's an occasional holiday from their daily responsibilities. For others, it's a welcome escape from a painful existence. For many, the attraction lies somewhere in between those two extremes.

Neither end of that spectrum is right or wrong. There is no better or worse. It's disingenuous to categorise alcohol and paracetamol as polar opposites of cocaine and LSD. Recreational use, drug addiction and sobriety are all as worthy of discussion as the other. To exclude any substance or lifestyle choice from this conversation would be a failure on my part, just as I believe it has been a failure on the part of Australian society to snuff out or shrug off any attempts to discuss the use of illicit drugs with a clear head.

As will become apparent throughout the following pages, I have some first-hand experience with substances. But I am a nobody – an interlocutor, a messenger boy. It is far more interesting, I think, to hear true stories about drug use – both good and bad, productive and destructive – from the mouths of those who know what they are talking about, from musicians who've made all that great music that's enhanced our lives throughout the years.

Maybe they *were* real fuckin' high on drugs at the time.
So what?

Andrew McMillen, Brisbane

STEVE KILBEY

At the age of thirty-seven, Steve Kilbey found himself at a crossroads. He'd become a pop star fronting The Church, a band whose song 'Under the Milky Way', the lead single from their fifth album, *Starfish*, became a worldwide hit in 1988. He'd made quite a lot of money: he had a house and a recording studio in Sydney, a couple of cars, a load of instruments and some cash to spare. He wasn't filthy rich, but he was certainly very comfortable.

By this point, Kilbey considered himself a worldly drug user: he had started smoking pot in his late teens, tried psychedelics soon after and bought his first gram of cocaine after making his first record, *Of Skins and Heart*, in 1980. Eleven years later, he was recording for a new project named Jack Frost with his friend Grant McLennan, a fellow Australian pop star best known for his work with Brisbane act The Go-Betweens. One night, while out at a bar and feeling an empty sense of unhappiness at the life he'd earned, despite his success, Kilbey was taken aback by McLennan's proposal: 'Let's get some heroin.'

'It came right out of the blue,' Kilbey recalls in February 2013. 'It was the last thing on my mind. I went, "Oh, here's $100, get me some too." No one had ever offered it to me up until then. All the other drugs you might get offered, but no one ever says, "Hey, want some heroin?" It's not like that. If you've got a stash, you don't offer it. You don't really go around turning other people on. It's not the sort of thing you advertise.'

When McLennan made his proposal, Kilbey thought to himself, *Yeah! That'll shift things around a bit.* 'As a teenager, I'd been hearing how bad marijuana was; people were being arrested and chucked in jail [for using it]. And then, when I started smoking it,' he says, 'I thought it was the most benign, pleasant thing that doesn't seem to have any real drawbacks. I wrongly assumed heroin might be the same. I thought it might be the victim of really bad press, and that all the perils had been exaggerated.' He pauses for a moment, then laughs. 'And I believed that for a little while, naively.' He had no idea that his first taste of that substance would come to define the next eleven years of his life.

'I loved it. The moment the fucking stuff hit my nostrils, I was like, "Wow, this is what I'm looking for,"' he says. 'All my life, I'd had my conscience going, "You're a cunt, you're a horrible guy, you don't deserve what you've got. You did this and that, and your mum and dad didn't love you." All this stuff. And then, the moment that first line of heroin hit my nose, it all stopped. I was sitting there going, "Oh, I'm all right. I feel kind of cool. I feel like people could like me."

It stopped that whole dialogue instantly, and I felt warm and cosy and happy.'

He acknowledges that not all heroin dabblers experience this instant affinity for the drug; some try it and think it's horrible. 'But for me,' he says, 'it was like' – he snaps his fingers – 'something I'd been waiting for my whole life.'

Kilbey wasn't the kind of guy to wait around for his friend to call his dealer; nor was McLennan reckless enough to give him direct access to the source. Perhaps the more experienced user had wisely recognised the sudden enthusiasm that Kilbey had developed for something in which he'd previously shown no interest. Kilbey says of McLennan, 'Sometimes he became addicted. He got little habits, and then he'd refrain, but he wasn't an addict.' He found McLennan's caution frustrating, because he refused to introduce his dealers. But the wealthy pop star saw no reason to hide his fondness for this drug from anyone. Around this time, some 'bad characters' started hanging around a house in Surry Hills that Kilbey had rented, which doubled as a recording studio. 'Some of them were heroin addicts,' he says. 'They were buying heroin for me. Eventually, I met some dealers. I was off and running.'

One of those characters was a doctor who had been deregistered due to her addiction. One day, Kilbey was snorting a line. In response, the doctor clicked her tongue and shook her head. He looked up, surprised. 'What's wrong?' he asked. 'What a waste,' she replied. Kilbey didn't understand; he thought he was using the drug efficiently. She beckoned him over, found a vein on the back of his hand and injected him. It was then that Steve Kilbey decided he wasn't going to waste any more heroin.

'For a while, it seemed to me like, "Wow, how good is this? I've got a doctor very carefully doing all the right things, talking to me about my veins and my arteries, finding different veins and showing me how to do it. This is really legit,"' he says. 'So I learnt how to shoot up. *Bang.* I was off, and on the downward spiral.'

It wasn't just the drug and the process of injecting it that gripped him. 'I was fascinated with all of it. I'd go round some idiot's house, and someone would be saying' – here he adopts a nasal, strained voice, imitating a junkie – '"Ahh, Jim is fuckin' getting sixty mils of methadone now."' His face perks up brightly, mimicking intense interest. '"*Really?*" The junkie would reply, "Yeah, they said he can have more takeaways ..." I was interested in all of this bullshit: who was in rehab; who was in jail; who was selling; stories of the great heroin of the past, from fucking Thailand or wherever. It was all I lived and breathed, this fucking rubbish world.'

He defines that year of his life, the beginning of his heroin habit, as 'a slow erosion'. Kilbey's creativity didn't falter, though. 'At first, I was super creative. I wanted to re-create the drug through music; I was trying to re-create this kind of languid, floating, deep, dreamy feeling.' This goal was best captured on The Church's 1992 album, *Priest = Aura*, a remarkable record that remains a fan favourite among the band's twenty full-length recordings. On the opening track, 'Aura', Kilbey sings, 'Where can a soldier fix himself a drink? / Forget the noise, forget the stink / And the opium is running pretty low / 'Cause when the pain comes back, I don't want to know ...' In 'Nightmare', the penultimate track on the re-release, he sings, 'I wanna consume, I wanna smoke up a forest / Shoot up a river, run up the bill / I want women and men / And when the whole damn thing is over / I want it all back again / Yeah, maybe I'll be happy then …'

'That was a good one,' he says of *Priest = Aura*. 'That was the honeymoon. That's when you can hear it; you can hear it's working. You can hear that I achieved that thing. And then it went downhill after that. For ten or eleven years, I still made records [on it]. But I struggled a bit. When the gear arrived, I'd get so stoned I couldn't work, either. Working with people, producing records, I spent a lot of time on auto-pilot going' – here he slurs his voice, imitating a barely there shell of a stoner – '"Yeah, great, great, mate. Yeah, that's a great take."'

The alternative was worse, though, when the drug was *in absentia* and the singer was hanging out for a fix. To demonstrate, Kilbey stands up from his couch, visibly shaking, and paces back and forth in an agitated state. He picks up my recorder from the coffee table and whispers into it, '*Where are you?*' Whether this is for dramatic effect or a genuine accident, mistaking it for a phone, I'm not sure; he apologises, puts it back down and then mimes talking on the phone, pacing back and forth again. '*Where are you? Are you coming? Are you coming?*' Still acting, he talks to an imaginary record producer, pretends to play it cool – 'Yeah, I'll be there in a minute. I'll come in and work for half an hour. Just give me half an hour …' – then resumes his agitated whispering. '*Where the fuck are you?*'

He drops the act and sits down as if nothing has happened. 'So it was never the best place, but nonetheless I did work,' he states matter-of-factly. 'And I had to keep working to make money, for the gear. I don't think the records I made during my heroin phase are the best records I ever made. The band were never very fucking happy about it, but there was not much they could do, either. They couldn't really kick me out. Whoever was there just had to put up with it. They became tired of, "Hey, can I borrow $100?"'

It's an understatement to describe Steve Kilbey as a gifted conversationalist. The tanned, silver-haired fifty-eight-year-old radiates intensity and engagement in the topic at hand. He is articulate, self-aware and funny. He uses simple adjectives such as 'idiot' and 'ratbag' at unexpected moments, which add to the humour of his storytelling. After he lets me into his bright, two-storey apartment off a quiet street in Bondi on a Thursday morning, I cast my eyes across his full bookshelves and striking artwork hung on the walls. Besides being known for his music, Kilbey is also a talented painter, with a small studio in his upstairs bedroom. Out the window is a view of the nearby hills; the ocean and Bondi Beach can be seen from the balcony.

Kilbey soon makes clear his problem with the volume of my voice. 'Listen, after forty years of rock and roll, I'm a bit deaf,' he tells me as we sit down in the living room. 'So speak loudly if you can, 'cause my ears are ringing so loud that to me you sound like ...' – he mumbles incoherently to illustrate the point. 'All the consonants are disappearing between my *woooooo*,' he says, imitating the high-pitch noise that he now lives with. 'So you have to really enunciate it.'

'Tinnitus?' I ask, loudly.

'Screaming tinnitus,' he replies. 'Oh well. They told me I'd go deaf, and I did.'

Partway through our interview, his partner, Sam, introduces herself, and spreads some avocado on rice crackers for both of us to munch on.

His slow erosion continued throughout 1991. 'At the beginning of the year, I was a confident, smart-arse, moneyed-up guy; by the end, I had a lot of people starting to realise I was on the gear,' he says. 'I was attracting a lot of ratbags. I'd used up a lot of my money. I'd gone through my "easy cash" – whatever was lying around – and then I started to cash in my super, and my long-term savings. I started rapidly running out of money and hocking guitars. Within a year, I was starting to go downhill; within two years, I was a mess, and everybody knew it. I was fucking up tours, borrowing money – stuff like that. It just went down, and down, and down. Of course, junkies were flocking to me like flies to fucking sugar, because I had money. I wasn't really watching the ball. I'd go, "Hey, go and get me two grams," and someone would come back and they'd fleeced a gram out of it. I didn't care; I'd say, "Oh, all right, yeah, sure." It was ugly and sordid.'

Heroin addicts share an adage among themselves: every habit is worse than your last. Every time you try to quit, then relapse, the effects will be felt more deeply and strongly than ever before. Steve Kilbey tried to quit. He'd tell himself that he wasn't going to use anymore. Then he learnt what heroin withdrawals felt like. 'It's a nightmare,' he says. 'There's not much worse that you could find, probably, other than chemotherapy or something like that. They're just the most terrible thing. Whatever you fear, whatever you were running from when you were using, that fucking devil comes back in spades when you're hanging out. Every rotten thing you could imagine that could happen to you, feeling bad in every single way, that's what happens when you're hanging out. You're so anxious and desperate to make it stop.'

Another adage: after a while, heroin users are addicted to the drug not because they're trying to get high but because they're trying to avoid the low. A shift in brain chemistry takes place. 'You move into a stage where you're in constant dialogue with the heroin: it's constantly saying, "You better sort this out, mate, or you're going to be sorry,"' he says. 'When you're not using, when you've run out, there's this threatening fear of, "What's going to happen if you don't get a fix?"'

This stark contrast between the highs and lows of addiction fascinated Kilbey. He'd be desolate in the absence of the drug, clutching his aching head and body, thinking to himself, *The whole world's going to end, my girlfriend and children have left me* — his partner took their identical twins to Sweden at the end of 1993 — *I've got no money, I've hocked all my guitars* … But then he'd 'fix' himself, fully aware of the irony of that term. His eyes would brighten. The dark cloud would lift. *Ah! Things aren't so bad! It's all right!* Watching him act out this seesawing emotional state, a by-product of chemical dependence, I'm struck by his vivid portrayal of the agony and the ecstasy.

He remembers the 'incredible power of going from being totally in the black — being physically, morally and spiritually bankrupt, at the nadir of withdrawals; you're sweating; you've got diarrhoea; you're spewing; every bone and muscle and sinew in your body is aching; your head's screaming. And then, in one second, you put this needle in, and the fuckin' moment that stuff hits the vein it's like this thing comes up.' He sighs, mimicking the relief. 'It runs right up your body, until, within a minute, you're like, "Wow, I feel good now." So you've gone from the worst to the best in one second. That's a feeling of power over yourself, that you can do that.'

Friends and family tried to stop him. There were attempted interventions, where loved ones would tell Kilbey, 'Listen, I don't like you using this stuff. If you're going to use it, I don't want to be a part of your life.' And the heroin, he says, would reply, 'See ya! All right! Bye!' It didn't matter who attempted to intervene, the drug came first. 'There was never no choice,' he says simply – a rare ungrammatical sentence from a well-spoken man.

At one point, his mother – 'an old English woman, who's drunk ten cups of tea every day of her whole life' – even phoned with an offer: she'd give up drinking tea if he kicked heroin. 'She was looking for an addiction trade-off,' he says. 'But even that – nup. Nothing was going to stop me.'

A move to Sweden, to be closer to his twin daughters, didn't help the situation: it was easier than ever for Kilbey to score. 'In Australia, you had to know a dealer,' he says. 'It was always this hassle; you'd have a dealer, but they'd [eventually] get busted. Or you could go out to Cabramatta [in Sydney's south-west]. But in Stockholm, I bought a flat right in the middle of the city. One train station away was Central Station. You just fuckin' turned up at Central and there were always like a dozen dealers down there, with really good, fuckin' white heroin. So I just went crazy with the shit.'

He had a few run-ins with the local constabulary there, too. 'I got busted in Sweden a couple of times. They didn't really know what to do with me.' This statement amuses me, so I press him on the details. 'Well, they'd catch me with a little bit of heroin, and they didn't know who I was. I used to say, "Oh, I'm just here for a visit." I didn't tell them I was living there. I used to show 'em my passport, and they'd keep me in jail for a while. The cops were really stupid there. These big, blond guys would come in' – here he adopts a bad Swedish accent, and starts yelling – '"*We do not like drug users in our country! We do not like this! We want you to go away!*" And I'd reply, "All right, I will, just let me out and you won't see me again." A few months later, I'd get nabbed again. "Yeah, I'm leaving, I'm leaving now." So they never took it any further, luckily.'

He pauses, remembering one close call in particular. 'There was so much fucking luck involved,' he says. 'Once, I bought like fuckin' six grams on the street. This cop was running up, the dealer was running away. I took these capsules and threw them on the ground.' He mimes tossing a few vials onto the street a few metres away, then standing there innocently, minding his own business. 'These cops came up, and they were looking around *everywhere*! They went through all my pockets; they were looking everywhere. I could see these six fucking capsules lying on the ground, but they didn't look! Then they went, "He hasn't got anything," and went away, and I just went over and picked 'em up, put 'em in my pocket, and went home. It was like *some miracle!*'

Luck doesn't last forever, though, as Kilbey found out while on tour in New York in October 1999. 'I wasn't even a junkie at this stage,' he says. 'I was in an in-between stage. A friend of mine rang me up and went, "Man, there's some good fuckin' smack down in Alphabet City!" So I went down there, I bought some smack, and a cop seen me buying it. I went to jail for the night.'

As a result, Kilbey missed a Church show scheduled for a Tuesday night on Manhattan's Lower East Side. 'More than two hundred fans waited at the Bowery Ballroom on Delancey St for the 10pm start,' wrote Michael Cameron in *The Daily Telegraph* on 7 October. He went on:

At 10.35pm lead guitarist Marty Wilson-Piper nervously walked up to the microphone to reveal the news. 'I'm not sure how to say this, but we have a problem,' Wilson-Piper said. 'Steve isn't here. In fact he won't be available tonight, he's been arrested.' The band had not heard from Kilbey for more than eight hours, drummer Tim Powles later explained. 'He failed to show for a 4.30pm sound check, but we're at the end of the tour so no one was really bothered,' he said. By 10pm, when the lead singer and bass guitarist did not arrive, band members began to worry. At first they started calling hospitals, before finally locating the veteran pop star.

The following day, Kilbey had a court appointment. His legal aid was evidently a fan of The Church. 'He came in and said, "I know who you are, mate. I'm going to sort you out," Kilbey tells me. 'He went up and told this sob story: "My client's a musician, he's under a lot of pressure, he's away from home, he's become addicted to drugs as an entertainer, he's really sorry …" The judge was like, "Well, Mr Kilbey, I know they don't like heroin down in Sydney either, so I don't know why you're coming to New York and using drugs. This is your first offence here, so I'm just going to give you a day's community service."'

As *The Australian* put it:

> After a five-minute hearing, Judge Carro agreed and sentenced the Australian to serve one day's community service – ordering him to return to the same court room on 8 December where, if he remains clean, and carries out his community service, his police record will be expunged. Kilbey is to report to the Metropolitan Transport Authority later this month for a day's cleaning detail on the suburban A-train.

Kilbey maintained a sense of humour about the incident: a *Daily Telegraph* article from 8 October describes him emerging:

> from room 103 of the Manhattan Criminal Court slightly dishevelled but otherwise unfazed over his experience with the US legal system. ... He said being picked up for drugs in New York was a rite of passage for Australian musicians. 'A drug bust is something every aging rock star should have under his belt,' he said. 'Nick Cave and I are in great company.'

('That's right!' he says when I remind him of this quote. 'It wasn't bad for business. I made the second page of *The Australian*. That's one of those things, isn't it? "Get busted?"')

At the time of his arrest, Kilbey was living in New York with an American and another set of twin daughters, about an hour's train ride away from the community-service appointment in New York City. 'So I went there,' he says. 'I'm cleaning up this railway track with all these other ratbags. Talk about a place to meet new connections! I'm working with this old black guy, about eighty. He goes' – here he adopts an American accent – '"Hey, man, what are you fuckin' in here for?" I went, "Scoring heroin." He said, "Oh, you like heroin, do you?"' Kilbey told him the story about being caught by the fuzz in Alphabet City. 'Oh, man, you're a fuckin' idiot!' his new friend replied. 'You want to score with me after this?'

The pair of them went to Harlem, and again Kilbey received a memorable lesson from a worldly drug user. He watched as the eighty-year-old, with his $100 in hand, wordlessly pushed through four black guys standing on a corner – he stands up to demonstrate this point, imitating a confident strut – then returned to Kilbey with the drug in hand. 'It was the most incredible thing!' he says. 'He'd walked through there without saying anything, without looking at them, without any hands changing money, anything at all. [Yet] he'd given them the money, told them how much he wanted, and he'd come out the other side.'

The pair snorted at his house in Harlem, then Kilbey got a guided tour of the neighbourhood while being introduced to 'all these really authentic people' as 'This is Steve, he's a great friend of mine'. 'So that was my day's community service,' Kilbey says. 'Going and fuckin' scoring more heroin. What an idiot.'

How Kilbey shook off his eleven-year addiction is a curious tale. While planning to leave Sweden and again set out for America, he stopped injecting the drug and switched to snorting, and bought a bottle of methadone that he mixed with cough syrup. 'When I got to America, I tapered down on the methadone until I was just having an eighth of a teaspoon full,' he says. 'When the methadone ran out, my body had tapered off enough so I didn't get any of the severe physical effects; I just had a long period of profound depression and anxiety. I felt like I was a hundred years old. Just to stand up and walk up a step was so much effort. I was so tired, but I couldn't sleep – insomnia. But my last withdrawal wasn't that bad, because of the methadone.' As a substitute for heroin, Kilbey believes methadone works because the body 'doesn't seem to latch onto it' as strongly as the other substance.

He describes the interior monologue that went on during that time. 'Your body is going, "Give me heroin!" and you go, "I haven't got heroin, try this!" And [the body] is like, "Okay, that'll do!" You have a bit less [methadone]. "That'll do, that'll do." And eventually you escape that incredible, spectacular withdrawal, and you go more into a kind of purgatory, numb, nothing.' This is because when you use heroin, Kilbey says, your body stops making endorphins. 'Because you're giving it the artificial endorphin, it stops. So when you stop using, it takes a while for your body to catch up – about four or five weeks before it starts making them again. And in that period, you find out what an endorphin-less life would be like.'

While in the United States, living in a small town with the mother of his second set of twins, Kilbey couldn't find heroin. He didn't expect to, either, which is why he'd planned ahead with the methadone. Upon returning to Stockholm four months later, though, he immediately visited Central Station, took the drug home and had a snort. Something strange happened. Instead of the warm, 'cushiony' feeling he'd known for over a decade, he felt the opposite: itchy; restless; headache; sickness. It was the first time that he'd had a bad reaction to the drug.

'It was almost like the smack had said, "I'm tired of you. I don't want to do it anymore,"' he says. 'Or something happened. The universe, or God, or whatever [had previously] said to me, "You're a guy who's been riding high his whole life. You've never lost. Now, here, at thirty-seven, you've got all this money, you've always been a success, you don't understand anybody at all – try this for eleven years." After my eleven years in fucking hell and purgatory, it's like the universe went, "All right, we've knocked a few rough edges off you. Right, you can come out."' He describes this outcome not as his decision to give up heroin; instead, he says, 'heroin gave up me'.

Since that moment, around 2002, Kilbey has had the occasional taste. 'I think probably last year I had a snort,' he says. 'And nah, it doesn't do it for me. I have no temptation. I'm just not interested anymore. Look at it like a woman you were once madly in love with. Occasionally, you go round her house and spend the night with her, and you always walk out in the morning going, "Fuck, what did I want that for? That was awful!" It's like that. So I'm not sitting here now going, "Oh god, I wish I could have some heroin." If you put a fuckin' bowl of it on the table, I'd go, "Oh, I don't know what to do with it."'

As our eighty-minute conversation starts to wind down, talk turns to other substances. 'I think there's only one drug on this earth I haven't tried yet,' he says. 'And that's ibogaine, which is a drug that's made from a bark in Africa that pygmies take at their initiation. I think that's the only substance I haven't had.' We discuss dimethyltryptamine – DMT, for short. It's a psychedelic drug whose duration is quite short when smoked – around fifteen minutes – but whose effects are said to be profound. I've yet to try it when I meet Kilbey. I ask whether he liked it.

'I loved it,' he replies. 'That's an amazing drug. It's not really a drug; there's some drugs that you shouldn't put in the category of being a "drug"; they're more like something else.' He stands up and fetches a canvas from a pile stacked against the wall, near his television. 'I did this painting here, called *DMT Download*, after smoking it. That's what it felt like.' It's a self-portrait of the artist surrounded by eyes and seven flaming pyramids, with a mysterious figure lurking at the centre of each structure. Smiley faces and yin-yangs feature throughout the painting's border.

He launches into an impassioned description of what he saw – 'I smoked it, and there were all these pyramids in my head going round. Instead of the pyramids being made up of bricks, they were made up of either music, or art, or mathematics' – and how he tried to capture it visually. 'Immediately after I'd had that, my art and my music had this great leap forward,' he says. 'See, I take drugs, and then I try and bring back these experiences into the world, for other people, so they don't have to take the drugs. It's like, "I died for your sins, so you didn't have to go through it."'

He opens his laptop and begins showing me an art exhibition that he staged in Yellow Springs, Ohio, in 2008, entitled *The Empty Place: A Modern Australian Psychedelic Vision*.

The twenty-one paintings were inspired by taking DMT and ayahuasca, he says, the latter being a psychoactive brew that originated in South America. I'm no art critic, but I like what I see: bold, colourful borders, striking human faces – including a few more self-portraits – and a recurring theme of blue, human eyes that surround the characters, all-seeing. His work reminds me of the American psychedelic artist Alex Grey, best known for his work with the American rock band Tool.

As Kilbey clicks through the images, commenting on each one – 'This is one of my best friends who's still using. That's a shot of her having a fuckin' fix. In the background, there's a soap opera going on TV'; 'I could see this woman communicating with me. *Medicine Spirit.* That was my attempt to draw her' – it strikes me that I'm in the presence of an unrepentant drug fanatic. Kilbey's enthusiasm for the topic is so bald, his experiences so vast, his ability to articulate altered states through art and conversation so refined, that it's quite fascinating to be in his presence as he narrates a lifetime of drug use.

I chuckle to myself at this thought, then ask, bluntly, why? Why do you like drugs so much, Steve Kilbey? 'I heard that the main drives of a human being are shelter, food, the need to procreate and the need to alter our consciousness,' he replies. 'I've always needed to alter my consciousness. When I was a kid, I did it by reading books about swords, sorcery, magic: *The Lord of the Rings*; Greek mythology. I just wasn't happy in this mundane world. I'm still not, really. I started smoking pot: "Wow, yeah, this is really altering my consciousness." Every drug that came along, I wanted to abuse it and make music, and somehow reproduce that feeling.

'Up until 1914, the whole world was pretty happy with people altering their consciousness. And then some fucking idiot in America realised, "If we make drugs illegal, we can immediately disenfranchise a whole load of fucking people: blacks, Jews, artists, the poor. We can immediately arrest them."' He's talking about the *Harrison Narcotics Tax Act*, which was the beginning of the end for what we still class as 'illicit drugs'. 'Up until then, you could buy heroin, cocaine, opium: whatever you liked. It wasn't a moral issue. If your neighbour was doing opium, you didn't give a fuck. And then suddenly someone found out a way to make it a moral issue, for their own agenda. Not because they cared that it was bad for you, but just 'cause it was a way of keeping a certain element of society under control.'

And that moralising has persisted for a hundred years now, I offer. 'Mm–hmm,' he says. 'But it's falling apart right now.' Yeah? 'I believe it is,' he replies. 'They can't hold onto it. Prohibition hasn't worked. The "war on drugs" hasn't worked. A lot of people are realising that. We're in a period now where it ain't working. In America, they're starting to legalise pot. Portugal has legalised everything. They've seen a downturn in drug addiction.'

In 2000, Portugal put 'Law 30/2000' in place, and it became legally effective from July 2001. This policy eliminated criminal penalties for drug users: possession of a small amount of heroin, MDMA, amphetamine, cocaine or marijuana is a misdemeanour on a par with illegal parking. What constitutes a small amount? Less than ten days' supply of each drug: one gram, one gram, one gram, two grams or twenty-five grams of leaves, respectively. These substances are all still illegal in Portugal, so it's not quite true that 'Portugal has legalised everything', but possession has been decriminalised. Portuguese drug users aren't viewed as criminals – they're sick, and potentially in need of medical help, not jail time. Anyone stopped by police and found to be in possession of drugs in excess of the aforementioned small amounts is viewed as a dealer and charged in court; anyone carrying underweight drugs is told to report to a 'Commission for the Dissuasion of Drug Addiction' – consisting of a social worker, a psychiatrist and an attorney – within the next seventy-two hours. If a user isn't caught again within three months, their case will be closed.

'We let people have booze, cigarettes, wars,' Kilbey continues. 'We let them have fluoride in the water, and all the rest of it. Why not let them have smack? People used to take it, and it wasn't seen as a problem. If you lived in 1890 and you were an opium fiend, that was your problem: to take it, and to find out how to stop taking it. It was nothing to do with the law. There weren't people wagging their fingers at you. It's just something that you embarked upon. It had its joys and perils, just like anything else.

'Now, I'm not going to sit here and go, "Oh, kids, look what I did to my life because I was a drug addict. Please don't be like me. Please be Mister Straight." I don't believe in that, either. I think we have to grow up and look at why drugs are illegal. It all goes back to this guy who started this whole thing in 1914. This wowser, puritanical agenda; the white man [attitude] of, "Let's disenfranchise all these drug users." It's nothing to do with protecting people. They don't give a fuck about you.'

Kilbey points to his fit, muscular, tanned body. 'Look at someone like me,' he says. 'I'm sixty years old, almost. I've been using all kinds of drugs all my life. I've been smoking [weed] forty years. I'm probably as fit as most thirty-year-old guys, and healthy. I'm a vegetarian. I do yoga. I don't drink much alcohol. Someone should fuckin' have a look at me. I'd like to put myself up and go, "Hey, you tell us how bad marijuana is. *Check me out*, for a guy who's been smoking chronically his whole life – seven or eight joints a day – and tell me: what's wrong with me? Where's all this damage that you're telling me that I should have?"'

He's getting a little worked up now, really getting into a groove. I can't wipe the smile from my face. It's a joy to behold. 'I'm much healthier than some guy who's sat there drinking beer and eating steaks,' he continues. 'I'm still going on stage, running around, and playing. I think it's becoming obvious to people that the whole thing about drugs was a fucking lie. I think this period we're going through, it's like the Witch Trials. It's like fucking burning witches at the stake, or having slaves. I believe one day people will, in some enlightened time, look back at this and say, "You know they used to throw people in jail for five years for smoking marijuana?" *Why?* What the fuck have you done except disobey some fuckwit in authority? That's all it is. People are realising that taking drugs is a medical issue; it's a social issue. It's nothing to do with the law.

'I'm paying my taxes. I'm raising my kids. I'm playing gigs; doing interviews; writing articles; being on TV shows; judging cake contests; swimming; bushwalking. I'm going bushwalking tomorrow. I'll be smoking dope the whole time.

So where's the fucking problem? I'm a pretty model citizen. I've written the most popular Australian song of the last twenty years' – 'Under the Milky Way', that is, as voted by music critics and fellow musicians in *The Weekend Australian Magazine* in 2008 – 'I play shows all around the world. I donate my money to charity. I'm involved in the community with the school. I'm a trustworthy guy, a good guy. And I happen to take drugs.'

He pauses, choosing his words carefully. 'I just don't want people to believe the hype, that if you take drugs you're necessarily an evil villain. You might be a silly person, or a weak person. But you're not a bad person.'

WALLY DE BACKER

One week after claiming three Grammy Awards and becoming the first Australian to win 'Record of the Year' since Olivia Newton-John in 1975, I meet with Wally de Backer in the sleepy Mornington Peninsula town of Balnarring, an hour south of Melbourne. Those awards – 'Best Pop Duo Performance', 'Best Alternative Album' and the aforementioned – capped a two-year touring cycle off the back of the 2011 Gotye album *Making Mirrors*, during which the thirty-two-year-old has had plenty of time on planes and backstage at multi-thousand-capacity venues with his band, yet precious little time to himself. Throughout it all, de Backer has kept his head. Since he first appeared on national radio in the mid-2000s, he's always given the impression of being among the most resolutely normal, well-adjusted musicians to emerge from obscurity. It helped, too, that international fame found him at age thirty.

We first met in 2009 at a Brisbane music conference, and we've kept in contact since. It was a joy to watch de Backer ascend the peak of Mount Pop throughout 2012, and it's a pleasure to see his unmistakable smile and thin frame loping towards me in red jeans and a vintage 'Life. Be In It.' shirt. After eating breakfast at a favourite Balnarring cafe, where a couple of locals stop to congratulate him on the Grammy wins, I follow his beaten-up white van to a brick house on a quiet street. There's a healthy vegetable garden out front, blooming with leafy greens.

The first thing I notice upon entering is a strange contraption I've never seen before. It's an inversion board, I learn, used for muscle-balance therapy. De Backer's sister lent it to him after recovering from a horrific snowboarding accident that left her immobile and in agonising pain for months, until she discovered this alternative therapy via Google. He straps his feet into the board and demonstrates how it's possible to fully invert oneself, feet pointing skyward, head near the ground; a full-body stretch like nothing else. He encourages me to give it a shot, and I do. It's the strangest feeling, willingly being upside down for a couple of minutes.

The board stands between the kitchen, a piano and an old arcade-game cabinet. His eyes light up when I accept his challenge to play a few rounds. While the machine powers up, he tells me that he bought it with some friends when they were twenty. It's fair to say that a few things have changed in his life in the intervening twelve years. We laugh about how, in the last few days, he's gone from the American music industry's seat of power to playing *Super Street Fighter II Turbo* in the midst of a Victorian heatwave.

De Backer rarely finds anyone to play against him these days; apparently, he's too good at the game. I find this to be perfectly true. The man has skills. He favours the sumo-wrestler character E. Honda, known for the deadly Hundred Hand Slap; I try my luck with Blanka, Dhalsim and Vega, my three favourite fighters as a child. He's memorised all of Honda's special moves, and, after some frustration, he eventually executes each of them, decimating my inept brawlers in the process. In this moment, I'm nothing more than willing cannon fodder. I might have won a single round, but he resolutely schools me in all three games.

In the living room, an impressive set of shelves holds a true collector's hoard of CDs, vinyl and books. He shows me his collection of foreign copies of *Making Mirrors*; the perfectionist in him can't resist pointing out that some of the Asian editions totally fucked up the inner-sleeve artwork. He shakes his head in dismay. In the bathroom, there's a stained-glass version of *Making Mirrors'* iconic cover art, based on artwork that his father created as a younger man. De Backer is touched that his dad went to the effort of learning how to blow glass purely in order to re-create the image and present it as a gift. A plush Muppets toy is propped up near the window, looking out towards the road. We sit on his couch as he unwraps a coffee-table book of album covers that he recently bought at the Museum of Old and New Art in Tasmania.

I soon learn that, to Wally de Backer, illicit drugs represent a world that he knows very little about. 'I feel like someone on the outside, with no idea what's going on inside,' he tells me. He first tried smoking marijuana around age ten, when a childhood friend – the one who made de Backer's parents frown, pegging him as a bad influence – cut up some of his mother's garden hose and made a Coke-bottle bong for the two of them. 'I took a few tokes, but I probably didn't feel like I'd really inhaled,' he tells me. 'I think I was fearful enough that I didn't really inhale, because I wasn't really sure what was going to happen [to me].' The pair of them walked from Eltham, in Melbourne's north-east, to Eltham North, where de Backer's after-school drum lessons took place. 'It was a good half-hour walk. He was pretty toasted from my memory, because he was giggling and laughing, and just being a dickhead.'

This early exposure was a one-off. As an adolescent, de Backer avoided drugs almost entirely, through a combination of willpower and by virtue of his social circle. Once, he drank a bottle of Jim Beam with a friend 'in like three minutes, then hurled all night before blacking out. That experience on some level probably turned me away from alcohol,' he says. At parties in his teens, he'd observe older kids smoking bongs and rolling joints but didn't feel compelled to partake. 'If anything, my thoughts weren't on drinking alcohol, or getting smashed, or trying to take drugs – it was more about trying to find a girl I thought was interesting!'

De Backer says that drugs have always been something 'other' for him. 'I've always been intrigued by them, but I think that my relationship to doing drugs – or considering doing drugs – is that there's always been some combination of fear, and at other times a conscious denial. As in, "Nup, that's not me. I don't need that, so I'm not interested." Especially when I was younger, there was a certain sense of arrogance, or setting myself apart; trying to define myself socially as someone who didn't need to do drugs, because "I'm better than that". Because I didn't need it.'

Not that de Backer looks down on those who choose to 'get smashed', or who feel like they need to use. He tells me that he harbours no condescending feelings towards drug users, whether they do pot or 'hard drugs'. 'In fact, if anything, I'm a bit more fascinated by it,' he says. 'I feel like, as I get older, I'm more intrigued to consider recreationally using drugs, to see what the experiences could be like.'

He relates a story about one of his managers, John Watson, slowly coming to terms over the past two years with the fact that de Backer is someone to whom clear organisation, structure and routine are all incredibly important – yet there's another side to de Backer that's drawn to surprise and chance. 'I'm almost rabidly interested in the possibilities of the unexpected, and not trying to hold on and harness my life – but within a very clear, focused context!' He gives a half-laugh. 'For me, it fits that, if I was ever going to investigate drugs, it would actually be quite conscious. I'd go, "Oh, I'm thirty-five years old. I'm going to try heroin!"' This time, he laughs properly, before adding, 'I've thought about it!'

He follows that comment up, however, with one that reinforces the thirty-two-year-old's decision to steer clear of substances. 'But every time I think about that, because it feels like such an "other" world, I feel like there's so much in my life already that I feel stimulated by, and interested in. Whether it's music, film, books, art; even very simple things like riding a bike, enjoying good weather, going down to the beach, enjoying nature. I don't feel a "lack" that has ever made me feel like I so desperately need to try those things, because it's a side of life that I'm missing out on, that I *need* to experience. But there are moments where I think, "Well, it'd be interesting to see what it feels like."'

Though Gotye has been a household name for the better part of eighteen months when we meet, thanks to the hit single 'Somebody That I Used to Know', de Backer cites access and finances as potential impediments to his hypothetical heroin dabbling. 'It's the investment, partly, that keeps me from more actively considering,' he says. 'Maybe I'm just genuinely not interested enough to find good-quality drugs, and to not be worrying about the possibility of that one time you decide to dabble, you have a bad experience, and maybe damage yourself. I don't feel like I have the energy to bother with the possibilities of things going wrong, versus what I might be missing out on.'

De Backer says he's never really accepted the common, media-led narrative that illicit drug consumers are selfish law-breakers who deserve to be punished. 'I have a much more "fair" approach to people. I have a liberal idea of how people should be allowed to explore their own lives, as long as it doesn't affect other people adversely,' he says. 'I'm fascinated by some people – "creatives" – who seem to have reached some of their creative breakthroughs because of their experiences from drugs. There's a part of that I feel attracted to, possibly that I'm denying interesting experiences that could actually unlock some part of myself that I haven't discovered, or that I'm keeping locked away.'

I ask de Backer to elaborate on that idea of liberalisation, and how that contrasts with how illicit drug use is portrayed in Australian culture. 'I think a lot of the problems that are associated with drugs do come from certain aspects of the criminalisation of them,' he replies. 'Bad-quality drugs; doing drugs to extremes in private, and not in a place where anybody else [who] cares for you is aware of it, [so they can't] potentially even evaluate how it's affecting your life, or how it's affecting you as a person. So, in that regard, I kind of feel like if the law and society were more open-minded ...' He pauses. 'It's hard to know. Obviously, lots of people smoke [cigarettes], even though the negative outcomes are well known. I'm trying to imagine a society where everyone comfortably accepts people shooting heroin if they do it in a clean, limited way, and whether that could actually be acceptable, or good, for people or society.'

I bring up the decriminalisation situation in Portugal, which might be just the sort of society de Backer is trying to picture. 'We were going to go to Portugal on our tour, but we had to cancel a show,' he says. 'So we didn't get to go there. The guys in my band went to Lisbon and had a great couple of days hanging out there. But that's interesting. I had no idea that they were trialling that anywhere in the world.'

As you can imagine, I tell him, every drug advocate in the world applauds Portugal for being a progressive country where taking drugs is seen simply as another aspect of life that some people choose to explore, and where problem drug users are offered medical treatment and counselling. It's my belief that this compassionate approach is a far more mature way to deal with drugs than the criminalisation tactic favoured by decades of successive Australian governments, which seems to barely work at the best of times.

'I think I believe that, too,' replies de Backer, who was born in Belgium. 'Especially the idea that you start to focus on other aspects when [a topic] is not taboo anymore. I have memories of my parents noting the style of drinking in Australia, which they thought connected a bit with the fact that they perceived a lot of kids were never allowed to have a beer or wine growing up. Whereas, when I was quite young, I could always have half a glass of wine to try it, or some beer, with my mum and dad. It wasn't a thing. In Europe, there's seemingly less of a culture of binge-drinking, of hitting a certain age and needing to "seek relief in" and explore [drinking].'

Based on our discussions so far, I wager that de Backer was never the kind of wayward son who was out all weekend, getting pissed with his mates, causing trouble. 'My parents are very open-minded, so I think I had a lot of freedom,' he replies. 'Like I said, I had a couple of experiences where I drank way too much and had terrible hangovers. Not a good night. That was enough for me to not even really want to drink too much at any stage. I've never been drawn to alcohol aesthetically. I don't really like the taste of a lot of wines or beer. I enjoy some wine or beer with meals, here and there. Sometimes, it really hits the spot. But rarely do I feel like I need to drink [alcohol], or like I'm not just happy drinking water or fruit juice.'

What about pharmaceutical drugs and prescription medication? Where do they fit into his life? 'I've always been quite "anti" that,' he says. 'I think that's very much related to my mum being very sceptical about mainstream medicine, and of doctors. Partly because, right before I was born, nurses came and told her that the doctor was planning to use her as a guinea pig for some experimental drugs to induce her. So Mum and Dad went to another hospital. She's always been the first to tell me, "Don't go to the doctor. What are they going to do? Check you out, give you some antibiotics? They'll make your body weaker."

'I think I've taken a lot of that on. I've never been one to go, "Oh, I've got a headache; I'll take a Panadol." I'll just go, "Gee, I'm feeling really shit; I better cancel work or go lie down, spend some hours in bed, have a nap.' Or just not look at the computer anymore. That seems to have served me pretty well. A good example is when I got gastroenteritis coming out of India. We were there for less than forty-eight hours, and I ate only at the hotel, but stepping on the plane to go to Tokyo, I was like, "Oh no!" I spent ten hours throwing up, shivering, with a fever – terrible. Worst plane flight ever.' He shakes his head at the memory.

'When I got to Tokyo, they insisted I go to quarantine,' he continues. 'I had to see an airport clinic, because they might not let me on the flight to LA. They thought maybe I had malaria, or something like that. So the doctor looked [at me], went, "I think you've got acute gastroenteritis," and gave me this cocktail of prescriptions: antibiotics, antibiotic-resistant pro-biotics, anti-nausea medication, and some other kind of powder that was meant to stabilise stomach activity. They had all these disclaimers about, "If you're allergic to this, don't take this, you might have this kind of reaction." I looked at them all and went, "Yeah, not going to take any of these." I kind of went [to the doctor] just out of going through the motions, in case there was something I had to prove [upon arrival] in the States.'

Not that de Backer discounts all medical advice as a matter of course: he plans to visit a doctor soon after our interview, to get a check-up after a solid year of globetrotting. 'I can still feel my stomach's a bit upset; there's obviously still bugs in there working their way through,' he says. 'But I often don't think doctors are right to prescribe something like that so quickly. I might be wrong. I certainly took antibiotics in Europe when I had those three rough shows, and that's probably one of the reasons why I got better so quickly. I realised, "I can't afford to be like this for two weeks – that'd be pretty shit." So I don't have a hard line about it in those situations, but generally I think the body's really remarkable at fixing itself. If you have a hunch about what's put your body in a situation where it's responding negatively [and it looks like it might be through] overwork, being stressed, or sitting in front of screens too much, I just do the opposite and take it easy.'

At this point, I confess to some pharmaceutical abuse of my own. This interview is taking place on a Monday morning, and I've spent the previous two days at the All Tomorrow's Parties festival in the western Melbourne suburb of Altona, taking in loud rock bands such as My Bloody Valentine and The Drones. I've had less than four hours of sleep before driving an hour south, through peak-hour traffic, to de Backer's quiet part of the world. I knew that fatigue would be an issue ahead of time, so upon waking I took a prescription drug called modafinil. It's usually prescribed to narcoleptics and sufferers of shift-worker sleep disorder, so my use is certainly off-label – I fall into neither of those categories – but, after writing a story on 'smart drugs' for *Rolling Stone* in mid-2012, I had some experience with it, including one work week where I was awake for seventy-nine out of ninety hours after taking the drug on consecutive days. I certainly felt like shit towards the end, but as a stimulant it's undoubtedly effective.

The easiest way to describe modafinil is that it makes your brain forget that you're tired, for around fifteen hours – that's how long a user will typically feel its stimulant effects. There's no real high associated with it; it simply allows you to operate at normal capacity despite fatigue. The US military has tested it on fighter pilots, to keep them awake on multi-day missions. It's a potent drug that I use sparingly, and only in this case due to being sleep-deprived. I didn't want to be in an irritable mood or risk a car accident due to tiredness, so I popped a pill. As expected, it did the job, and it's kept me focused and functioning throughout an important interview.

'Here's a contrast for you,' de Backer replies. 'I once asked if I could take a fifteen-minute power nap in the offices of Warner Bros Records in LA, right before I met the CEOs and everyone in the company. I was like, "I'm so tired, I can't do this right now – can I just lie down on your couch for fifteen minutes and take the meeting then?" They were a bit weird at first, but they allowed me to do it.' He laughs. 'I have huge responses to power naps. I also knew I didn't want to sign with them, so I wasn't too annoyed [with myself] if I pissed them off!'

I've found that modafinil is beneficial during long flights and when in transit; rather than battling through that half-awake, half-asleep limbo phase familiar to many travellers, one pill will guarantee at least fifteen hours of consciousness. 'I could probably do well to consider doing that,' de Backer replies. 'I've always been a bit "anti" that, too. My manager John likes saying, "You really should take a sleeping tablet on this flight, considering that you've insisted on not flying business and you're in a seat in economy with the band, and you need to arrive fresh." I'm like, "Nah, I know flying is kind of shit, but I'll just respond how I respond." I'm not into taking a sleeping tablet.'

The theory behind 'smart drugs' and 'cognitive enhancers' is they help you to improve your memory and overall focus so you can be more productive and high-performing, simply through the regular act of taking particular pills and supplements. As I found in my *Rolling Stone* story, 'Building a Better Brain: Wired on Nootropics', there's a hefty dose of marketing bullshit behind that theory, but it's still a tantalising idea. 'That implies regular usage, which I probably wouldn't be willing to do,' de Backer replies. 'I think I'm just not into the idea of relying on any outside things that then become part of your expected way of life. I'm just not into the idea of addictions. For me, any kind of reliance on anything feels like some level of addiction, something I feel that I want to avoid, or that I should be able to avoid. It's a vaguely Zen Buddhist type of thing.'

As our hour-long conversation draws to a close, de Backer suddenly remembers his most recent drug experience – a worthy bookend to his first tokes from a Coke-bottle bong, aged ten. 'When we were in Taipei recently, we went to this gorgeous little family restaurant,' he says. 'The cuisine was just amazing. We had a fantastic dinner, wandered outside, and then Ben, my [sound] monitors guy, says to me, "Hey, Wally, try this." He gives me this little green nut. I didn't know what it was. I didn't even ask him. I just popped it into my mouth. He said, "Chew on it, don't swallow the juice – spit them both out." I'm like, "Okay!" I started chewing, then I'm like, "What is it?" One of the promoters says, "It's kind of like a natural marijuana." So I ended up, for the next three hours, being a bit weird and unsettled. At first, it was quite a cool feeling. I'm forgetting what they called it now. Some kind of nut.'

A betel nut? I ask. 'Yes, betel nut,' he replies. 'Have you had them before?' I haven't, but I've read that it's a type of opiate that's abused in Papua New Guinea, among other places. In Port Moresby, there's orange juice all over the ground from workers spitting it everywhere. 'There you go,' says de Backer. 'I must say it was an amazing feeling for like half a minute, where this warmth just went all the way up my whole body. Then I felt quite unsettled. I wasn't prepared for it. I felt like we'd just had a nice dinner – "Here's a dessert!" or something.' So Ben sprung it on you? De Backer laughs. 'Yeah! We still had a great night, because we went to the night market and there were all these amazing foods to try, but the whole time I was kind of walking with [my girlfriend] Tash, hand in hand, a little bit going, "What's going to happen? Am I having the wrong reaction to this thing?"'

It's an internal dialogue common among first-time users of any drug: comparing the new sensation to your idea of normality, as the curious mind attempts to classify the effects. 'It was kind of odd,' de Backer says, thinking back to that night, brow furrowed. 'But it died down slowly, over the course of a few hours. That was my recent drug experience. There you go!' He perks up again, flashing that warm, disarming smile. 'I don't know if I'd try betel nut again. It wasn't that great. If it could be like that first warm feeling, more consistent, that'd be pretty good. That was a good feeling.'

JON TOOGOOD

Shihad's Jon Toogood reached a point in 2001 where he could no longer listen to music. He found himself having to make a clean break with the one thing that, up until then, had always been a sure bet to soothe and thrill his mind. Alone in a recording studio in Melbourne, listening back to the music for a song called 'Run', which would later appear on the 2002 album *Pacifier*, the lead singer and guitarist broke down crying. The realisation that he was critically unhappy hit him like a fist. He decided on the spot that he didn't want to listen to music – a decision that, as a career musician, had some deep ramifications. He told his bandmates that he was out, and caught a plane to his parents' home in New Zealand. Anxiety attacks rocked his mind and body even on that flight home, after vacating a situation that he found intolerable.

Silence was Toogood's soundtrack throughout that period, which lasted for six months. 'It was so weird,' he says as we walk and talk. 'I couldn't listen to all my favourite records;

I couldn't listen to anything to do with music. I was sick of anything to do with the music industry. And that included music, which had always been my saviour. Music had always been the way to make myself feel better, but then it turned into the thing that gave me anxiety attacks.' The forty-one-year-old stops in his tracks. 'Whoa, that's so cool! It's like a pukeko!'

We are looking down at a small, black-and-blue bird with long, orange legs and a red beak that occupies the edge of a water fountain in Brisbane's Botanic Gardens. Plenty of other bird species are making the most of a sunny Thursday in April, as are dozens of humans drawn in by the peaceful allure of the green surrounds. I have never heard the word 'pukeko' before. 'Oh, they're called "pukeko" in New Zealand,' says the frontman, gesturing down at the water hen as it searches for food. He looks up, taking in the gardens. 'Oh, this is nice.'

There's a stark difference between the Toogood who saw no choice but to escape the music industry and the one who sits beside me on the lawn, occasionally tugging absent-mindedly at grass strands. This Toogood is still leading Shihad, which is currently tasked with supporting heavy-metal titans Black Sabbath throughout their Australian and New Zealand tour. The Toogood of twelve years prior couldn't bear to hear a single note of his favourite Sabbath records, let alone energise a crowd while powering through a solid half-hour of his band's heaviest material, as he does at the Brisbane Entertainment Centre later that night.

The story of how one of the southern hemisphere's most engaging rock frontmen came to hate music is harrowing and fascinating. 'I think I burnt the candle at both ends,' he says.

'And I was changing the chemistry of my brain on top of that, to try and fix this fuckin' leaking ship. It was just making the holes bigger.' But this is a story that takes some time to tell, and it's one that begins over tacos and burritos.

After taking a circuitous route through the Brisbane CBD – which is peopled with thousands of people out to see marching war veterans and their families, as today is Anzac Day – and meeting Toogood in his hotel lobby, I go with him to Guzman y Gomez, a Mexican food chain. After ordering, I offer him the seat that looks out into the bustling hall, and it's a good choice: as I learnt while interviewing him for *Mess+Noise* eighteen months earlier, he's so hyperactive that it would've been torture for him to be facing the bare brick wall, as I was.

Toogood is looking curiously at the beers and margaritas that sit atop neighbouring tables. 'I thought at licensed premises you had to be of a certain age ...' he begins. I interrupt: 'It's Anzac Day! Different rules!' He laughs and says, 'It's Anzac Day! Let's have four shots of tequila next to the three-year-old. Fuck it!'

So begins an enlightening, hour-long conversation that is peppered with expletives and salted with Toogood's enthusiasm. I get the impression that this is not a man who has much to hide; on the contrary, it often seems as though he can barely wait to get the next words out. Dressed in black jeans, brown shoes and a red-and-black striped shirt, the singer's famously lithe body is starting to fill out as he ages. He's not so much the skin-and-bones Shihad frontman of decades past, but he still certainly looks to be in great shape. Grey hairs are beginning to poke through his short-cropped black hair.

'Luckily for me, I did work out that I have an addictive nature very early on,' he says near the beginning of our conversation. 'I like to feel things intensely; I like things with lots of salt, lots of sugar, lots of colour.' He eyes off the full tray of food that a waitress carries towards us but delivers to a neighbouring table. 'I like to experience things deeply, whether it comes to music, art, theatre. Drugs have been a part of that in my past. You get off stage and that feeling is like, "I feel like a fucking *god*," you know? "I feel *awesome*! How do we keep that rolling?" Usually, you keep it rolling by taking drugs, because it's an instantly accessible way to replicate that feeling, that high that you get off doing something as weird as getting in front of a room full of people and smashing out your music.'

Toogood was fifteen when he first smoked pot, and found that it afforded him a deeper understanding of the art form that first entranced him as a two-year-old. 'All of a sudden, I wasn't just hearing the bassline, I was hearing the harmonics that would go with the bassline. I'd hear the vocal line that would go with that bassline, and the guitar line that would go with that. I'd also hear the drumbeat. I'd hear all of it. It was like a revelation!' he says, his eyes lighting up at the memory. 'It made me see all these other layers that I would never have seen before.'

When I ask whether pot was easy to come across when he was growing up, he chuckles and nods while chewing a soft taco. 'I live in New Zealand – there's green shit everywhere! I saw everything change when hydroponics came in. That's actually when I started being less creative, because everything became so much stronger. I got far less done. I'd smoke a spliff that was hydroponic, and then I'd find two hours later I'd been, like, looking at a computer screen and working on a kick-drum sound. I'm a fucking songwriter; I shouldn't be doing that! I know my limits with that shit now. I know that a quiet toot puts that nice, sparkly, magical edge on everything, and I can hear what I need to hear, and then I can also deal with reality.'

Drug experiences were referenced in Toogood's early lyrics; he singles out 'Screwtop', from the band's 1993 debut album, *Churn*, as being about a frightening acid trip, 'having my ego blown to smithereens, realising it's not even about me, and putting my mind back together again'. (First line: 'Should we debate significance, or would it leave us too small? / 'Cause it could take some time to linger, pushing us to a fall'.) He describes that kind of trip as one 'where you realise it's not all about you, and you thought it was. It's a necessary thing to learn, but when you learn it in fucking one hour, after not even knowing that that existed, it's quite frightening!' He laughs.

He begins ticking off the band's early albums: '*Killjoy* [1995] – just a lot of pot. The "fish" album [their 1996 self-titled release, whose cover art featured fish trapped in a net] – too much pot. That's when it changed into hydroponics. That's why that record is quite *slow*.' He laughs. 'But luckily for us it has "Home Again" on it, which is one of our signature songs. But that record suffers from smoking way too much pot in the studio. And then, what happened after that?' He pauses, momentarily forgetting the band's biggest hit, released in 1999. 'Oh, *The General Electric*. That's really serious. That's work. But I still would've smoked pot along the way.'

A documentary released in 2012 entitled *Beautiful Machine* – also the name of the band's seventh studio album – captured the four members reflecting on their twentieth anniversary. It's a compelling film for Shihad fans, naturally, but I'd recommend it to any music fan, as it's a well-realised portrait of a high-achieving rock band whose career has been marked by almost as many lows as highs. In *Beautiful Machine*, Toogood says that, when *The General Electric* became a hit, Shihad found that people were throwing free drugs at them.

'Musicians don't hardly pay for our fuckin' drugs,' he tells me. 'They're just *there* – especially once you start getting a profile; they're there *all the time*. Because what we do is something that people want to be a part of; they want to have a bit of that "magic" in their lives, so you'll tend to be surrounded by people who don't know how to express that, but can afford to pay for the drugs to be around it. And so they almost live vicariously through you, and pay you in things that are fun at the time, but maybe *you* pay for in the long run.'

I ask Toogood what kinds of drugs he found surrounding him after the success of *The General Electric*. 'There were lots of pills,' he replies. 'Lots of E; a little bit of speed here and there. But pills. And pills were weird with me. I really did love that "lovey" feeling; I loved that connection. And I'm not sure if it was because of my previous experiences with acid, where I did have bad trips occasionally. Because it [the ecstasy hit] came in waves, and you were getting higher and higher, I'd get frightened that I was just going to go into the stratosphere and never come back again. I'm a bit of a control freak. I like to know where my feet are. Even though I do like to feel things intensely, I still ... I like to be in control of my mind as well. I like to know where I am.' He pauses. 'I developed anxiety attacks from taking too much E.'

This connection is alluded to in the film but it's not quite as clear cut as what Toogood has dropped onto the table between our now-empty food trays. Yeah? I reply. 'Yeah. I think it was from a fear of losing control of my mind. I was just filling my body with adrenaline all the time and burning myself out. There's a psychoactive element to that drug. It's messing with the chemistry of your brain, so I think ... my brain didn't like it, after a while.'

Were you taking too much at one time, or doing it too regularly? 'Too regularly, over a small period of time,' he replies. 'Unlike acid, where if you had a bad trip, you'd have to douse yourself in orange juice and Valium to bring yourself back down four hours later. At least with ecstasy, if I started to get that anxiety, I would just get the fuck out of where I was, have a few breaths, have a laugh with somebody I knew, and then I'd be okay again. But then all of a sudden I'd start developing those anxiety attacks out of nowhere, even when I wasn't on it. I became a very unhappy man.'

In the years immediately after *The General Electric*, the band was attempting to write a hit follow-up while playing around a hundred and fifty shows a year. Even those who dislike Shihad will credit them as a fantastic live act, and much of that can be attributed to Toogood's enthusiastic showmanship. Within a few songs of their set beginning, he'll inevitably be shirtless, his skinny frame brandishing an electric guitar, sweating and singing his heart out, crowd-surfing, ascending balconies and facing his bandmates, eking out chords from fifty metres away. Zero affectation or pretension; one hundred per cent earnestness. Every time I see them perform, I can't help thinking, *This is what Jon Toogood was meant to do with his life*. It's rare to see a musician so utterly enveloped in the moment, yet Toogood seems to inhabit that role wholly, every single time he steps up to a microphone. A born performer.

'I give everything when I'm on stage. I was fuckin' doing that every night, destroying my body, and destroying relationships as well,' he says of their peak touring regimen following that album. 'I lost a couple of great fuckin' techs along the way, who loved our band and actually loved me as a person, but got sick of having fucking guitars thrown at their heads in the middle of the show. And having to fix broken guitars every morning. So I was burning up. I was doing everything I could to show every single fucking audience that we were the best fucking band they'd ever seen. That takes its toll. 'Cause you fuckin' give it, even when you haven't got anything. And then if you're taking drugs on top of that, it's like …' He exhales through his teeth. 'I just didn't have anything left in me, I don't think. So I just burnt myself up.'

Toogood became scared shitless when the attacks started happening even while sober. He thought he'd soon become one of those 'could've been' rock stars who ends up in a mental hospital. 'I thought, "What if I never correct this? What if this is what it's going to be like for the rest of my life? I'll always have these uncontrollable anxiety attacks; I won't be able to function,' he says, the fear of that reality still evident in his eyes as he relives it. 'I wasn't functioning. I had to stay home. Or, when I had anxiety attacks, I had to walk, and I'd walk for fucking miles, and people would have to walk with me.

They'd be *knackered*.' He laughs. 'And I'd be [like], "Come on, let's keep walking." I felt like I had to get away, but there was nothing to get away from. I was just trying to get away from myself.

'I honestly thought I'd lost my mind. And it wasn't because I was thinking of anything too weird; it was just because I'd be sitting around, and out of nowhere I'd feel like there was a fucking tiger sitting there, wanting to eat me. That feeling of fear, you could feel it running through your body, like poison. And, actually, it was reminiscent of the feeling … this is the reason I don't like cocaine. When cocaine runs out of your system, that's the most empty feeling I've ever felt in my life. That's why I always go …' – he inhales through his teeth – 'when I see it. 'Cause I always go, "Yeah, that's going to be fun, but the comedown is going to be so fuckin' awful."'

Our Mexican has long since been demolished. I suggest we go for a walk, and Toogood happily complies. He calls his guitar tech to discuss the set list for tonight's gig. 'We may do "Empty Shell" there at the end tonight,' he says as we weave through a crowd at the store entrance. 'It's all "D" [tuning]. Hopefully, if you give it a good tweak, and I don't smash anything out of tune, I could do it all with one guitar.'

As we walk down Albert Street towards the Botanic Gardens, I prompt Toogood by saying that the band were based in Melbourne around that time, having made the move across the Tasman Sea following the success of *The General Electric*. 'I was the only one out of all the guys that had my partner living in another fucking country, as well,' he says. 'I was staying on couches, staying with friends. Everyone else had their own little home lives going along. I was in a volatile relationship, yet I still missed my partner, and her daughter. I felt alone.

'Which suited me when I was doing the "rock thing". I was so fuckin' driven, it was just like ... ah, fuck, I just became a cartoon of myself. I was living that fantasy. It's unsustainable. Anyone who lasts will tell you, I'm sure, that you do need to come back down to normality. I just spent too much time out in fantasy-land. I'm not cut out to stay there forever. I need some stability. And I just didn't have that in Melbourne. So I was writing away with the guys, and just being unhappy and getting nowhere. When I knew there was a problem ... I mean, I was fucking dousing myself with Nurofen and shit like that; I'd go through a packet of twenty a day. It was fucking my stomach *completely*, just to not have to deal with the fact that I was really fuckin' lonely, and in a lot of pain.'

His bandmates would sometimes watch him pop the pain pills, perhaps saying among themselves that it wasn't a great idea, but Toogood was so determined to get on with it, to write another hit record, that he wasn't really open to his friends' input.

As we stop at a set of traffic lights, standing behind a father and his young daughters, he says, 'I was getting increasingly worse. I mean, like most sensitive, arty kids, I definitely had my moments of sadness and stuff, but never depression or anxiety to that extent. So I didn't really know what it was. I was just going, "Oh, it'll come right, it'll come right." But it was just getting worse. I remember listening back to what became that song "Run" on the *Pacifier* record, which I still really love, a lot ...' Cue emotional breakdown, the return to his parents' place in New Zealand, and six months of thoroughly uncharacteristic silence.

The film *Beautiful Machine* captures another formative drug-related experience from Shihad's early career: their manager, Gerald Dwyer, died of a morphine overdose alone in a hotel room on the same day that the band played their first main-stage set at the Auckland Big Day Out festival in early 1996. Toogood and I discussed this earlier, while waiting for our food to arrive. 'Luckily, with heroin, we had first-hand experience. I'm sure Gerald didn't want to kill himself – but he did. That was *horrific*, you know? But you've seen the movie; one band went, "Fuck it, let's keep going [with using heroin]," he said, referring to Head Like a Hole, another New Zealand hard-rock band managed by Dwyer. 'The other band went, "Let's never have anything to do with that drug again." And, luckily, we were the one that went *nup*.'

He continued, 'There's never a good heroin story. There isn't a happy ending with that shit. You either get beaten up, mugged, one of your best mates steals your bike ... it's all fuckin' seedy as shit. There's bad karma that follows that drug, that always ends in the gutter. And for every record that's great that you wrote on heroin, the next fucking six are going to be shit. And they're going to get progressively worse. And less and less people come to your fuckin' shows, and all of a sudden you're a fuckin' junkie with nothing.'

Toogood has decided that drug use of any kind is all about pain deferral. 'Especially the opiates. Even the other way around – cocaine and shit like that – it's pain deferral 'cause you're turning yourself into Superman for an hour. But why do you want to turn yourself into Superman? 'Cause it feels better than being who you are. But, sooner or later, you're going to have to face the fact that you are who you are.'

He gave a hollow laugh. 'Unless you stay off your head on coke, and die of a heart attack, 'cause you can't sustain that. Sooner or later, rock stars have to grow up.' Another laugh. 'They fuckin' do. Otherwise you die. And everyone goes, "Fuck yeah, the best rock star's a dead rock star!" But fuck that, man! I want to be seventy; I want to have kids; I want to see the world; I want to do other things with my life. Just because I love music and I play rock and roll doesn't mean I have to die to be relevant. Ultimately, it's relevance to myself, and that's it.'

While we sit on the lawn at the Botanic Gardens, Toogood casually picks at the grass strands. He is amused by the nearby ibis. 'It's like an old man's head!' He laughs, pointing at the bird's tiny skull. 'They're definitely not pretty.' He tells me that his period of silence and convalescence at home in New Zealand was managed with the assistance of Valium to calm the anxiety, a counsellor to help him work through the psychological effects, and a healthy diet, including the removal of all stimulants. Toogood kept smoking cigarettes, though, as he had his entire adult life. Having recently quit that packet-a-day addiction, he has been enjoying his new-found ability to cope with the physical demands of a Shihad show. 'I probably have more stamina now at shows than I have since I was a kid,' he says proudly.

I smile and reply that he's never struck me as someone low on stamina when it comes to performing live. 'No, but I mean, I'd do the show, and then I'd be backstage and like …' – he imitates wheezing hard to catch his breath – 'I'd be *fucked*. Recovery time would be a while. Nowadays, I get off stage and it's like, "Cool, what the fuck's happening? Let's go out!"' And I give it just as much [on stage] as I ever did.'

There is one quote from a talking head in *Beautiful Machine* that I'd like to run by Toogood. 'Music without drugs is not music,' says Karl Walterbach, founder of German label Noise Records, which distributed *Killjoy* in Europe. 'Some of the best music you listen to is drug-induced. It's symbiotic; you can't separate it. It just belongs together.'

Toogood pauses for a moment, staring off at the scenery, then says, 'I tend to think that this is true to a point. I mean, I just saw the Bill Hicks movie recently [*American: The Bill Hicks Story*]. He's got that whole skit about how "I'd rather hang out in hell, because at least they made all the good records. All those records you loved, they were made by people who were really fucking high on drugs." But for me – yeah, I was high on drugs writing some of the more successful [Shihad] records, but it was only ever pot. It wasn't heroin. I would've had trips that informed those records. *Churn* and *Killjoy*, definitely. But mainly it's been pot, and psychedelic drugs.'

We are momentarily distracted by two birds making a scene right in front of us, apparently over territorial rights. One of them runs right at me, causing me to flinch, which makes Toogood laugh his arse off. 'That was fucking *awesome*. It was so close! You got attacked by the Australian version of a fucking pukeko!' I regain my composure and say that I'm glad he mentioned that Hicks quote, as I'm thinking of using it at the beginning of this book.

'Hey, fuck, it connects you,' he replies. 'That's what it was like for me with pot: it connects you to that place that those ideas come from. It's a quick way of doing it. There are ways of writing songs straight, though. But you've got to be open to it. You've got to be in the right fucking place. You've got to be ready for it to come through. I mean, fuck, I don't know where the big Shihad songs came from. They just came. When I looked for them, they were there. I tended to find them easier when I was stoned. But I have written songs when I've been straight. Like [the song] "The General Electric"; I was totally straight. That's a fuckin' *huge* riff, you know? But it was just right place, right time. And I was maybe open to receiving. 'Cause creativity's a fucking weird one. You have to: a) set up the fucking space to be able to receive the information; b) create the space in your mind to receive the information; and c) have the fucking will to do it in the first place. I don't believe it has to be with drugs. But I do think that they do make those things accessible.'

The fact that Jon Toogood has been sober for two years – besides the occasional toot on a joint while writing – offers him clarity and perspective on this entire topic. His sobriety came about after he met a woman who didn't take drugs or drink alcohol. He found that, because his best friend didn't do those things, and he had fun with her without drugs, he didn't see much point in doing those things anymore. So out went the cigarettes, cold turkey; booze, too. With distance comes reflection. 'Because I haven't done [drugs] for a little bit, it's made me go, "What was it about it?" he says. "What was it about it that I loved? 'Cause I'm not saying that it's not fun. It's fuckin' great fun. But, like I say, sooner or later you do have to face yourself. Whether it's now or in five years, or whatever the fuck, you will have to face yourself. And the longer you put it off, the harder it is.'

It's at this point, as our conversation winds down, that I ask an inelegant question: I prompt the singer to tell me about his life now, with his partner who 'doesn't do anything'. 'She's great,' he replies, then reacts to my terrible phrasing: 'Oh, we do plenty!'

I quickly apologise, saying that I didn't mean it in a negative sense. 'No, no, I know.' He laughs. 'It's great. She's challenging me. I go and help her volunteer; she volunteers at this place called AMES on Wednesdays, which helps boat refugees get medical help, and help with lawyers trying to fuckin' sort out their visas and shit like this before they get sent to Nauru. These are people on home detention who are basically people who gave their life savings to some fuckhead in Indonesia, hopped on a boat that could've not floated, but they're getting away from something so atrocious that they're prepared to do that, and then they're treated like fucking dogs and criminals when they get here.' He half-laughs at the ridiculousness of it, then goes on to stick the boot into the politicians behind those policies as 'disgusting, despicable, opportunist racists'.

Volunteering at AMES – Adult Multicultural Education Services – has exposed Toogood to a sector of society that is essentially invisible, unless you're paying close attention. 'It's really making me go, "Oh right, fuck, everyone's the same. Everyone just wants their family to be safe, everyone wants to find a fuckin' roof over their heads where they're not fucking threatened,"' he says. 'Some of these people are Muslims, some are Hindus, some are Buddhists, some are atheists. They're from everywhere. But I go and help out there on Wednesdays with her, and that just makes me get over myself. When I'm fuckin' freaking out about whatever's going on in my life, I just go there and think, "Fuck, [my life] is fuckin' sweet."'

This is the first time that the singer has had a sober force in his life. He is, clearly, loving it. 'I like to be present,' he says. 'I like to take responsibility. It's the long game rather than the short-term high. My fucking god – even getting through a day without a cigarette [years ago], I would've patted myself on the back. I haven't smoked a cigarette for two years; I haven't drunk for two years. I never gave a fuck about alcohol anyway, but I don't wake up with hangovers, I'm clear-headed, and I like it. I like being in control. I still beat myself up; I've still got fucking shit I need to work on. I'm very quick to judge myself, and I think a lot of artists do that, 'cause we're in the business of putting our ideas and our innermost thoughts and fuckin' feelings into something and sticking it out there for people to either like or fuckin' *hate* intensely. Most people don't have to do that.'

He pauses, checking himself. 'I'm not saying that "woe is me", 'cause I chose to fuckin' do that. But it doesn't make it any less painful, when someone doesn't like what you really love intensely and what you've put out there, you know?' He laughs. 'So it's a fuckin' strange job. It's a weird job. But I think for me, now, I just need to be straight to deal with it, and work through it.'

PAUL KELLY

Prior to 21 September 2010, Australia had never known a champion for the recreational use of heroin. That night, on national television, the singer and songwriter Paul Kelly stepped in to fill that space, much to his initial reluctance and increasing discomfort. During a prime-time interview on ABC TV's *The 7.30 Report*, host and veteran journalist Kerry O'Brien pursued a sustained and aggressive line of questioning towards the fifty-five-year-old's drug use in much the same way as he'd grill a politician over failed legislation or weasel-word mistruths.

'I thought I had something to say about heroin that was different to the usual narrative,' said Kelly on camera. 'I mean, the usual story of heroin is either a tragedy or redemption. You go down with it, you don't get up; or you go down and you come up, and you've got the redemption story. I just thought there was another story there.' And what is it? O'Brien asked. 'That, you know, people do use "hard" drugs recreationally and not all the time; that people can use drugs like heroin without having a habit. I never did. And that, at some point, you weigh up the costs against the benefits and at some point you think, "The costs are getting too much; I'll stop."'

O'Brien devoted a touch over five and a half minutes – roughly a quarter of the twenty-two-minute unedited interview, though the version that screened nationally was shorter – to the topic of Kelly's heroin use. Throughout that time, the singer appeared somewhat dismayed that an interview about his book and musical career was being railroaded by this obviously minor, sidelined part of a life well lived. In his 2010 memoir, *How to Make Gravy*, the singer deems the topic worthy of just four pages out of over five hundred and fifty. By the end of this line of questioning, as O'Brien wore him down, Kelly practically bristled when asked what advice he'd give to viewers who might consider experimenting with the drug. 'I wouldn't say anything at all. I think the last thing the world needs is pop singers giving advice,' he said, stony-faced. 'I'm certainly not someone who wants to give advice to people I don't know.'

It's nearly three years later when we meet on a Tuesday morning in late July 2013. Melbourne-based Kelly is five shows into a unique twenty-eight-date national tour where, in the first half, he leads his band through a full performance of his nineteenth studio album, 2012's *Spring and Fall*, before a second half brimming with crowd-pleasers. I'm half-heartedly inspecting tourist brochures in the lobby of the Oaks Hotel in central Brisbane when a familiar voice says my name – a statement, not a question. We shake hands. He's wearing red jeans, black shoes and a navy hoodie advertising Sydney hip-hop label Elefant Traks. In the lift en route to the thirty-ninth floor, I compliment him on his hoodie. 'From the man himself,' he says with a smile, referring to the label's co-founder Tim 'Urthboy' Levinson, whom Kelly picked as an unconventional tour support act.

When I remark how it must be strange for an energetic hip-hop performer like Urthboy to be playing to a seated audience, Kelly replies that Tim and his band have been playing more of their slower, ballad-like songs, such as 'The Big Sleep' and 'the one about the roller-coaster', referring to 'Orphan Rocker'. It's been tough-going for the younger performer before Kelly's older audience, but he seems to be savouring the challenge. My parents saw the tour when it visited the Moncrieff Theatre in Bundaberg the previous Saturday; I pass on their thanks to him for visiting the regional Queensland city where I grew up. It was there that I saw Paul Kelly perform for the first time, too, in May 2004. Then, as now, for a credible rock band to visit Bundaberg is a rare treat indeed, and one not lost on my music-loving parents. They introduced me to this man's music at the age of nine, with his greatest-hits compilation *Songs From the South*, released in 1997. His songs have never been far from my mind or ears since.

Pride of place on the coffee table in Kelly's room is a slightly battered red Sherrin football, flanked by a pair of running shoes and a guide to the local sights and surrounds, the latter likely placed there by hotel management. An avid AFL fan fond of kicking the footy at any opportunity, Kelly tells me that he's been enjoying the Queensland leg of this tour as it involves driving down the coast and not having to worry about how to fit the ball in among his checked luggage.

This hotel room is his temporary base between a show at the Gold Coast Arts Theatre tonight, Lake Kawana Community Centre tomorrow and Brisbane's Performing Arts Centre the night after. A MacBook sits open at the desk. The dishwasher cycles noisily in the kitchen. I sit on the couch after he clears some dirty clothes from it; Kelly places a chair directly across from me and sits with a tall glass of water held between his knees, his brown eyes sizing me up. His thin figure is framed by the bright sunlight that filters into the room through a white curtain, giving him something of an angelic appearance.

Kelly first used heroin in Adelaide circa 1976, at the age of twenty-one, yet the only reason we know about this is because he was bold enough to reveal it to the world, unprompted, in his 2010 memoir. 'I'd been quite anxious about the heroin chapter in the book,' he tells me. 'I'd written it and I'd talked with my editors about whether to leave it in or keep it out. And I sort of held my decision until pretty late in the piece. I said, "I'll just let it sit there, and I want to reserve the right to take this out." They were great. They said, "That's totally up to you."' The only other person he discussed the matter with was his partner at the time, Sian Prior.

One of Kelly's self-imposed rules while writing the book was that if he could find a way to write about a subject that differs from the usual discourse, then he should keep it in. 'Also, for me, it was a matter of genre; if you're writing an autobiography, you need to have a certain amount of frankness in it,' he says. 'Otherwise, a memoir with too much hidden or veiled or not spoken about would be a failed memoir, I think. I mean, you need a certain amount of truth-telling, or putting stuff on the table. And heroin had been in my life for so long;

[it was] a part of it, even if it was a shadow part of it. So I thought, "If I leave it out, it'll be one of those memoirs that squibbed it." That was the decision for putting it in.

'Another reason I'd written about heroin in the first place was what I said to Kerry: I think the narrative around heroin is often the same old one you hear over and over again. You go down to the pits of hell with it, and then it either gets you or you climb out of it. It's this sort of damnation/redemption thing. And [the idea] that heroin is something that you get totally enmeshed with; that it's not something you can keep at arm's length or use recreationally. I just thought I had something different to say about it than other stuff I'd read, so I thought, "I'll see what I can say." That's why I started writing the chapter, and followed it through.'

As we talk, and Kelly stumbles over *ums* and *ahs* and long pauses, working out how best to articulate his thoughts, I come to realise that we share a writer's sensibility in our inability to adequately explain ourselves in speech. My mouth tends to bumble over inelegant phrasing and half-baked metaphors, but before a keyboard – where there's a backspace key, and more time to consider exactly how I want my message to be imparted – I make much more sense. Kelly seems to share this trait; his sentences on the page are beautifully formed, a sharp contrast to the comparatively inarticulate expressions and half-finished thoughts that occur to him during our hour-long conversation. Perhaps this is true of many people, but it's only while talking to Kelly that I'm struck by this realisation. It's also true that he is my only interviewee to have previously written about this topic at some length, and it's for this reason that I'll also quote some of his written thoughts about heroin – *the one for me; the recreational drug of choice*, as he called it in *How to Make Gravy* – in italics throughout this chapter.

It was those initial sessions in Adelaide with his older, more worldly friend – referred to in the book as 'T' – that solidified in Kelly's mind a healthy respect for the drug. *The pretty, billowing bloom of blood in the glass tube preceded, by a slow second, the nauseous, freight-train flood of pleasure.* This was not something to be mindlessly used and abused; instead, it was something to be savoured. With 'T', there was a ritualistic, ceremonial nature to it all. 'He treated it like a bit of a sacrament,' Kelly recalls with a laugh. 'I was straight into shooting it up. It was the old-fashioned glass syringes, and there's a whole lore; there was the "Lux Rose", and the "Blue Lady", all these different names for the types of hypodermic syringes. It was classic "boy stuff". The gear is the main thing. He was getting pretty good quality. I think he might have been getting it through chemists' busts.'

You had no hesitation with using needles? I ask. 'To me, if you were going to use heroin, that was the way you use it,' he replies. 'It seemed to be much more effective. There's probably a certain amount of carelessness there, but always, even when you were sharing needles, you'd share one of them but you'd go and boil it for a while in the kettle. Among people I was with, it was never just "use a needle from the person next to you". Or you'd get little plastic syringes of your own.

'I was in a house for a while with people that were using it regularly. It was a point of pride for me not to be; I just didn't want to use it regularly. So I didn't. One, I didn't want to be addicted. And two, I found it was always to me like a recreational drug. It was not a drug for work. It wasn't a drug for playing on. It wasn't a drug for writing. And I wanted to do all that.' *Great ideas, images and schemes swell in the mind like clouds in the sky, and then, like clouds in a drought, move on without dropping rain.* 'So it was really something that I would use after a long, intensive period of work, or a week of gigs, or a few weeks in the studio, or a day off. That's the pattern I got into.'

Like a treat, I offer. Kelly nods. 'Heroin was my treat,' he says. 'I tried to keep it that way. And then, if it wasn't around for months, or a year or two gap sometimes, it wasn't really something I had to go and find. So it went on like that for a long time. And then at some point, I think in the mid-nineties, I got the warning bells. I don't know whether it was just because it was easy; it wasn't hard to find. And maybe because I'd gotten older and seen friends of mine who were also casual users – suddenly, they weren't casual anymore. They'd suddenly become serious about it. And I still carried on for a few more years, thinking, "I'll be okay." My usage crept up without it becoming habit-forming, but that was when the cost-benefit analysis came into play.' *To keep it as something to want, not to need; a thing of joy rather than necessity. That was the theory, anyway.*

Only on a few occasions did this private life seep into the writer's public notepad, and not in any of the bold, joyous pop hits that he's best known for – instead, quieter, more introspective deep album cuts: 'Blues for Skip', from the 1985 album *Post*; 'Little Decisions', the closing track from the same album; 'Coma', from *Professor Ratbaggy* in 1999. In his memoir, it's the latter song that Kelly attaches to his chapter on heroin, entitled 'Me Or It'. Sian Prior played clarinet on that track;

she is the one who gave Kelly the ultimatum for which the chapter is named. *I didn't take heroin because I felt bad or because I had an unhappy childhood. I just liked it.*

It was in the late 1990s that Kelly approached Spencer P. Jones – who was playing guitar in his band – with a quiet offer to help with securing a place in rehab, sensing that his friend was sinking in deep waters. 'He was really supportive,' Jones told me of Kelly. 'He's not judgemental. It was one of those situations where Paul's not hypocritical. He was definitely there for me.'

When I repeat this quote to Kelly, he says, 'Generally, I'm not that interventionist. I like people to figure that stuff out for themselves, but if someone's in my band and I think their behaviour is starting to impact their work, I'll have a word. And Spencer's been a friend for a long time. We've been friends when we weren't in bands together. If you see friends and you think they might be heading for trouble, you try and point it out. There's not much else you can do.'

Jones also told me that he and Kelly had 'a little bit of a drug-buddy thing going on for a couple of months', some time prior to that chat. The band leader had the self-awareness to put an end to that soon enough. 'I remember being well aware of the danger,' Kelly says, 'because, usually, I was the only guy in the band that liked heroin. So I used to go off and it was completely my private life, on my day off. But I had someone else in the band who liked it too, and to me that was [something] we had to be really strong about, you know. I didn't want to be starting to do it with him, because you start encouraging each other. I wanted to draw the line there. He understood that, and we did that.'

Kelly summarises that ethos with, 'Do what you want to do on your day off,' punctuated by a short laugh.

The singer knew from the very beginning that heroin was a powerful drug. 'And maybe that's part of the attraction, but it's part of the reason I really wanted to treat it very carefully,' he says. 'And, most of the time, I did. That's why I always wanted to keep it to occasional use. My philosophy was: if you don't respect the drug, the drug won't respect you.'

He pauses, then says, 'That's all very well and good, but I think it's an insidious drug. It can sneak up on you. It's like cocaine. It changes your brain enough [that] it can make you delusional. You think you're fine, and you're not. I think that's its power.' During periods where Kelly felt that he was using too much, too often, he was struck by the strange feeling that his choice was making 'groove marks' in his brain, like those on the surface of a vinyl record. *You feared [they] would turn into ruts you wouldn't be able to climb out of.* 'So that was another reason to stop, because I felt it might start rewiring my brain,' he says. 'The brain is so plastic that I'm sure it did, and [that it] could keep doing that.'

As his relationship with the drug wore on, Kelly found that his recovery time increased in parallel with his age. Eventually, it became a simple equation: the comedown would tend to last twice as long as the high. If he bought enough to use for an afternoon and a night, it'd be two days wiped out due to basic depression – 'just feeling *blah*', as he puts it. A weekend binge would result in four days of the same emptiness, essentially killing his week. *Too many days of dread. Weeks disappeared and lists stayed uncrossed.* 'So, if you're a weekend user, you're actually not getting anything done,' he says. Were you counting this cost as it was happening? I ask. 'Yeah, but I was still thinking, "I'm just going to cut back …"'

Heroin rewires your brain. It's a beautiful brainwasher that makes you believe the dumbest things. 'I eventually did stop when the woman I was with said, "No occasional use; it's me or nothing,"' he says. 'I'm really glad she said that, because I did stop. Once I did, I could step back and say, "Oh yeah, you had more of a problem than you thought you did." I went to a counsellor a couple of times. I found that pretty useful. The most useful thing she said was, "Write a list of the reasons not to take it, and look at it."'

Was it a long list? I ask as Kelly gets up to refill his glass. 'No,' he replies immediately from the kitchen sink. 'About six [reasons]. But they were good reasons,' he laughs. In *How to Make Gravy*, his list of nine New Year's resolutions for 1998 included 'learn more about wine' and 'read more history', and ended with 'give up heroin'. 'Yeah, well, that wasn't too far off,' Kelly says when I remind him of this. 'About 2002 [I stopped]. So I obviously knew it was a problem then, and that I should stop it completely. It was starting to nag at me.' The desire to have it? 'No, that it was sort of encroaching too much. Like I said, I was always aware that it was not really good for work. It changed my behaviour, and people around me were aware of it. Of course, I worry about my children knowing about it all. It's a bit risky. Then you start thinking, "I'm heading towards fifty. Why am I still doing this?"'

There was great satisfaction to be had in getting the balance right, however; in taking a Goldilocks dose of heroin, as it were. 'For me, it was a social drug,' he says. 'If I took too much, it wasn't, but if I took the right amount, I was more loquacious, relaxed. I thought I was being more charming [than usual], but probably other people thought, "What's he on?"' He laughs. Then he explains that what he pursued was a feeling of wellbeing, above all. 'And when you feel wellbeing, you're sociable. You're pouring the drinks. You're cooking the dinner. Nothing was too much trouble.' *You were Ray Liotta in* Goodfellas – *buying the gun, crossing town watching the helicopters, giving instructions over the phone on how to make the bolognaise sauce – without the paranoia. Master of the universe.*

As a child, drug use seemed like 'some far-off, far-fetched' universe. Kelly's parents drank beer and wine – very rarely to excess, though he noticed that the face of his father, John, would become flushed after a few beers at big family gatherings. 'But I never noticed any great change in behaviour or character,' he says. The sixth of nine Kelly children, Paul watched his older brothers leave school and start studying at university around 1969, when he was fourteen. 'There was a lot of counter-culture philosophy and action going on; pushing against the system,' he says. 'Both my brothers were involved in hunger strikes against the Vietnam War. They and their friends were smoking pot. They had a garage out the back [of the house]; I could smell it. So that was around. I didn't get involved in it then.'

He did three years later, on Lameroo Beach in Darwin, having recently turned seventeen. The idea was to travel around the country with a mate for a year. 'We went to Darwin first and we stayed with his brother for a while, and then we lived on the beach for a few weeks,' Kelly says. 'I remember we brought the pot in a little matchbox. It was classic; I still remember thinking, "This isn't working ..."' he says with a fond laugh. 'Then we went for a walk back up towards the town, and then everything got really freaky.

'I never really took to pot in a big way. I found it quite powerful. It made me antisocial, really, and quite introspective. But, later on, playing in bands, a lot of musicians I've worked and played with use pot quite regularly. I found it really hard to smoke pot with people I didn't know, or out among strangers, 'cause I would start to feel too self-conscious, or just wouldn't feel that safe. But with people I knew, it could be quite pleasant. We used it more in the mid-eighties with the Coloured Girls and those guys. But I could never use it before a gig. I'd lose my way. To be performing, you need to always be one step ahead, in a way. I'd be in the middle of a song, and pot would break that.' He laughs.

Sitting back with a joint could be 'a nice unwinder' after gigs, though, or after finishing a recording. 'It makes music sound so great,' he says. 'So, for a while there, I would enjoy pot for listening to music – but among friends, or at home, not long before bed, as long as I didn't have to do anything for which I would have to be functional. But it was really great for enhancing the enjoyment of music.' He pauses. 'I don't really even do that much. I can't remember the last time I smoked a joint. It's never something I've sought or gone out of my way to buy or to find. If it comes my way when I'm in the right situation, I might have a toke,' he says with a wry smile.

As they entered their teens, the Kelly children were offered wine diluted with water with meals at home. At the age of thirteen, Kelly moved into a cellar room, which would later provide him with his first experience of being drunk: in his final year at school, he nicked a bottle of fortified Frontignac wine and started finding his limits, working out when to stop. 'There was a period where I was drinking in my twenties where I would wake up the next day and I couldn't remember how the night had finished off. That scared me a bit,' he says. 'That was a bit of a wake-up call, having those blackouts. So drinking's always been there. I still drink, every day; not a day would go by when I wouldn't have a drink. But I don't drink that much anymore.'

He had to make the mistake of drinking too much before playing shows, too, to learn that it wasn't such a good idea. 'I remember one time in Melbourne, in the late seventies, taking Mandrax before I played.' I've never heard this term before. 'A "mandy",' Kelly replies. 'They were around a lot. Serepax, Mandrax, Rohypnol, barbiturates. And evidently I don't remember much about it. I think I sang everything about half a bar behind the band.' He laughs. Speed was common, too: usually snorted, sometimes injected. 'There was a period of using that quite a bit, especially with the long drives, or as a party enhancer,' Kelly recalls. 'I didn't like to use it too much, because the after-effects were too horrible. Too "flat"; trouble sleeping.'

The double album *Gossip*, which featured the singles 'Before Too Long' and 'Darling It Hurts', was released in 1986 and became Kelly's breakout hit. With success came interstate gig bookings and regular travel between Sydney and Melbourne, the five-piece band eating up those nine hundred-odd kilometres while buzzed on Victoria Bitter and Sudafed – white cold-and-flu pills that contained a yellow nucleus of pseudoephedrine. *The speed kept you sober and the beer took the edge off the speed.* 'When I think about it now,' he says, 'the idea of taking speed actually makes me feel a bit sick in the stomach. I don't really have great memories of that. The cost of taking speed always seemed to outweigh the benefits.'

I get the sense that the young Paul Kelly wasn't held back by any barriers; anything within reach was up for grabs. 'Yeah, I was pretty interested in trying things,' he says. 'That was my philosophy of life: to try as much as I could, to experience whatever I could.' *Like Arthur Rimbaud, we wanted to taste all poisons and distil their essence.* 'I tried acid, and mushrooms, but only had them a couple of times in my life. Again, I find they're too full-on, so it didn't really appeal. I had ecstasy a few times; we used to call it "attack of the friendlies", because you would be best friends with strangers, and give them your phone number, and have deep and meaningful conversations. And the next day, you'd think, "What the hell?"' he says with a laugh. 'So I didn't really stick with that. That seemed a bit false. And, again, the next day was weirdly flat. Anything that takes you up is going to take you down. That's the cost, the pros and cons you've got to weigh up all the time. At some point, the downer outweighs the up.'

It took little more than a promise to a woman and a clean break for Kelly to quit using heroin. *I threw out certain phone numbers, said goodbye to all that. I thought about 'it' every day for a long time. Less now.* This jars with the popular perception that it's the hardest drug of all to kick; that relapses are common; that substitutes such as methadone and Suboxone are required to ease the body and the brain back towards sobriety. Perhaps this is why Kerry O'Brien grilled Kelly so insistently during that *7.30 Report* interview.

'I was expecting Kerry to ask about it, so I was sort of prepared for that. I didn't expect him to *keep coming*,' says Kelly. He kept coming, all right. 'I felt pretty awful after that. It's not his fault; that's his job. But I felt underprepared. I should've realised he was going to keep coming. But then, when he started asking me, "What do I say to my kids?" it gave me the perfect out, because I'm not on there to talk about how I talk to my children, which I told him.'

He never watched the interview afterwards. 'I'm probably doing this,' he says, wringing his hands in mock anxiety. I tell him that his hands are fine, but his facial expression goes from a smile to almost a frown towards the end of the questioning, especially when asked about his kids and giving advice to potential heroin users. When I remind him of his line about how the last thing the world needs is pop singers giving advice, he laughs.

'I got some criticism from people I know saying, "You made it sound too attractive, and that's irresponsible,"' he says. 'They might be right. Like I said, maybe the damnation/ redemption scenario is ultimately correct, because I never managed to keep it happily recreational all my life. At some point, I could feel the danger looming and had to get out.' With a small laugh, he says, 'I wouldn't recommend it.'

While he maintains that his usage was always closer to recreational than dependent, and that he didn't experience physical cravings for the drug or feel sick in its absence, the mental draw could be remarkably strong. 'That was probably when I realised I was thinking about it too much,' he says. 'Once the little thought starts going in your mind – "It'd be nice to have some …" – you just cannot get rid of that thought. That was the most insidious part, the mental thing. "It'll be fine; just one little one will be fine."'

The reason why heroin is so bad, Kelly says, is because it's so good. 'People get dragged into it because it's very attractive, so I thought I had to write about why I liked it, how it made me feel, and why I liked to use it. So that's what I did: I tried to describe it as accurately as possible, the way that I used it, which is quite true for a lot of people. Not everyone who has heroin and continues to use it becomes an addict straight off. I knew quite a few people that would just take it occasionally. Some of them were doing this over twenty years – the same sort of period as me. All those people ended up getting into real strife with it. I don't know anyone successful who successfully continued to do it.

'Maybe, looking back, I might have made it seem easy, because once I decided to quit, I just quit. I didn't have a relapse, like lots of people. It was as simple as that; I quit all use completely quite cleanly. I write about that fairly matter-of-factly in the book, so that might give the impression that it's very easy.' Logic suggests, however, that just because it was easy for Kelly doesn't mean that it will be for the next person.

In sum, the singer says he's 'pretty much done' with drugs. What do you see in the rear-view mirror? I ask. Fond memories? 'Fond and regretful; a bit of both,' he replies. 'It was risky behaviour. I also probably feel a little bit lucky. Maybe a bit relieved.' When I tell him that I'm curious to try heroin at some point, he replies with a gentle laugh, 'Good luck.' But I'm cautious, of course, I assure him. 'That's the main word,' he says. 'If you don't respect them, they won't respect you.'

BERTIE BLACKMAN

Her first thought was that she was having a heart attack. One night, on tour on Queensland's Sunshine Coast in early 2009, the twenty-six-year-old had a sudden and terrible feeling: she couldn't breathe. Severe chest pains were accompanied by shallow breaths. She was scared, and so were her bandmates. Next stop: the emergency department of Noosa Hospital. The diagnosis: inflamed cartilage rubbing against her ribcage. The cause: overexertion on and off stage; drinking too much alcohol too often, and feeling invincible as a result. Yet here was concrete proof that the young musician was doing serious damage to her health and that perhaps it might be a good idea to rethink things.

Anyone who saw Beatrice 'Bertie' Blackman perform in the years leading up to that health scare would have found her to be one of Australia's most arresting rock frontwomen. Night after night, she'd be slugging from a bottle of Jameson between singing into the microphone, thoroughly inhabiting the loose, hedonistic image that rock history has conditioned us to expect, if not demand. Blackman's body became conditioned to the abuse: she could drink a bottle of whisky each night, then hop in the van the next morning, inured to the ill effects. And off to the next city she'd roll, to do it all over again.

When the Sydney-born singer's half-brother saw her drinking whisky on stage a couple of years prior to that Noosa Hospital incident, he reported back to Bertie's mother using a particular noun with a long history in the Blackman family: *alcoholic*. 'It's a big word for me, because when I think of "alcoholic", I think of my dad,' she says. 'In a way, I did feel like I needed to drink to cope with my nerves and anxiety. I'm sure my father drank for a lot of reasons, but he was painfully shy, and maybe he suffered from anxiety, too. He was kind of self-medicating.' Like father, like daughter – at least, for a while. 'I did get pretty good at hiding it from my family,' she says. 'I didn't wake up and start drinking first thing in the morning. But it was part of my day.'

Victoria Bitter in a can conjures up a nostalgic smell for Blackman: it reminds her of waking up to her father passed out in the morning, and observing the detritus of his workplace. Charles Blackman was a painter who worked late into the night. He'd start drinking at around 3 am and be out of his tree by 7 am, when his daughter would arise just as he'd be winding down. Her parents fought a lot because of his drinking. Blackman's mother confessed that she was something of a teenage alcoholic, too: at age fourteen, she'd go through a bottle of gin every weekend. But she had outgrown that habit by the time she met Charles five years later.

He hadn't outgrown drinking heavily, though, and as a result Blackman was surrounded by alcohol from a young age. This early, consistent exposure had an interesting effect on her. There was one party where the curious youngster took sips from plenty of guests' drinks, felt the woozy effects for the first time and woke up sick the next day, but otherwise she steered clear of booze until her late teens. 'When everyone else was drinking, I wasn't interested,' she says. It was a similar story with pot and acid. 'I found it all a bit boring, I guess because I'd been around it so much. When it's accepted, in a way, it's not like I needed to rebel in any way against it. And then, as a result, I'm not a drug addict!' She laughs.

We are talking in a light-filled building that looks out onto a spacious home owned by Blackman's manager, Mark Richardson, at Arthurs Seat, seventy-five kilometres south-east of Melbourne on the Mornington Peninsula. Featuring a desk, a sofa, a heater and all manner of musical instruments, this is where the slight thirty-one-year-old with messy, black hair has holed herself up while working on new material. It's a quiet, picturesque spot that's far removed from the clamour of inner-city Melbourne, where Blackman lives.

Abstaining from alcohol as a touring musician takes an incredible amount of self-control. Emerging artists are offered free drinks in lieu of payment; all the way from inner-city-pub circuits to stadium shows, booze-filled riders are the norm. 'It really is part of the lifestyle of being a musician,' Blackman says. 'There's a lot of alcohol there. When I got into my twenties and was playing lots of gigs, I went through a stage for a while where I did drink too much. But it's because you spend so much time at pubs. You're waiting around for six hours to play gigs, there's just nothing else …' She pauses, catching herself on that excuse.

'It's not like there's nothing else to do,' she clarifies, 'but when it's around and everyone else is doing it, you kind of just fall into this pattern of doing that. And then I started drinking on stage, out of a whisky bottle. Then I found myself drinking the whisky rather than drinking water, and by the end of the gig I'd be really, really smashed – and not really realising it, or doing it on purpose.' The Jameson-slugging rock-chick image: was that an emulation of another performer she admired? 'No, I just thought it looked cool!' She laughs.

The health scare at age twenty-six put paid to that habit. There was another reason: concern that she was developing a reputation for it. 'I also just didn't want to be seen as "trashed on stage",' she says. 'I didn't want to be known as that kind of person, because there are certain musicians who I know as being heavy drinkers, and people go, "Oh, they're just drunk again …" When you're around people and you see them roll their eyes: "Oh, wasted again. And it's 11 am." It's like trashing a tour bus: it just gets a bit old.'

Blackman attributes her increasing reliance on alcohol throughout her mid-twenties to her anxiety disorder. 'It started off being associated with gigs,' she says. 'I'd vomit fifteen times before going on stage, not be able to eat, and then vomit a bunch of times when I got off stage, because I was so exhausted. And then I found myself drinking more, as a result of that, to try and cope with the nerves. It's something a lot of people automatically do; if you have a stressful day, you have a glass of wine, and it does relax you a bit. It's a numbing agent.

'But then, as the anxiety got worse, I would start drinking earlier in the day if I was playing a gig that night. I think my body got confused between a creative adrenaline and a nervous adrenaline – the whole fight-or-flight thing. When the body starts to get confused about the reasons why you're feeling that anxiety, it's all in your head. It spins out of control.'

Her mental state worsened to the point where Blackman was forced to cancel several shows prior to the release of *Secrets and Lies* in 2009. For a time, she couldn't leave the house. The thought of performing her music before a crowd sent her into panic mode. Blackman took six months off to work through coping mechanisms.

During the first session with her psychiatrist, he counted the number of breaths she was taking in a minute. 'He said that I was taking three times the amount of breaths that you should normally, which meant that I was basically in a constant state of hyperventilation,' Blackman says. 'My body was constantly in that fight-or-flight state, which meant that it was very easy to trigger me off into feeling panicked, or feeling like I needed to have a drink to deal with that.' She was diagnosed with anxiety disorder and depression, but it took her a month to start taking Zoloft, the antidepressant that she had been prescribed.

'For the first few months, I felt ashamed to call my mum and tell her about that,' she says. 'It felt like it was a taboo thing to do. I had to be secretive about it.' This is a curious contrast: Blackman's mum was relatively comfortable with the idea of smoking marijuana when her daughter was growing up, yet Blackman felt that she had to hide her use of antidepressants. 'I wanted to be strong, healthy and successful in my life, and happy,' she says. 'You feel like you've failed, in a way, feeling [depressed], because you let it all get the better of you.'

Yet the reality is that you can't easily change how your brain works, I say. 'No,' she replies. 'And if you have anxiety disorder, you're predisposed to it. It's the same with depression. It's always going to be there. Once you figure out that you will be living with it for the rest of your life, in one way or another, you go, "Okay," and you just figure out the way that's best for you to be able to live with that, and deal with it. You know that some days during the week are going to be harder than others. You just have things set in place to help you deal with that.' She pauses, then says with a laugh, 'Preferably not being drugs!'

Besides those that have been prescribed, of course. For Blackman, the Zoloft worked. 'It was lucky; it only took one go, thank god,' she says. 'But it took my body four months to get used to the drug. Taking just crumbs [of a pill] at a time would really affect me. I was really ill for a couple of weeks, feeling worse than I [already] did. I have a sensitive constitution. But, after that, it's been really helpful for me. The lifestyle that I have, of having to be "on form" all the time – with gigs and press and being creative and all that stuff – there's a lot of pressure you put on yourself. In the end, it's helped me cope. It didn't take any of the feelings away. They still kept appearing; they still appear now. I'm much more happy within myself now than I was then. But that comes with a bit of wisdom – getting older, learning about yourself.'

Her psychiatrist worked through cognitive therapies that addressed Blackman's anxiety, including inducing 'safe' panic attacks and instructing her to write down all of her feelings before and after hyperventilating. The singer would do this five times in a row, until she got to a point where the impending-doom sensation became more manageable. This brain-retraining exercise was incredibly valuable to her, to the point where nausea remains one of her few triggers for anxiety. What she found strange after being prescribed these drugs to manage her mental health, though, was that some people would ask whether they could have a Zoloft, or a Valium, for the purposes of recreational abuse. To which Blackman would reply, with a raised eyebrow, 'No, I need that ...'

I ask whether she was concerned that the Zoloft might wipe the edge off her creativity – her life's work, and her main source of income. 'Yeah,' she replies. 'And I have been on high doses of Zoloft where I just didn't really feel very creative at all. But I've been on Zoloft now for five years. I mean, I've made records in that time.' This is true: two excellent indie-pop records, in *Secrets and Lies* and 2012's *Pope Innocent X*.

'My therapist made sure that I told him if I was ever feeling like I wasn't creative, [so that] we could change the dosage, because he didn't want that to numb [me] out,' she says. 'But I think with the kind of medication that I'm on, it's not like lithium or anything like that, where it really dulls you out. With all medication, it really should bring you back to a level like this ...' To demonstrate, she moves her hand from down near her knees to her midsection, signifying a happy medium.

She pauses, then says, 'I did go through a few moments of feeling really suicidal, and not being able to be in control of that anxiety, and the constant panic attacks and stuff. And because I was experiencing them for a while before I got any help, as well.' I ask her if this is pre-medication. She nods. 'I realised I'd probably been experiencing the panic attacks heavily for around two years before I went and got any proper help,' she says. 'I did try a lot of other types of therapy, like meditation, psychologists, counsellors, yoga; I tried everything before going to a psychiatrist, because I knew that by going to a psychiatrist they would probably prescribe antidepressants. Stubborn,' she says, following a sheepish chuckle.

At the time of our meeting in June 2013, however, Blackman tells me that she is experimenting with reducing her dose of Zoloft. 'I don't want to be on it anymore,' she says. 'I'm at a stage where, right now, everything isn't hectic, so I feel like now is a good time to try and get off it, because if I feel like I can cope [now], everything's cool. I don't think it'd be a good time to wean myself off the drugs if I was in high stress. I don't think I'd be strong enough to cope with that. So where I am now is pretty good; I'm being very creative.' The room in which we speak seems an ideal means to that end: it contains a bass, guitars, keyboards, amplifiers, a drum kit and a fat notebook that the songwriter looks to have half-filled with ideas for a fifth album.

It's only since she began taking medication that Blackman has felt comfortable with speaking about these highly personal matters of mental health and illness. 'But since feeling more in control, I quite enjoy talking about it,' she says. 'The more you can help other people with it – to make it easier for them than it was for you – the better. If I'm open about it, then young musicians might feel like they're not alone. I wish that I'd known about anxiety when I was a bit younger.'

I ask whether she has ever spoken about these matters with her father, Charles, who is one of Australia's best-known visual artists. 'No, I wish I'd been able to,' she replies. 'My dad has Korsakoff's syndrome, which is alcoholic dementia. He's had that since I was fourteen or fifteen. Before then, he was in and out of rehab since I was about ten. I feel sad sometimes that I haven't been able to communicate with him about his drinking, or why he drank. A lot of things about his past, certain decisions, and stuff like that. It's obvious that he's suffered, 'cause no one's an alcoholic that's really happy.' Then, with a rueful smile, she says, 'Or not that I know of.'

So, given her journey to mental health, where does illicit drug use fit into Blackman's life since she began taking antidepressants five years ago? 'Cocaine will appear every now and then, and I'll have a bit of that,' she replies. 'I've never been a big ecstasy taker. I took it a few times; I think it was at Schoolies that I took it for the first time, and it was really great! But then the next time I had it, it was just not good.'

For anxiety-related reasons? She nods. 'It always induces some kind of anxiety,' Blackman says. 'For me, it's a couple of days of really feeling chemically right out of whack. It's not worth it for me. And my inner dialogue starts up [while high]: "Don't act like that, you're being obvious, people know that you're on drugs." Or I'm thinking, "Why are they all having a good time on it and I'm not?" It's an unpleasantly self-conscious situation. But I am around it occasionally, and I don't frown on it or anything. Recreational drugs in a safe environment are cool. I mean, they exist. It's just that I make the choice now to not partake, because I know that, for me and my mental health, it's not good.

'Plus, there are only so many nights of talking crap to people that you can do, before it just becomes really boring.' She laughs. 'And then it just becomes something that keeps you awake, and it's like, well, for what? 'Cause now everyone's just talking crap to each other. Nothing productive is going on.' Blackman says that, although she first smoked pot at age eleven, she has never been able do it with much success; it makes her 'curl into a retarded ball', unable to function. Early attempts to emulate Hendrix by smoking a joint on her lonesome and writing music at age fourteen proved disastrous, inducing one of the singer's first panic attacks.

This physical reaction may be a blessing in disguise, however. 'I think, in a way, it's good that I can't function creatively on drugs, just because of my bloodline: my father, and then my mother's father was an alcoholic as well,' she says. 'There's a lot of alcoholics in my family, so I'm very conscious of [having] an addictive kind of personality. It's more the escapism, really. And I like that, because of what I do. I live up in my imagination a lot of the time. Any excuse to remain there is good for me – though I've been enjoying earth a little bit more lately.' She smiles.

For Blackman, recreational drug use has always been a matter of satisfying her curiosity. The first experience with each drug is subject to close internal observation, as she learns first-hand how it works, and how it makes her feel. This curiosity has a limit, however. 'I won't ever try heroin or acid, or any of those dirty, chemical drugs,' she says. 'I did have magic mushrooms once, in Thailand, on a beach. It was magic-mushroom thickshake. That's the only hallucinogen I've ever done. It was a very strange six hours. That was the most out of control I've been on a drug, in terms of having literally no control of how my body was feeling at all. I didn't like it so much in that way. When I got over it, I was like, "Well, I'm never going to do that again!"'

She pauses as if hit by a sudden realisation, then laughs at herself in retrospect. 'I mean, it probably wasn't a safe environment to try something for the first time! Some strange drug given to you by a stranger on a beach in a foreign country!'

Heroin is off her to-do list because some friends of the family have a history with that drug. It didn't end particularly well, though she does tell an unpublishable story about being taken on drug runs by her babysitter as a small child – which she only learnt a few years ago, much to her surprise. 'Street cred!' She laughs. 'Sitting in a pram in a crack den! God …' Blackman shakes her head. 'The way that I think about heroin is that, if I tried it once, I'd be addicted to it, and I wouldn't have any control over that,' she says. 'That's not [based on] fact; I just think that's what's going to happen to me. You just look at the people that are hooked on it; it's just awful. It seems like you enter that world, and people find it really hard to get out of it.'

'Acid' is a word with poor connotations in her world, too. 'I don't really want to put it in my body,' she says. I ask her, What about 'LSD'? Does that sound better? 'It does!' she replies, perking up, her voice raising in pitch. 'Because I go, "Yeah, I'd probably try that!" For me, it's definitely got to be pitched in the correct way.' She laughs. '"LSD" sounds like a French name, like it's melted in some sugar cube. I'd probably be like, "Yeah, okay. I'd like to try LSD once." A pure, proper thing.'

I tell her that I took acid for the first time two days prior to this interview. I went to a driving range with some friends, who were all sober. The long, green field topped with white balls was a great locale for tripping. I thoroughly enjoyed it. 'Awesome,' she replies. 'That's great. I like the idea of doing stuff like that, because if you're in an environment that you know you're going to be in, and you're around people that you know really well, I think social experiences like that can be really interesting.'

As a student of the 'independent, artistic' International Grammar School in Ultimo, Blackman was shown videos from a young age about the effects of different kinds of drugs. She recalls a documentary that investigated whether cannabis is addictive, based on academic research. 'I must have had really good teachers,' she says. 'And I guess I just presumed that everyone else had that.

'I certainly think the younger you get children knowing about how drugs will affect you – what they are, what they mean, and what's in them – the better,' she says. 'Obviously, not [teaching] a four-year-old, but as soon as you're old enough to understand. As soon as I was old enough to take a drug, which was the age of eleven, I was engaging in that. I think people should know exactly what they're putting in their body. It's your decision, because you're doing it.'

I didn't have a sensible, responsible drug education like Blackman's. I wish that I did. At Bundaberg State High School, there was complete silence about drug use in all subjects – even health and physical education, which seems like it would have been the best place to raise the issue. As a result, my education was cultivated slowly, in piecemeal fashion, from a series of unreliable sources: hearsay, pop culture, friends.

'I think it's natural for everyone to be really curious about drugs,' Blackman says. 'You took acid on the weekend. People should go and do it. I would never say "don't take drugs" or anything, because I still occasionally do it. I think if you have an education, then you know to a point what you're doing, and what you're putting in your body. If you're damaging yourself, or wanting to go down that path, you'll find whatever you can to do that. But it all stems from whether or not you're happy in yourself.'

MICK HARVEY

Amphetamine is best known as a drug of alertness: snort or shoot a line of speed and you'll be awake far longer than the body can usually tolerate. The avoidance of sleep is one of its major benefits, especially for creative people who feel compelled to spend their time on this earth productively, rather than being laid out in bed for one-third of every day. But the drug can be used medicinally in this sense, too, especially if you're in a band where others are burning the proverbial candle for days on end. As Mick Harvey found, using amphetamine was sometimes the only way to keep up with Nick Cave and the Bad Seeds, the band that he co-founded and managed.

In the mid-eighties, while based in Berlin, the guitarist would look around the studio and realise that his bandmates were invariably loaded on one substance or another. He'd partake in half a line of speed and stay up for two days. 'I don't know why they would keep going back and taking another line every two hours,' he says. 'There was no need whatsoever!' Sometimes, the group would spill into a bar at seven in the morning and rage on. All of this was fun to Harvey, then in his mid-twenties, who thoroughly enjoyed being part of a band perceived then – and now – as one of Australia's edgiest rock groups. Speed was incredibly useful on those occasions, but its medicinal purposes only stretched so far. 'I certainly never had a desire to continue to take it every day, or to deliberately go and find some and party,' he says. 'I just didn't really do that.'

Those six words evoke the popular characterisation of Mick Harvey as a quintessential 'straight man'. He just didn't really do drugs, we've been led to believe, even though he was a founding member of two bands known for consumption: the Bad Seeds and its preceding incarnation, The Birthday Party. Regardless of the truth of Harvey's own intake, the perception of excess that surrounded these outfits wasn't exactly bad for business, either.

'To some degree, there were aspects of what was happening that was feeding into the creative work, in an odd way; not always in a *good* way,' he says of the latter band's output around 1980. 'And [feeding] into the whole mindset and attitude of the thing, which was the public image around it. We were being kind of rebellious, kind of "on the edge". When the balance was right, it would actually work in our favour. I could see that. There were some nights where the degree to which certain members of the band were "out of it", but we were still able to play really well, would create a very, very unusual vibe, a very dangerous kind of atmosphere. It was really exciting; they were just amazing shows. But you couldn't harness it in any way at all. It was completely random.

It wasn't like I thought, "Oh, if everyone would just clean up, the band would be better." It actually wouldn't have been.'

Cocktails of heroin, alcohol and speed were flowing through the veins of several musicians, adding to the unpredictable nature of each Birthday Party show. 'I wasn't part of that,' says Harvey. 'Just as well. I mean, if everyone in the band had been doing it, it would've been ...' He pauses. 'At least there were a couple of anchors there.' With Harvey on guitar and a dependable percussionist locked onto the beat, the others could freewheel and improvise wherever the mood or mix took them. 'There was a wild side to what could be going on that was pretty amazing sometimes,' says Harvey. 'And I could see that, so I wasn't *anti* what was going on, particularly.'

On stage, intoxication could be an asset. This was rarely the case in any other situation, though, particularly when Harvey became manager through necessity – 'there was no one else there to do it', he notes – and began learning on the job, as it were. The pressure would build within him until, at a crucial point, he'd have a meltdown and blow his lid at those who surrounded him. 'Things would be happening that were getting absolutely preposterous,' he wryly notes. The stoned band members would look up in shock, slurring to each other, 'Oh, what's the matter with Mick?'

'I'd just *lose it*, and nobody would understand,' he tells me. 'They'd just think I had a really terrible temper. It was like, Christ!' He sighs in frustration at the memories. 'God! The stuff I'd been putting up with; it was almost *unbelievable*. I mean, I used to have quite a bad temper sometimes. But they had no notion of what I'd been putting up with.'

Sitting there, hour by hour, some of the band members wouldn't be thinking about their behaviour of the past few days that might have been problematic for a manager whose job it was to corral them into action to meet studio deadlines, board flights and buses, make it to the sound check. 'After they all "cleaned up" – and Nick hates that term, so I'll continue to use it,' he smirks, 'some of them would go through the twelve steps [rehab program], and sometimes they'd come and apologise to me about stuff they'd done.' Harvey would inevitably respond by muttering a dismissive *whatever* under his breath. What was he meant to say to that? He wasn't sure.

'Usually, they'd get to that phase, and then just start abusing me about how I'd [reacted], which was really charming,' he says. 'I'd have to explain, "Look, I know that I lose my temper with you occasionally, but what you don't understand is that it was over a long period of time. That was the way I handled it, by not getting angry, just coping with it for a week at a time, and then cracking. I know it wasn't the best way to handle it, but it's the only way I could do it."'

There is a pause in conversation while we both consider those words. Suddenly, Harvey bursts out laughing for the first time. 'I don't know what they made of that!' he exclaims. 'I've got no idea. They just remember these incidents where I'd be angry at them, yelling at them about something, and they'd see no correlation.' He laughs again. 'It's just unbelievable.'

Mick Harvey owns a studio in a nondescript laneway in North Melbourne. As I arrive at the gate, I happen to meet with a passing mailman, who can see that I'm heading into the property. He cheerfully hands me a few letters, which I take in to Harvey. 'You've got mail!' are among the first words

I say to him. This entrance throws him, I think; we don't properly shake hands and say hello for a couple of minutes, instead making small-talk. This icy reception is in line with my expectations, for reasons I can't really place: I had supposed that Harvey might be a difficult interview subject, and these first few minutes set that tone, as we both hover awkwardly in the kitchen-cum-living room.

But, soon enough, the fifty-four-year-old with striking white hair and piercing blue eyes reveals his true nature. Warm and friendly to a fault, he shows me into the adjoining rehearsal room, which is stacked with an impressive array of instruments and amplifiers. A drum kit is set up at the far end, beneath a striking, enormous artwork by Italian painter Michelangelo Russo. Harvey had been puzzling over a computer prior to my arrival: his twelve-year-old son uses a machine in the music room to play video games. He's in the midst of downloading a zombie shooter called *Left 4 Dead 2* using Steam, a software platform with more than its fair share of quirks. I never thought I'd be sharing Steam grievances with Harvey within minutes of our meeting, but that's exactly what happens.

During our interview at a kitchen table beneath a set of fascinating pinhole photographs, Harvey makes clear that it's not as though decades spent in a social milieu rooted in heavy drug use is a barrel of laughs, not even close. 'It had some really negative effects on me,' he says. 'It's not like I was unscarred by it.' He recalls an ABC Radio interview on the *Conversation Hour* in the mid-2000s where he was asked how he managed to stay sober while everyone else was high. 'That's a popular history – that I was "straight as a die" while everybody was [not],' Harvey tells me. 'I didn't even say, "Well, actually, sometimes I might have been taking something too, or drinking heavily" – which is true, eventually. I just said, "Oh, you're assuming that when you're around people using like that, you don't get damaged or affected by it."'

To Harvey's surprise and dismay, the *Conversation Hour* host began laughing and said something inane: 'Oh yes, rock and roll!' or words to that effect. 'He just completely missed the point of what I'd said. I was sitting there going, "What's the matter with this guy?" He just wanted to wade into the "sex and drugs and rock and roll" circus, and thought it was really funny.'

Like a punchline, I offer. 'Yeah,' Harvey replies. 'I was trying to make a really serious statement about how the people who aren't using drugs get very adversely affected by being around it, because I was the "straight guy"' – he uses air quotes here – 'across the journey, and was having to deal with that. Everyone says, "I don't know how you coped all those years." And I used to go, "Oh, yeah, I don't really, either." And eventually I realised that I hadn't coped, that it affected me really badly. The eighties affected me really badly, being around that for a long time. It took me quite a while to get realigned, to get back out of that.'

He finds it difficult to pinpoint exactly how he was damaged over that period of prolonged exposure to self-abuse by the people around him. 'It was just that association, I suppose,' he says quietly. 'They have those groups for co-dependents and people like that. I don't think I was a co-dependent; I think I was only really there because of the band. I wasn't along for the journey just because I wanted to help people on drugs, or be around [them] because I actually liked being around them, or something. I didn't, at all. I suppose it just damaged my soul more than anything, really, just having to cope with that for years and years. It really took me a while to back out of that and patch myself up.' He pauses. 'And to feel okay about it.'

Within The Birthday Party, and later within the Bad Seeds, Harvey was not only manager but also bandmate and – importantly – friend to those men. I ask whether it was difficult to separate those roles at times. 'Yeah, it was,' he replies. 'They were all intermingled, I suppose. The Birthday Party broke up; the Bad Seeds started in late '83, and I started another band [a third incarnation of Sydney rock group Crime & the City Solution]. So I was in two bands then, through to the end of the decade. Both were filled with people with drug or drinking problems. And living in Berlin in 1986, it was pretty out of control. All-night bars; speed sent over from Stasi laboratories to corrupt the youth of West Berlin; people with heroin problems ... It was pretty wild.'

And fun, too. Let's not overlook that. If it wasn't enjoyable, why would he have stuck around? 'It was a fantastic social milieu there,' Harvey says, smiling. 'A lot of great friends; a lot of creative activity going on. It was really exciting. But there was this backdrop of a whole lot of weird stuff; people with drug problems; people being really out of it, a lot of the time. That was just the territory I lived through in the eighties. And it did affect me, over time, adversely.'

We won't detail certain musicians' numerous attempts at 'cleaning up'; those are their stories to tell, and theirs alone. All Harvey can do is reflect on how he dealt with those matters at the time, and how they now appear in the rear-view mirror.

'As much as they may have been sitting there thinking I was judging them quietly, not saying anything,' Harvey says of his former bandmates, 'I was not judgemental with people who were using drugs. I was judgemental of some of the behaviour after a while, when it was just completely useless.'

And it's not as though Harvey was a teetotaller who steadfastly refused the experiences that those around him were attracted to. He tried heroin. 'I didn't really like it!' he says with a laugh, after deliberating on the question for a few moments. 'It made you feel a bit sick and delusional about how great everything was, while doing absolutely nothing. It just seemed extremely indulgent to me.'

Up the nose it went, never directly into the vein. 'I've kind of got "hyperdermaphobia",' he says. 'I'm hopeless with needles; I can't go anywhere near 'em.' These days, he's more able to cope with injections, as his high cholesterol requires regular blood tests. But he could never watch his friends shoot up. 'It becomes part of this mythology of the drug-taking; this fetishistic thing, with the needles and stuff,' he says. 'I find it gross, actually. It's really grotesque.'

By the time the Bad Seeds were in a London studio recording *The Boatman's Call* in 1996, Harvey was fed up. The judgement was starting to creep in; the drug abuse had gone on too long. It was beyond a joke; instead, a sad fact of life and an impediment to creativity. Having recently lost his father to a heart attack, aged sixty-nine, Harvey was in a delicate state. The sight of some of his peers being stoned every morning had worn thin. A kind of catatonic world-weariness set in. 'I just didn't need to be there, wasting my time,' he says. 'I just sat in the TV room until I was asked to come in and work on a mix.

I wouldn't go anywhere with them until I was actually asked to come in, 'cause I just couldn't cope with it. I don't know if that's being judgemental, actually. I was just not coping with it. I just didn't need to be around it anymore.'

The problem was not so much the consumption but the fact that the lines between the band members and their personal lives had long since become blurred. As a result, it was quite hard to separate the two. 'If loads of your friends are in these situations, you're talking to half of them about their drug problems, and trying to help them as best you can – which usually [involves] hours and hours of conversations that lead nowhere,' Harvey says. 'It's very, very draining.' Combine that fact with the common issues that surround drug addiction – money problems, dishonesty – and Harvey found himself saddened by the erratic behaviour of those around him. 'It's a really hard thing to deal with over a long period of time. It upsets you.'

He and his wife, Katy Beale, were together already in Berlin, and have remained strong since. But that union was not without its challenges. 'I think it affected our relationship indirectly, because we were around these people that we had relationships with, which impacted back on [us],' Harvey says. 'Then I'd be off on tour half the time. It really created enormous instability inside our relationship. When I finally came out of all of that, it was like ...' He pauses, sighs, then says, 'I just wanted everyone to get better. It was then another decade of struggle with people sort of getting better, and then relapsing, and getting better ...'

'Draining' doesn't seem close to the right word for it. 'I had to find my own stability, and my own course [as to] where I was going, despite anything else. It took a while to realign all of that,' he says. At the heart of this process was the realisation that the actions of others were out of Harvey's control. Little by little, he was able to disassociate from their behaviour. Luckily, he says, almost every person in his life affected by drugs was someone whom he'd known prior to those substances intervening in their friendship.

This is important: if you only ever know someone as a drug user, it certainly colours your perception of them. Harvey knew what these people were like deep down; he could discern that their drug use had added another layer of complexity to their relationship. Whether those layers were positive or negative, he found the inner strength to weather those storms. 'I'm just glad that it's really not around now,' he says. 'I still know people who've got their issues – some people still have heavy drinking problems – but a lot of the drug problems in my age group, people have moved on from it, for the most part.'

Harvey himself moved on from Nick Cave and the Bad Seeds in January 2009, ending a thirty-six-year-long collaboration with the band's frontman. 'They've had to deal with it or they've died,' he says. 'It's one or the other.'

I mention Rowland S. Howard in this context: the distinctive guitarist who joined The Birthday Party in 1978 later formed These Immortal Souls and became an accomplished – if chronically underappreciated – singer and songwriter in his own right. Howard died in December 2009 at the age of fifty from liver cancer, a complication associated with hepatitis C, which was likely contracted from sharing needles earlier in his life. Ultimately, his liver gave up. Since the two had worked closely together for decades, most recently on Howard's final album, 2009's *Pop Crimes*, I ask Harvey whether he views his early demise as a waste, knowing how talented he was.

'It's difficult,' he replies quietly. 'I'm oddly kind of Buddhist in some ways. I just tried to treat it in terms of, "It's what's happening." We would have rehearsed here with him a few times' – he gestures at the adjacent music room – 'around the time of *Pop Crimes*, when we were doing shows. J. P. [Shilo, who played bass and violin in the final incarnation of the band] would see Rowland deteriorating. He'd go, "It's really sad," and I'd be like, "Oh." I mean, it *was* sad, but I couldn't sit there and look at it that way. It felt like that would be me indulging. I just felt like – well, he's got what he's got, and he's still trying to do what he can with his abilities, and he might get better. Just accept what's there, and try and work with it, you know?

'He just had a physical condition in the end, where there were toxins in his system and his liver wasn't dealing with it. Every morning, he was almost getting a bit delirious with it. I couldn't do anything about it. And then he couldn't really play anymore. That was a real shame, and I felt really sorry for Rowland that he couldn't exploit the level of interest there was in his new work, because he'd really been in the …' He pauses, and sighs. 'He'd spent a long time being not really "in favour". He wasn't out of favour, but there wasn't a great level of interest in what he was doing for quite a while there.

'When *Pop Crimes* was in production, there was this huge new groundswell of interest. There were about fifteen years where there wasn't a lot of it. Rowland sensed that very acutely. It was a struggle for him to get people interested in what he was doing – which I know about from different projects that I've been involved in. When you don't get the buzz behind it, it doesn't really have a lot to do with how good the music is; it's just whether there's a willingness to listen. I've seen it too many times. But for Rowland, it was very frustrating for him, and then there was finally this groundswell of interest, and he wasn't able to take advantage of it – or finally get his "just desserts", or something,' he says with a mournful chuckle.

For as long as anyone could remember, Howard – forever rake-thin, with spiked hair and dressed in a smart suit – would perform on stage with a lit cigarette dangling from his lips as he eked out evocative notes on his Fender Jaguar. Harvey, too, was a lifelong smoker but gave up at the age of forty, some thirteen years prior to our conversation. 'I'm a nicotine person,' he says, even now. 'It's a really cool drug, actually.' He laughs as if he's just revealed an embarrassing secret. 'People would think, "Oh, what's it do anyway? They're just smoking and it's not doing anything."'

I admit that I'm one of those people: I've always viewed smoking as a dumb, pointless habit.

'It takes the edge off your emotions, which is really nice for a lot of people who are a bit edgy and prone to being emotional,' Harvey explains. 'It makes it all a bit easier to get through those difficult bits and pieces in the day. And that's why people, when they get aggravated or upset by something, they'll reach for a smoke, 'cause it just takes the edge off your emotions. I really liked that. In fact, for years I'd just be like, "Blow it over here; it's the only cigarette I'm going to get!" I didn't mind passive smoking at all!' He laughs. 'I wasn't one of those reformed, anti-smoking fascists.

'Any mind-altering drug has a different effect: making you happy, or slowing you down, or picking you up. They're all mind-altering substances, and so is nicotine. So it seems like people are just puffing away on this weird weed that smells, but they're getting a dose of this stuff that's helping them cope with their emotions.' Was it hard to quit? I ask. 'Yeah, it is,' he replies. 'People say, "Oh, harder than heroin!" I don't know about that – literally. The thing with smoking is that it's just so readily available, and so easy to go back to, so you really have to be vigilant and just decide, "Nah, I just can't have one." It's a little bit easier to have one than to go and score heroin, if you know what I mean. So maybe that's where the difference lies. But I can't imagine that it's actually a harder addiction to shake than heroin. It's certainly not as extreme a set of sensations that you're dealing with.'

Despite the wide-ranging conversation we've had over the last hour and a half, Mick Harvey ultimately takes the position that illicit drugs aren't necessarily the problem: instead, it comes down to the way in which people choose to use them. 'All drugs can have grave associated problems,' he says. 'First, they've been banned, and then they've been demonised.' Any change on this topic at a governmental level will require a spine, so to speak, and an ability to backtrack on the negative messages that Australians have been sold for decades. 'There's not the political will to do that – or even the awareness, perhaps. And, if there was [an] awareness, then how would they go about doing it? How are they going to change their tune to the public? It's a big job, to re-educate and re-inform.

'Because I've been so surrounded by [illicit drug use], I've seen a lot of the problems that come with it. But I've also seen a lot of people, as well, who've used in different ways and not had problems. So the point about banning it across the board is that then you remove that freedom of choice of those people, too. I mean, why does alcohol remain available when other things aren't? It's not a great drug, at all; [there are] quite an awful lot of negative associations with alcohol abuse, particularly health-wise. It's a shame that Western societies have closed it off so much and made it such a ridiculously complex and bitter issue, because it didn't have to be handled that way. But it has been, and now that's the way it is.'

TINA ARENA

To grow up as a child star is to be pre-judged. We humans tend to compartmentalise individuals at the earliest opportunity; it's a mental short cut that allows us to make broad assumptions about our peers and get on with our day, rather than fussing over nuances and small details. So it was for Tina Arena, who first appeared on the national television program *Young Talent Time* at the age of eight. The small girl with the big voice became a regular fixture on the show, ultimately staying for over six years. Arena was sucked into the vortex of the entertainment business – a decidedly adult playground. Pigeonholed as a singer, and little more than that, she had no choice but to mature fast in a fickle industry where chances are rare and careers can be snuffed out in the blink of an eye.

'Growing up, everybody thinks they know who you are based on one sliver, one little facet of your life,' she says. 'They think that they know exactly who you are. I was like, "These people don't have a clue about who I am." They didn't think that I would be able to think outside myself. But I was fascinated by so many different things. I was genuinely curious about human nature, and politics, and all sorts of things: love, multi-culture, languages, history, art, literature. So I spent a lot of time observing when I was growing up. It's been a great educator for me.'

The young performer learnt a lot about human behaviour on the job, as it were. She developed conversational skills and found the value of asking the right questions of the right people. An attuned intuition bloomed. 'I'm somebody that's pretty instinctual,' Arena says. 'I have unbelievable feelings, and feel people's energies as well. I know when someone is really comfortable and liberated, and when they're not.'

The music business afforded her glimpses of the hedonistic side of human consumption, too. 'There were people surrounding me that were doing things that I was really quite unaware of. I was in situations with people, famous musicians and so forth – who I can't name, for obvious reasons – but I'd look at [what they were doing], and I was like, "Oh …"' She laughs at her youthful naivety. 'I thought, "Well, it's their rapport." I was a little bit too frightened of it. So I just observed.'

It was in 1977, at the age of nine, that Arena first began to understand the effects that drugs could have on the human mind and body. Her mother, Franca, slipped a couple of discs in her spine in a car accident. For over a year, her mother was practically bedridden. 'Mum was taking a considerable amount of Valium to numb her pain,' Arena recalls. 'I do remember my mother being different: cloudy, foggy. It was only when I got a little bit older that I realised what Valium was, and its effects. I went, "Oh, okay, that explains why Mum was foggy."'

The Arena family were never big drinkers, and talking frankly about any kind of illicit drug was an impossibility. As Arena matured, however, her mother gave her some advice: 'If you go to a club, make sure you always keep your hand over your glass, because you never know. You could get your drink spiked.' Which proved to be a prophetic suggestion. 'As it turned out, I was about eighteen and did have one of my drinks spiked. That was somewhat of a disconcerting experience for me,' says Arena, perhaps understating the incident. 'But I was such a feisty young girl, and I was so street-smart, that I knew what was happening to me a little bit into it. I went, "Okay, this is something that I control. It doesn't control me." So I was very aware, pretty early on, about how to try and deal with that.'

While chalking that one up to experience, Arena thinks back to the night and says, 'Shit, that was pretty wild. I remember being together, though, because there were quite a few things that I remember of that evening. Fortunately for me, I didn't end up in any compromising moment – which is not always the case for young people.' She pauses. 'Shit, I couldn't believe I kept my scruples about that night. It was unbelievable. I must have been lucky, you know, because it's not always the case. I was eighteen years old; those drugs were around a long time ago, weren't they? I'm forty-five now.'

We meet on a Friday morning at the Emporium Hotel in Brisbane. It's July 2013 and Arena is touring as part of the Queensland Music Festival; later tonight, she will star in a Bee Gees tribute show entitled *How Deep Is Your Love*. A short woman with striking facial features, Arena is a charismatic interviewee with a forthright, passionate style of delivery. She doesn't mince words, and she also fixes me with an intensity of eye contact unlike anyone I've ever spoken to before. Wearing blue jeans, a grey overcoat and a colourful scarf, she removes a fat ring from her left hand and places it on the table, where it remains for the duration of our chat at a window seat inside the empty Emporium bar. She sips from a large coffee mug while a couple of young, male staff perform opening duties nearby.

Her Australian tours have been infrequent in recent years, as the singer has been based in France for over a decade. There, she essentially reinvented herself by finding success in the pop charts while singing in French. Her transformation has been so complete that many of her European fans are likely oblivious of her Australian roots; they'd certainly get a shock if they heard her natural speaking voice, which is peppered with expletives and distinctly Australian colloquialisms. But, considering her young fame and the roller-coaster ride of Arena's performing career in this country – her second album, 1994's *Don't Ask*, sold over two million copies worldwide, but she never again came close to achieving those sales – the relocation to the other side of the world makes a lot of sense. A familiar face to several generations of Australians, her occasional tours here tend to hold true to the adage that absence makes the heart grow fonder. Marketed as a rare commodity, Arena now likely yields larger crowds and higher returns than if she had stayed put for the duration.

Arena's double life, as it were, affords her a unique insight into the culture of her home country. 'It really frustrates me when I come back and I see the rapport that people have with alcohol,' she says, gesturing over at the array of half-drunk bottles behind the bar. 'It's perturbing. In this country, binge-drinking is a real problem. In a lot of European countries, alcohol is introduced to teenagers before they are eighteen; a glass of wine is presented to them with a meal that they enjoy with their parents. It isn't taboo. It's socially acceptable, and monitored under adult supervision, which I think is a more sensible approach. Anglo-Saxons tend to be unbelievably excessive, which is something, as a Mediterranean woman, I don't really understand. I have a very different rapport with alcohol. For me, it's something that is very much a part of a ritualistic thing: eating and gathering, discussion, and the beauty of different glasses of different flavoured wines that go with different plates.'

Arena attributes the Australian attitude to booze to two factors. 'One, a lack of education,' she says. 'And two, quality control. I do believe that we have a problem with the quality of what people are consuming. I instinctively feel that there's something wrong. It's a relationship between food and alcohol, and how the body responds with that association. Europeans have a very different metaphysical relationship with those two things. And even drugs, too; when you see them doing drugs, as I've seen in my time, it's a metaphysical thing. I think diet's got a lot to do with it. People don't pay a lot of attention to diet.'

Australians also put a lot of bad food into their bodies, Arena contends, and, given this country's growth in girth over the last two decades, it'd be difficult to argue otherwise. 'It's something that I observe regularly,' she says. 'Look at the size of people! You get visual confirmation immediately! Everybody says to me, "How come you're so skinny?" It's like, "Well, fuck, I don't starve myself! I never have!" I probably eat a lot more than people would think. I avoid copious quantities. I probably eat a little bit more consistently throughout the day, and drink a lot of water. I don't drink beer. Beer's not great; it bloats people. And I'm not about to do chemical drugs. It just doesn't interest me. But it's incredible, this fascination with them, and this psychological association that people have: that if you're a musician, automatically you are associated with drugs. There's a whole generation out there that have nothing to do with it. That don't care for it.'

Intrigued by this rather abrupt conversational turn, I ask Arena whether she is of that generation. 'I don't really care for it, but I know people of my generation that do take drugs,' she replies. 'I don't judge people who want to experiment with it, who want to understand what that may do to them – what they may feel, what they may think. I'm not interested in judging them. It's not my job to.'

Arena's own experimentation with drugs began in her mid-twenties. 'It was grass,' she says with a laugh. 'That was about it, really.' I laugh, too, because it's a rare treat to hear anyone call cannabis by that name. It reminds me of the street slang for 'police informant', which I learnt while watching *The Bill* in my childhood. 'It wasn't anything chemical, 'cause I didn't understand what the effects of anything were,' Arena says. 'I was very hesitant. I was a bit frightened of it, really. And, also, frightened because of the kind of personality that I have. Being a pretty strong character, it could be pretty easy to get addicted to this sort of stuff. Funnily enough, I had a strong enough sense to just go' – she clicks her tongue and gives a disapproving shake of the head – '*Nuh*. I'm probably better off staying away. So grass was what I really experimented with. I also saw how people couldn't function for days [with other substances]. I worked hard, was touring, doing PR; I love my job and was very focused on doing it well.'

I ask Arena whether she liked smoking weed. 'Yeah, of course!' she replies, smiling. 'It was something I liked. I liked the fact that it was able to bring me down. Somebody like myself, who is pretty "up"; it was about being the absolute opposite. They were the effects that I felt, and I understood it also enables you to scratch a few layers, and become a little bit introverted. And that was interesting as well. So I understood that effect pretty quickly. It was interesting. I was in control. For me, the sense of not having the control was deeply, deeply perturbing. Maybe I am a little bit of a control freak. I don't ever want to feel a situation being out of control. And, while I love serendipity, and I think that happy accidents are very important in life, I was never game enough to get myself into a position where I could lose all my sense of control.'

The singer educated herself when it came to the substances that dealers used to cut chemical drugs with, too, and that knowledge was enough to turn her off. 'It's not exactly something you'd really want to break down the door to put up your nose, or inhale, or swallow,' she says with a laugh. 'It doesn't particularly excite me, knowing that there's some sort of poison cut in something. What the fuck for? Who cares?' It's a similar story with the additional ingredients contained in cigarettes, I offer. 'Absolutely.' Were you ever a smoker? 'Absolutely. I've had my battle with tobacco. That's a *shithouse* addiction.'

Her father was a smoker, as was her mother, to a lesser extent. 'She gave it away early,' says Arena, who started smoking in her early twenties and tried to quit numerous times in the ensuing years. Given her remarkable and distinctive voice, I'm interested to know how smoking affected her singing. 'It can certainly take away the top part of your range,' she replies, taking a clip out of her hair and placing it on the table next to the ring. 'There's no question about that. Singing is a muscle, though, and it depends on how you train it. I've known a lot of singers over the years that are smokers, and that have still been able to sing. I think it depends on how much you smoke, too. I was never a choo-choo train. I've been fortunate enough to have an extraordinary command of my muscle, though.'

Switching gears, I hit Arena with a broad question: why do people take drugs? 'I've never really thought about that,' she says, pausing. 'To experience what it does to them, existentially, I think, 'cause it can do some extraordinary things. I think it may have been ecstasy that was apparently constructed to help couples that were having problems in their marriages. Interesting, isn't it? And then how it kind of veered off the path from there is amazing. But it was apparently something that was used in rehabilitation mode, to help couples sexually connect.' I can certainly appreciate that sentiment, I say, given its empathogenic effects. 'And if that's what their objective was, in the creation of that drug,' she continues, 'well – terrific.'

Arena is somewhat correct here: MDMA was first synthesised in 1912 by a German chemist who sought a substance that would stop abnormal bleeding. It was popularised, however, by the American biochemist Alexander

Shulgin in 1976, who dosed himself before introducing the drug to psychologists, as it was found to be useful during couples therapy for its ability to enhance communication, reduce psychological defences and increase capacity for introspection. 'The fact that it has now evolved and been so incredibly diluted is a tragic reality of today's society, and the financial aspects that come from the selling of drugs,' Arena says. 'Governments make all this revenue from alcohol and tobacco, but then, as a consequence of excessive alcohol and nicotine consumption, there are incredible burdens on our hospitals and medical systems. It's all very interesting.'

She leans forward and imparts her next words with urgency, her brow furrowed and her brown eyes unwavering from mine. 'I'm deeply saddened about what's happening to the generation today: what they do, what they take. The very little respect they have for their bodies, and the ramifications of what it is that they're taking.' You have strong feelings about this, I say. 'Yeah, I do,' she replies. 'Every time I come back to Australia, I open a paper, somebody's overdosed … And the fact that they highlight it in such a way; it's just absolute pandemonium. There seems to be a lot more aggression with drugs and binge-drinking today.'

I tell Arena that my interest in writing this book arose from a desire to shred the cloak of silence that surrounds this topic and to add to our collective understanding about what illicit drugs can do to people, both in a positive and negative sense. The goal is to provide a clear reflection, rather than smoke and mirrors. 'Look at the corporate world. I mean, you want to talk about prevalent drugs …' She exhales dramatically. 'There's a hell of a lot more drugs in the corporate world than there are in the music world, I can tell you. It's got a lot to do with the fact that the music world is certainly not a rich industry, [when compared] to the corporate world. They've got the money to be able to do what they want. Musicians don't.'

This brings to mind a theory that Phil Jamieson told me in the early planning stages of this book. The reason that we tend to associate drugs with musicians, the Grinspoon frontman believes, is their work demands that they promote themselves and their lives in order to sell products and remind the public of their existence, whereas real-estate agents, lawyers and bankers don't necessarily have to promote anything; they can live their whole lives without talking to a journalist. As a result, their use of drugs and their feelings towards the topic are never reported. 'Correct,' Arena replies. 'There are people I know that have nothing to do with music that would put any musician I know to shame. So this perpetual association is quite a fatigued story, I think. From a media perspective, it's really boring.'

She points at me. 'Why don't you go and have a look at the politicians that take drugs, and the corporate leaders that take drugs? Go and have a good look at our financial circles around the world. Has anybody talked to them about their drug use, or their rapport with drugs? No, because no one's brave enough to. However, the musician is always the one to be able to be picked on. It's rather boring.' She gives a cute little yawn to illustrate her point.

Right, I say, taken aback. I feel a little like a naughty schoolboy being lectured in the principal's office. Well, maybe that's my next book, Tina, I say, while she laughs. I'll let you know.

I regain my composure and ask whether she's given any thought to how she'll raise the topic of drugs with her son, Gabriel, who is seven years old at the time of our meeting. 'I think communication is really important,' she replies. 'I don't think it's something you can avoid. I'll cross that bridge when I come to it. I'm not at that bridge yet, but I will be, no different to any other parent. I'll be confronted with it, and I think that the only way I'll be able to deal with it is through sheer honesty, and by telling him everything unadulterated: my experiences, his father's experiences. He already asks questions like that: "Why do you drink? If you drink too much, you know it's bad." Alcohol, tobacco: he's very aware of those things, which is amazing. I think it's wonderful. I really hope that his generation will have enough interesting and intellectual distractions that they won't feel the need, that drugs will be a very passé subject by then.' That's quite optimistic of you, I say. 'Yeah, it is. Somebody's got to have optimism!' She laughs. 'I don't know. I hope so. It's probably not going to be the case.'

The conventional wisdom surrounding illicit drug use is that children are experimenting with drugs younger than ever, and that the substances themselves are becoming more powerful. 'That's all the more reason that this needs to be sincerely dealt with,' she says, leaning forward again. 'Why is the internet filled with ways in which to create drugs? Is it because it's information that should be free and accessible to all? Why are the important things that are coming into our country, from different sources in the world, not monitored a bit more? Unfortunately, I have a fairly cynical perspective on it. It's because, at the end of the day, there is so much money involved. And anywhere that there's money involved, there's something that's virtually impossible to stop. It's such an incredibly lucrative market. It's like a cancer. How do you get rid of it?'

I'm surprised by this sudden contradiction. So you want to get rid of it? 'Oh, it would be great if those kinds of drugs [could] be gone with, absolutely,' she says. 'There are absolutely drugs that I would like to see gone forever. There are a lot of drugs that are very dangerous and that kill a lot of people. They also cause the breakdown of families; children are exploited via drug trafficking – it's a very serious and seedy side. So, yes, it would be a better world without those drugs.'

I ask her which ones she is talking about. 'Heroin, ice: horrible chemical drugs,' she replies. 'The cheap ones that are on the street today, that are being passed through the mail, and that kids are getting online and on street corners for next to nothing. That's something that we need to address as a society a little bit more, I think.'

I tell Arena that I'm familiar with the website that I think she's referring to, where you can order and receive drugs via the postal system. 'Are you?' she replies, surprised. 'I'm not. I was being hypothetical, but everything else is on the internet – why wouldn't this be happening?' It's an anonymous online marketplace called Silk Road, I tell her. I interviewed users and vendors while writing a feature about the site for *Australian Penthouse* in January 2012. After writing about it, I began using the site myself to order drugs: cocaine, MDMA, acid. Because it offers easy access to almost every substance I could want or imagine, legal or otherwise, Silk Road has totally changed how I engage with this aspect of culture.

It's not a stretch to say that it has changed my life. Without Silk Road, my attitude towards illicit drug use would have remained ignorant and intolerant. I wouldn't be writing this book, and I wouldn't be talking to Tina Arena.

'But it's nothing that's controlled, either,' she replies, trying to keep up with me. 'So I'm just wondering, what on earth gives somebody enough courage to be able to take something like that from a website and just sort of go, "Okay, well, I don't know who's manufactured this. I don't know where it comes from. Am I prepared to [take it]?" See, I'm not prepared to do that. I'm not prepared to take that risk. I mean, I'm a mum, too, so it's really different [for me], you know. Maybe twenty years ago, had the website [existed], maybe I would have tried something. Now, I wouldn't have the courage to do anything like that. But with this generation ...'

She pauses, looking at me as if for the first time. 'I would imagine it's your generation, if I can ask you how old are you?' Twenty-five, I reply. 'It is your generation,' she says. 'Do you guys not have any fear about getting something sent through [the mail], ordering something online, receiving it and taking it?'

I tell Arena that I find Silk Road is a far more valuable source of obtaining quality drugs than finding some dodgy guy in a nightclub or an alley and taking whatever he sells me. That kind of transaction, to me, sounds incredibly archaic and risky, because a key feature of the site is a comprehensive seller feedback system – similar to eBay – and a popular discussion forum where users post reviews of products sent out by new vendors, often accompanied by the results of chemical safe-testing kits. Distributing quality drugs is in the dealers' interest. If they sell shit, they'll quickly get bad feedback, which is obviously bad for business.

'Right,' Arena says, intrigued. 'Who controls Silk Road?'

No one knows. There's a team of anonymous people who operate the site infrastructure and take a commission on all sales, but there is no overarching regulation. Given that it's a totally illegal black market, there is no equivalent of the Therapeutic Goods Administration (TGA) overseeing the products sold on the site. But, as a libertarian experiment, it works incredibly well – despite the original incarnation of the site being seized by the FBI in October 2013 and its alleged founder looking at serious prison time. (A second version of Silk Road was up and running within a month of its closure; many of the marketplace's features were redeveloped with a stronger focus on security, both for administrators and users.)

'Oh, I find that amazing,' she says. 'It's a topic that's fascinating, if something like that is controlled by a governing body of hopefully decent people, who are decent enough to know that whatever they make available for people to purchase is not going to kill them. Still, you can't control that, because you never know how a human body's going to react.' And everyone reacts differently, I offer. Arena nods. 'That's something that cannot be controlled. It cannot be policed. But I understand your point. I understand exactly what you're saying.'

Explaining to a global pop star twenty years my senior how I go about sourcing and consuming illicit drugs is not something I thought I'd end up doing when I first conceived of this book, but I'm thoroughly enjoying this moment with Arena in the empty hotel bar. Previously, all I really had ready access to was weed, I tell her, which I would smoke occasionally, but I was never motivated enough to seek out the contacts required to acquire other substances. With Silk Road, I have access to any kind of drug I want – yet with that relative ease of availability comes the responsibility for me to decide how much I take, and when.

At this point, Arena's manager politely interrupts, indicating that we have five minutes left before she's due at Brisbane City Hall for sound check. 'Done,' replies Arena, before again fixing me with her gaze. I steer our conversation to an earlier point she made about how her son, Gabriel, recognises that drinking alcohol is bad. I point out that I had a similar view towards illicit drug use up until 2012; I believed the normalised messages spouted by politicians and the media that, if you take non-legal drugs, you're a bad person who lacks control over your mind and faculties, and who deserves to be punished. I ask Arena how that sits with her, since her son seems to have taken on this idea that drinking a lot is bad.

'Bad *for you*,' she corrects me. 'I don't think Gabriel would be the kind of individual that would ever judge that person. He's seen his mum and dad have a drink; he doesn't think we're bad people. Again, it comes down to an intelligent form of education, which is something we've got a long way to go [towards]. It's a cultural thing. I think it's going to take some time to change that [idea] that people who have a drink are not bad people. We advertise things on television excessively. "Eat this." It's huge. Print and visual media [are] responsible. That's where the responsibility and the accountability starts, before you can even attack the individual psyche, and the individual's discernment.'

Sensing that the conversation is veering down an unexpected path once more, I prompt Arena further. If you're being exposed to those advertising messages, I offer, it's quite hard to push against that tidal wave – especially if you experience a constant barrage, all day, every day. 'Absolutely,' Arena says, leaning forward again. 'And lord knows people have been worn down. Somebody smoking a cigarette on the side of the road is completely ostracised.' She gestures outside to a man experiencing the very social isolation she refers to. 'Okay, it's not great to smoke, I know. But since when does that person need to be ostracised because he's smoking a cigarette? It's not illegal! And yet it's okay to have a hundred thousand people in a sports arena paying *x* amount of dollars to get in the door, to lose their minds for two hours, to *vacate* the aggression they've built up throughout their week, drink whatever, and walk out? That's fine. That's totally fucking acceptable, isn't it? That's where your problem starts.'

Sensing that she's really getting into a rhythm now, I sit back and let Arena take the conversational reins. 'I'm coming from a very different angle. You will never stop people drinking. Having a glass of something is a wonderful [ritual]; something you share. It's great. There's a lot of beauty and value in it. Yet what is in your glass? It's up to you to control how many you decide to put down. But, for me, the start of dealing with this problem goes back to the big lobbies, that are never held accountable. Food quality and control. Alcohol quality and control. Tobacco quality and control. Drug quality and control. Pharmaceutical responsibility. That's where it starts, for me. The rest – they can all talk till they're frickin' blue in the face. That's where the problem needs to be treated from.'

The decision-makers, I offer. '*Voilà*,' she replies, seeming to savour the word. 'And we've got a very, very big problem with the decisions being made on those levels, and in those subjects. People can go to the supermarket: "Buy this white bread, it's on special." For some people, it's the only thing they can afford. Fine. Well, if you as a supermarket chain are making this bread available, because you know that there's obviously a lot of people that can only afford to buy that white bread – as opposed to a spelt bread, or a gluten-free bread, which is much more expensive – make sure that the white bread that you're putting on your supermarket shelves is of decent quality. That's where the problem starts, for me. Whatever it is that you're selling on special – whatever beer brand, whatever alcoholic brand – what is in that bottle? What is in that can? Why are these companies not being held accountable? Fuck, that's so, so simple for me. Yet it's not them, it's *us* – the consumer – being slapped in the face every two seconds. "You've got to eat this, this is great for you!"' She exhales heavily, touching her forehead as if suffering from a sudden migraine. 'Sorry. That's kind of what I think about it.'

I'm glad to hear your thoughts, I say. 'You know, I would be so happy,' she continues, 'if every community and every suburb in the country had their local markets, where people could come in, set up a stall, and sell whatever it is that they've grown. "No, this hasn't been sprayed. There are no pesticides in it, no additives." If it's more expensive, it doesn't matter; it's worth it. You're helping somebody, and we're encouraging people to procreate in a very positive way. Agriculture is really positive. Look at the land we have, yet so much of our land is chemically infested. All these big chains are churning out this stuff, and then they wonder why we're an obese society? And we're also having our medical system saying to us, "You're too fat. We're not going to operate on you." Are you *fucking kidding me*? We've come to that point now' – she starts laughing in disbelief – 'where we're actually saying, "If you're a big drinker, a big smoker or a bad eater, we have the right to refuse to heal you"? *Man!*'

In a 2013 *Good Weekend* profile of the same woman that sits before me, journalist Tim Elliott wrote, 'As with many famous people, she cannot resist the opportunity to air her opinions uninterrupted.' This is a wildly divergent conversation from the one we were having five minutes earlier, but Tina Arena is on a roll and I dare not throw a stick in her spokes. Her manager hovers on the periphery of our interview. Perhaps he feels the same way.

There's a lot of problems along that chain, I say, nodding. 'Fuckin' hell,' Arena says. 'There's a *lot* of links in that chain that need to be greased, I tell you. So that's the way I think of it. I don't know; I may be completely off the planet. And that's okay.' I don't think so, I tell her, perhaps unconvincingly. 'People tell me I'm off the planet,' she continues. 'It's fine. I'll assume it. I don't care. But, you know, I care about what I put in my body. I care about what our family eats. And that's not to say that occasionally we won't do a McDonald's. Absolutely not; that's not the point. But on an everyday level, whatever it is that we consume, it's a responsibility that everybody needs to take stock of, from the manufacturers down. And that goes for drugs. It's the way it goes.'

By this point, all I can manage is a non-committal *hmm*. I certainly agree with what Arena is saying, but, given the purpose of our interview, I'm a little thrown. 'Is that an argument?' she says. 'Is that an interesting angle, or have I completely gone on another tangent?'

She laughs at the perturbed look I'm giving her, and says, 'Andrew, I'm sorry.' I regain my wits and reply that she's on the money, and that it's probably something I should be looking into. 'Well, I think so, darling,' she says with some tenderness. 'Without telling you what to do, because at the end of the day you're a journalist; I'm not. But I've spent a lot of time really thinking about this. I love food, and I have a very privileged life. It's something that I really don't take for granted. I live between two beautiful cultures, that have their strengths and weaknesses, like any culture on the planet. But they've given me incredible depth and perspective to be able to see what it is that we're doing, and I'm able to flirt between both of them.

'So I get to see, and love, the French for that history and that *dialogue*; asking the questions, and [saying], "No, we won't accept that." And you get to this side [Australia], and they take everything. Why? "Don't argue with them. It's not worth it. Don't contest this; don't contest that. Shh. Zip it." Since when? Do they honestly think that we're going to advance by continuing to have that kind of an attitude, to not ask ourselves questions? People want to do drugs; well, then, let's make sure that people do drugs responsibly, and that there are avenues where these people can get access to quality drugs, so then they can experience whatever they want to experience. It's totally their prerogative.'

And get help if they need it, I say. She nods emphatically. 'And get help if they god-damn need it. And don't tell them they're fucking losers. That, for me, is evolution. Not bandaid after bandaid; fine after fine; rule after rule. It's all right – you make the decision for me. *Great*,' she says sarcastically. 'And what am I – just a fucking shell, then?'

I'm impressed by this rant, and tell her so. 'I'm not a shell, baby!' she says with gusto. 'I am a human being. I have a brain. That's what I've been given, and I want to use it to the best of my ability. I'm not here for a long time, but, by god, I want to enjoy every moment that I can while I am here. That's the way I'm looking at life.'

And, with that, Arena smiles, shakes my hand and stalks out of the hotel to a waiting minivan.

TIM LEVINSON

New Year's Eve 2000. A hip-hop group named Dase Team 5000 is playing a show at a warehouse in the inner-city Sydney suburb of Alexandria. Completely improvisational in nature, the band is composed of a bassist, two rappers, three members poking at laptops and, occasionally, a singer. On this night, the group is down an MC, so a solo rapper is tasked with handling vocal duties. His birth name is Tim Levinson, but most in the crowd know him by his stage name, Urthboy. At the age of twenty-two, he is growing in confidence as a writer and performer; so confident, in fact, that he pops an ecstasy pill prior to taking the stage. This decision fits with the occasion: hell, it's New Year's. The mood in the room is euphoric, but it soon becomes apparent that there's one big problem: overcome by the effects of the drug, the rapper is unable to rap.

'I just resorted to wishing people a Happy New Year, and making terribly cringe-worthy sentiments of love to my new girlfriend, Anna,' Levinson recalls. 'It was the best thing that happened when I was a kid: I learnt enough to know never to do that again, because that was just a *baaad* look. But I don't regret it, because it was a great lesson to learn.' Luckily, there were two hungry MCs in the crowd of four hundred who were only too willing to relieve the faltering rapper of his duties. 'It was probably the only time I've been happy to see other MCs hitting me up for the mic in my entire music career!' He laughs.

Though his performance that night was rubbish, musically speaking, Levinson's outpouring of emotion towards his new lady evidently went some way towards sealing the deal with Anna: the pair married in 2003. When I visit their apartment in Sydney's inner west after the rapper picks me up from Marrickville Road in his white hatchback, we discover that a heavily pregnant Anna is wearing fewer clothes than socially acceptable. She isn't expecting a visitor, but averted eyes and a quick dash from the kitchen to the bedroom solves that problem with good grace. Her husband and I sit on a leather lounge and talk, while the afternoon light slowly fades and James Blake plays softly through the speakers. The New Year's Eve anecdote comes up after I ask Levinson – whose short-cropped, ginger hair is offset by a bright-green shirt – how taking drugs can influence live performances.

'It's terrible,' he replies. 'Weed's a shocker for me. Weed is one of those things where you can smoke and perform, and probably three times out of ten it'll enliven it; it'll make things more exciting. I know lots of people who smoke before every gig. For me, it's everything from not being totally clear, to second-guessing myself – a terrible thing to happen on stage – to desert mouth. That's happened many times on stage, particularly in the early years, when you're just partying. "Yeah, I'm going to smoke! I'm going to have such a good time!" We're playing to a sell-out Gaelic Club. There's like seven hundred people in the room, with The Herd, Hermitude or Urthboy'– three hip-hop acts that the performer has been associated with since their inception – 'yet you get out there and all of a sudden you feel like you're not talking clearly to seven hundred people. "When did this become a good idea?"'

Levinson grew up in the small Blue Mountains town of Wentworth Falls, over an hour west of Sydney. As a teenager, cheap booze, weed and freshly picked mushrooms were the favoured mind-altering substances. 'I remember one party in particular, where some feral came along and just had a plastic bag with a whole bunch of dirt and mushrooms in it,' he says. 'It was wet, too, because in the Mountains you have rain that just settles, so you'd have a consistent drizzle for two weeks. This guy had a plastic bag with all this dirt on the inside; it just looked like a grotty rubbish bag. You'd put your hand in, pull out some mushrooms and just eat 'em. *Bam.* Straight down.'

He only ever had a good time on mushrooms; with acid, same deal. 'I never had that much of a hankering that I needed to go and do it again, though, so I haven't since,' he says. 'When I moved to the city, there was such a thing as ecstasy. Never really in the Mountains; in the mid-to-late nineties, maybe there was ecstasy around, but we never came across it. And it was by the by, 'cause our economy was cheap wine and free drugs, like mushrooms or, every now and again, weed. Weed was really expensive. You can get a four-litre cask of wine for eleven bucks or something. That's *economical.*'

I'm amused by his word choice: 'wine', not 'goon', the euphemism widely used by generations of teenage Australian imbibers. 'Goonbag – totally. That's exactly what it was. I was just trying to add an air of sophistication about it.' He smiles. 'Four-litre cask wine, with my friends.' By the glass, held by the stem? 'Sometimes it's just more practical to hold it above your head and turn that little tap on,' he says, mimicking the action, then immediately shuddering at the memory. 'It was *disgusting*. And the worst was "fruity lexia",' he says, referring to a particularly sweet white wine. 'With that, it was as though you deserved to be drunk, because you worked for it. You'd try and drink as much as you could to just get over it, and then everyone would pull a terrible face.' He scrunches up his features to demonstrate. 'You know when you do that face? "I've just put myself through crap, so I better have a good time." That was the economy of scale at that time.'

Levinson was raised in a devout Christian household, where the ethics and morals around illegal substances were always black and white. His family weren't big drinkers. 'Alcohol was probably the only other drug that I was really aware of. There wasn't booze in the fridge until some parts of the family structure started breaking down,' he says. 'That was very symptomatic of that breakdown. But there wasn't wine drunk over meals; the parents didn't really do that.'

Levinson landed his first job at age fourteen, washing dishes at a local guesthouse located seven kilometres from the family home. He was working most nights of the week to earn coin: he'd go to school, then work 6 pm to 11 pm, and either ride his bike home or catch a train. On nights when he took the latter option, he'd spy used cigarette butts on the station platform and light them up. 'As a kid, I was just curious to see what smoking was about,' he says. 'Why were people smoking? I thought it was cool. There were these stubs on the ground, so I thought, "Oh, I could smoke those." Which, now, is just the most disgusting thing I can think of!' He laughs.

An absent father and a mother working long hours to support three children meant that the middle child of the Levinson family was on a long leash in his teenage years. Several of his good friends shared his broken family situation; at these homes, he saw adults using alcohol and marijuana to excess for the first time. 'By that stage, I think I was a bit more aware of it being out there,' he says, between mouthfuls of peanuts. 'But, aside from being a little bit curious, I never really had any really clear link to [drug use], outside of it just being "a bad thing to do".'

At the age of fifteen, Levinson and his friends would experiment with these new vices 'under the cover of darkness'. Their formative pot experiences were born from MacGyver-like ingenuity, improvising with tools and vessels. 'We'd bend a Coke can, stab holes in it with needles or something, shove [the weed] in the back and smoke a "can bong". It was horrible. Leaf weed. You're never really going to get very high off it, but I think I got high a few times.'

This ritual was always a roll of the dice for Levinson, though. 'I never really agreed with smoking,' he says. 'I would "green out", and not handle it very well. Some people can do it till they've consumed a whole room full of smoke, but I was one of those people who could smoke a bong once and I'd be okay, but still a little bit wired. The next time, I'd go green straight away: pass out, vomit, whatever. It seems that people fall into those two camps.'

Ecstasy was an occasional treat that only became available once Levinson moved to Sydney at the age of twenty. At $50 a pill, it was a big investment, but the young musician had some enjoyable experiences with that drug, particularly when combined with the ascendancy of the DJ in the mid-nineties. A hip-hop head at heart, Levinson says he never identified with dance or house music, but he'd occasionally take a pill and go to these events. All of a sudden, it'd be 5 am and the crowd would filter out into the sunlight, annoyed that the night had ended.

'All these "superstar DJs" like Roger Sanchez and Pete Tong started popping up and headlining huge events; people would pay a hundred bucks to go and watch a handful of DJs do a party,' he says. 'It just seemed it was what everyone did. It's so weird, looking back at it, that a type of performer can just be fortunate enough to go through a phase of time where the perceived value is so astronomical that it's just a truth.'

Pills were taken in moderation by Levinson, but some of his friends might take five or six in a night. I react with surprise at this dosage; to me, that amount of MDMA is outrageous. 'That's not even close to the extremities of consumption that I've heard,' he replies. 'What happens is, you have one, you're like, "This is crazy!" You have two: "I'm back sort of where I was." You have three: "This is not nearly the same hit as the first one. I'm just really trying to continue that hit." As they keep on going, obviously they're introducing more foreign substances, and who knows what that's doing? It's not actually getting that first high, but you're still chasing that first high, even though you can never get it back.'

He began to intentionally space out his ecstasy encounters months apart, to the point where two months became four, became six. 'I'd be like, "Whoa, I've only had three pills this year. I must be moving on! I'm really doing this moderation thing well!"' It was never a case of tapering off his usage due to abuse, though; more the fact that Levinson was rarely keen to seek it out. 'Unless you're in that immediate circle of dependence, where [a user] needs someone to share that experience with, to sort of justify their abuse of a drug – "Oh, come on, let's do this! We want to have a good time!" – you'll only come across it every now and then,' he says.

It's been years since Levinson has used ecstasy. He's always steered clear of heroin, having seen its effects a little too close to home. 'I've had some friends on heroin,' he says. 'I found them absolutely detestable, uncommunicative. I pitied them.' He pauses. 'It was almost as though the amount that I detested addicts, and their reliance on [heroin], overwhelmed any curiosity in it,' he says. 'I don't necessarily think I should be proud of that. Friends who were addicted are still friends, and you shouldn't turn your back on them, but I was young and there was nothing about their behaviour that lent any sympathy. I just did not like it at all.

'I find it very hard to tolerate people who have no consideration of others. I lose a lot of empathy. Despite the busyness that I sometimes get myself trapped in, I don't necessarily think it is always purely productive. When I get trapped into that busyness, I can sometimes lose what I think I naturally have: a decent level of empathy. I lose that empathy for people who do not have consideration of others. Even if it doesn't affect me, even if I just see the way they treat other people, I just think, "You're an arsehole." So drugs, quite often, are part of that. Once again, I don't know whether that is a very good thing, because being tolerant and patient for people who have disorders and drug problems is the "enlightened way", but I just haven't always found it that easy.'

His experiences with cocaine are limited to a handful of occasions. Levinson describes it as a cringe-worthy drug. 'There's nothing like feeling like you've got a licence to proudly talk like a helicopter mum.' He smiles. 'As if whatever it is that you've got to offer the world is now being communicated via some excessively proud parent, showing it off to whoever will listen. I had an experience on coke a while ago at a [music] industry event. A friend of mine had a little bag. He probably took a bigger slice [than I did], as people are known to do, when you're as elegant as a drunken punter in a toilet cubicle, stumbling into a satchy bag of white powder, [snorting] through a $50 note that's probably seen more hands than you'll ever see in your entire life. Hygienically, it's quite fuckin' terrible. But anyway, that's that world, isn't it?

'I was there with another industry person, who I was talking to because he was interested in our business [the independent record label Elefant Traks], and I was a little bit out of it. It was a night of celebration. My friend walked up to our conversation and awkwardly tried to join us. He didn't just come up and go, "Oh, hi"; he made this grand pronouncement about how he was going to join in the conversation ...' He pauses the story while we both laugh hard at this classic behaviour of a high person. 'At which point, both myself and this other guy sort of looked at him: "Glad to have you here!", like we were welcoming some sort of foreign dignitary – as opposed to some loud conversation over alcohol and really loud dance music.'

His high friend continued standing there in the party of three, talking excitedly, making all sorts of faces and carrying on in a manner that Levinson says he found 'brilliant. Because I had also had a line of coke, and I was standing there with him, just going, "You're exactly what I could be doing now, if I don't keep my guard up." It was a really good reminder, because nothing makes me cringe more than being full of myself. Not even that he was being overly full of himself; he just urgently needed to impart his "wisdom".'

I return to the $50 note he mentioned earlier, wondering aloud whether the poor hygiene of snorting through circulated currency from a nightclub toilet top might actually be worse for your health than the cocaine itself. 'All those compromises that you make in that moment,' says Levinson, shaking his head with a wary smile. 'I mean, it's the same as the weird decisions that we make in all sorts of ways. I'll quite often go to a cafe and look to the prices of the drinks and be like …' – he sharply inhales, as if clocking high prices chalked onto a blackboard – '"I'll not be too extravagant here. I'll have a coffee and I'll have food." Functional. Eating breakfast. I mean, I could have a piece of toast and survive, but on the road we like to go and eat at cafes. It's part of the little marks in the day that keep you sane. Breakfast. Eat well. Enjoy it. Sane. Go here, do this; sane. You're living outside of your home, you're staying up late, you're drinking, you're waking up tired. You're drained.

'Anyhow, you look at a cafe menu and go, "I won't drink that $6.50 frappé," but then, if you're at the bar, and drinks are $8 each and you're in a round, you buy four of them' – he snaps his fingers – 'without thinking. Obviously, you can't do that forever, but it's just not the same sort of thought process. There's a different approval metre that goes on. It's the same with drugs. Imagine going to a dinner with your grandma or something, and you go to the toilet and just start thinking, "I'm going to have this muffin; I'll put it on the toilet top and I'll rub it along it, then I'll chew on it …" – nothing would be more disgusting.'

He pauses. 'I'm trying to think of some sort of example that's not absolutely preposterous. And that is. As if you'd rub a muffin on top of a toilet!' I laugh and reply that I understand what he's getting at. 'That approval metre is dumbed down when you're trying to get high,' he says.

As Levinson is one of Australia's leading hip-hop artists, I'm curious about his views on where illicit drugs fit into that aspect of music culture. After exhaling, he replies, 'I think it's fairly uncelebrated. It's not anywhere near the glorification that it is in the States. There's no question about that. There's no "sizzurp"' – otherwise known as 'purple drank', or cough syrup – 'or "Purple Pills",' he says, in reference to a popular song by D12 that mentions almost every illicit drug under the sun.

Why? I ask. The rapper points to the possibility of the culture's gatekeepers playing a part in that. 'I'm talking about Triple J and those types,' he says. 'They have a little bit of a "tut-tut" approach to it. I'm not saying that's a good or a bad thing, but it just means that it's not encouraged. Any young group desperate for attention and acclaim are no mugs: they're going to pick up on what's cool and what's not, what's condoned and what's not. I have no doubt that a bunch of these artists that have made a bit of a name for themselves would've probably put out more "drug songs" if that was what Triple J was playing.'

And yet, he says, you'd have to have your head in the sand to not pick up on local hip-hop's obsession with booze. 'In Australia, *we* are all about booze,' he says. 'And no one's tut-tutting anybody for celebrating booze culture. That's the great elephant in the room. Booze culture is just encouraged almost everywhere you go. Celebrated when you make a fool of yourself; celebrated when it's just part of daily life; celebrated when it's given cultural importance. I mean, booze in Australian culture is just king. If an act talked about excessive alcohol consumption, the only thing that would happen would be a bit of a wink, a roll of the eyes, and ...' – he clicks his tongue while shaking his head disapprovingly, but smiling. 'But if it's a harder drug, people will be lining up to talk about the "moral degradation of this music".'

There's a line from 'Keep It Relevant', the second track from Urthboy's 2004 solo debut, *Distant Sense of Random Menace*, that I'm curious about. 'All day with the biro / With or without hydro / Filling up the rhyme book,' he rapped, referring to hydroponic cannabis. Does smoking pot help him write?

'I've come to think that, for me personally, weed is more of a crutch, something to justify creativity,' he replies. 'Sometimes, it does facilitate the creative process, but quite often it's more psychological. You start using it as a carrot. "I'll smoke this, then I'll work on music." Particularly during busy times, it's a way of kicking you up the arse to get you into that spot. That doesn't necessarily mean because you smoke you start writing productively, though – quite often the opposite. It is an individual's question to answer.

'Smoking can sometimes facilitate writing, and getting your head into that space. It can throw an idea in there that you haven't thought of before. There's no question. So maybe it's not just about if it makes you write better; it's a matter of how you balance your motivations. I'm not really sure I can be so sanctimonious to say that that's a crock of shit, you know? That I don't need that, or that no one needs that. I think it's just different for everybody, and sometimes I think it's been really positive. But when people say "I need weed to be creative" or "Weed's really good for creativity", I've never really had any clear proof of that. You can't say that's a fact when you write really good stuff without smoking. Trusting your brain to be able to create solutions for songwriting problems ... Fuck.' He pauses. 'To ever suggest that weed is an essential ingredient in that process is almost to give up on your own abilities.'

The light has faded in the hour and a half we've been talking. Towards the end of our conversation, we're sitting almost in the dark. Outside, it's just started raining. James Blake continues playing softly through the speakers. I ask how illicit drugs fit into the life of the thirty-five-year-old father-to-be.

'I don't really think of drugs in any other way than I think of lifestyle choices that have consequences,' he replies. 'That sounds a bit ambiguous. For example: you drink processed milk and eat meat that has been mass-produced with hormones and different human-generated technological developments in order to be able to sustain the demand of a growing society. Animals live off land where the soil is not as nutritionally rich as what it once was, so the standard of the food that we're eating is very different from what it once was. There's no argument there. So we all make lifestyle choices in these areas. Some of them are condoned by the powers that be; some of them aren't. So, while [drugs] are unregulated, you're taking a gamble whenever that happens. What you're finding, often, is that that gamble is the issue. Not that lifestyle choice [of] "I want to have coke", or "I want to do this thing that, in moderation, is probably a hell of a lot more harmless than drinking, which is socially acceptable".

'So I don't have any strong objections to their existence. No way. Not a chance. I still find people who are addicted to drugs a turn-off, but I feel that's a different issue. I don't think those addictions should be lumped in with the actual thing that they're addicted to. You can be addicted to a fucking phone.' He holds up his iPhone as if swearing an oath in court.

'I'm more addicted to my phone than I am addicted to any substance, and I know that,' he says. 'It doesn't mean that they're comparable, necessarily. But there are all sorts of different addictions. There are addictions that we condone, we're cool with; there are addictions that are symptomatic of the breakdown of society. I don't think it's my right to cast judgement on that too much. If you're addicted to drugs and don't have social awareness, or consideration, that makes you an arsehole. If I'm on my phone, and I'm not paying attention to a social environment that demands my attention, if I'm not being present for people, well, there's an element of me that's an arsehole. And I have to be honest about that. I just spoke to my wife the other night and said, "I'm going to make an effort to not just be everywhere with my phone." It's actually something of significance to our relationship. She doesn't even give me a hard time [about it]; I recognise it in myself.'

That fateful New Year's Eve gig with Dase Team 5000, where Tim Levinson learnt never to take ecstasy before taking the stage, was a gift. Not just because he ended up marrying Anna, but because it was a formative experience in terms of his own life; a cautionary tale that he can share with other people, whether they're hip-hop MCs or not.

'When it's bad, there's almost no alternative but to warn of those consequences,' he says. 'You'd be neglecting your own duties as a good human to not try and warn people that this might happen. I can understand why people take real hard-line approaches to drugs. But, for the vast majority of people, it's a round peg in a square hole. It doesn't quite make sense to the lives that they're leading. So people need to be able to experience these things, and learn from them. There are going to be people that don't learn; [some] people's lives are going to be ruined from it. But that doesn't necessarily mean that it's a more logical solution to take a blanket approach to it and punish other people.'

LINDY MORRISON

One step above sideshow alley. That's how Belinda 'Lindy' Morrison describes the crooked lens through which many Australians view professional music-makers. 'The public doesn't like musicians,' she says, fixing me with hard eyes. 'Seriously. Really. They don't have a good perception of musicians. They don't understand how much work goes into making a recording, for a start. How much time, how much skill is required, how much money, all those things. Like, somehow or other, musicians' time has no value. And you know why? Because they're "having fun"!'

This is the sort of attitude that drives Morrison insane. 'This is what I've tried to change,' she says. 'People's perception of musicians, and the whole drug thing. That's why on the [Support Act] website, I've got testimonials about real stories and case studies. I've not used the ten per cent of people that are "drug-fucked".' Morrison accompanies this description with air quotes. Ten per cent is the figure that she puts on the Support Act beneficiaries who apply for help while harbouring conditions associated with drug and alcohol abuse: Korsakoff's syndrome, hepatitis C, liver disease and liver cancer chief among them.

It is February 2013, and Morrison sits in an armchair in her pleasant Clovelly apartment, in Sydney's inner east, her piercing blue eyes levelling with mine throughout our conversation. I settle into an adjacent couch, while down on the street a steady stream of traffic works its way past the open balcony door. A former musician herself, most notably as drummer with Brisbane-born pop act The Go-Betweens from 1980 until their break-up in 1989, the sixty-one-year-old has devoted six hours a week since 2000 to the role of national welfare coordinator for an initiative named Support Act. Founded in 1997, the non-profit organisation's mission is to raise funds that provide relief for Australian music industry workers who face hardship and illness.

'I think there's a real prejudice against people with hep C that's unwarranted,' she says. 'One of the things that I'd like to do is see that prejudice changed. [I want] hep C to just be seen as "bad luck" – they picked up a virus. But people think those who've got hep C must have been ...' – here she pauses, before smiling – 'junkies.'

It's not a pretty word, filled as it is with plenty of negative connotations. The reason Morrison smiled before saying it is that, earlier in our conversation, she had begun saying, 'I've had junkies steal from me ...' A second later, she quickly corrected herself by replacing that loaded word with the softer, less provocative phrase 'people who use heroin'. When I remarked on her specific use of language, she replied, 'I'll tell you why, because everyone's got a picture of what a "junkie" is. So when I say "junkies", they'll be thinking I'm talking about a specific down-and-out person, who is sitting in a gutter in the Cross hitting up, or selling their body in [Kings] Cross, or going to the hit-up centre. I'm not talking about that. I'm talking about people who just use heroin, and get away with using heroin for their lifetime, or for a great part of their lifetime. They are "junkies", because they're addicted to heroin, but they don't fit the stereotype. But still, in terms of all that manipulative, emotional-havoc-wreaking behaviour that they do around them to their peers, and their families, it's exactly the same.'

Born in Sydney in 1951, Morrison never discussed drug use with her parents due to the stark generational gap between them. 'From 1968 – when I was seventeen years of age – times changed forever,' she says. 'Our parents were Stone Age in their thinking. They were raised before the war; they'd gone through the war. The whole hippie revolution, the whole advent of the pill, the whole anti-Vietnam War demonstrations, the whole fight against racism, particularly in Queensland – it all just took them completely by surprise. There was no discussion ever about that sort of stuff.'

The head of the Morrison family, Ion, was a doctor, and he instilled in his four children one key message that stuck with the youngest daughter: never use needles. 'He said that to us on numerous occasions as we were growing up,' Morrison says. He supplied three compelling reasons: you could overdose; you could get an air embolism; or you could get a blood disease. 'This is in the 1950s and sixties, he's telling me this. "You'll get a blood disease." He knew nothing about HIV, and he had no idea of the scourge that hepatitis C would be on my generation of musicians.'

Her father's warning worked. 'That affected me so much that I never used a needle. Ever,' Morrison says. 'When everyone around me was hitting up, I was sitting there, taking marijuana. I was made fun of for that. People would say, "You're not prepared to take the risk! We take risks!" It was seen to be much more "worldly" to take heroin, to hit up with heroin. I was seen as "straight" because I stuck with marijuana. But that's because I was seven years older than them all.'

An anecdote from David Nichols' 2003 book *The Go-Betweens* is illustrative of that era in Morrison's life, when she was touring with bandmates Robert Forster and Grant McLennan, and living in a share house in London with Nick Cave, frontman of post-punk band The Birthday Party:

> Morrison was well on the way to realising her ambition of leaving Brisbane and Australia. Overseas travel had been the reason she'd wanted to hitch her wagon to Forster and McLennan's, despite their perverse immaturity ... At twenty-eight, she had made a third career change, and this time it would be something that took her beyond the narrow confines of Brisbane political scenes and the Bjelke-Petersen government's overbearing manipulations. Forster and McLennan were a decent gamble.

Morrison told Nichols:

I used to be the one responsible for cleaning the house
because no one else would. I found some heroin of Nick
[Cave's] – I could never afford heroin, I was broke all
the time – in an envelope in the kitchen, and naturally
I just took it. Anyway, Nick came home that night and
of course I was really stoned, and Nick said, 'How come
you're stoned?' Because I was the one who was never
stoned. And I said, 'I found some on the kit—'

'You knew that was my heroin!' He went completely
berserk about how I'd stolen his heroin, and I said, 'I
didn't know it was yours. I found it on the kitchen floor.'
But for months afterwards Nick was saying, 'You stole
my heroin, you stole my heroin.' And I was *so* happy
about it.

While pot was Morrison's drug of choice during that time,
she did snort heroin a couple of times. Did it appeal? I ask.
'Yeah, I mean, it's like having a lovely warm bath. But it's
just ...' She pauses a moment. 'Useless. You can't exercise on
it, you can't have sex on it, you can't think on it. You can't do
anything on it. It's just pointless. It's like sitting in a bath. You
can read in a bath, I suppose, but there's not much you can do
in a bath. You're sitting in a room and everybody's in a bath,
on their own. I just never quite understood it. It's the feeling,
I guess, that beautiful warm feeling. People would say, "You
don't feel anything. It takes away all pain." That's what Grant
used to say. And ... I guess that was it. I just didn't have that
much pain.'

She compares the drug's uselessness to alcohol, recalling that, in Melbourne in the early 1980s, all of the bands in the local scene would congregate at someone's place and bring in crates of beer. Nothing was more boring to Morrison than that. 'I couldn't understand why people would sit around drinking beer, and getting fat,' she says. 'It's just not my way to have fun. I had a different experience growing up. "Fun" was about doing something that was going to have a beneficial effect in some way. Like going for a really long walk or playing creative games. Sitting round getting stoned was such a waste of time, on heroin, because it wasn't like you were having any epiphanies. Maybe the epiphanies you had on marijuana were bullshit anyway, but at least you were actually thinking.' Morrison does note, however, that her alcohol consumption has increased with age. Towards the end of The Go-Betweens' existence, she began enjoying it for the first time — a late starter, as she points out.

'I often make myself not drink, because I think I drink too much,' she says. 'I won't drink at home, alone. I set myself rules now. It's easier as you get old to start drinking. Something happens.' Why is that? I ask. 'I guess [because] we can afford it,' she replies. 'And it's socially acceptable. It's a socially approved manner of "relaxing".' She contrasts that against marijuana, pointing out her belief that it wouldn't be a good look if she was smoking nowadays. 'Besides, marijuana makes me totally paranoid now. I found that, after I had my daughter, I was never able to smoke again, because I became convinced when I had a smoke that something terrible was going to happen to her, and I wouldn't be able to deal with it.'

There's another reason behind her illicit drug abstinence, though. 'I was building up a reputation in the music industry, in the work I was doing, as someone who was completely responsible,' she says, referring to her work with Support Act, for which she was awarded an Order of Australia Medal in January 2013 for 'service to the Australian music industry as a performer and advocate'. 'People need to know that that's the person I am now. I couldn't afford to be seen to be a drug-taker. And, also, it was bad enough that when I go out to social events, I can get very loud and boisterous, and "hilarious"' – the air quotes make another appearance – 'when I've had a few drinks. I can put people off anyway, by just being a loud drunk, so I don't want to put people off any further by other flaws in my personality.' She smiles. 'I'm very conscious now of being respectable. And I don't think that you can be respectable if you're seen to be a drug user.'

I ask Morrison how she has approached discussing drugs with her twenty-one-year-old daughter, Lucinda. 'Well, I told her the whole "don't use needles" story,' she says. 'I've told her friends that. I do that with all my students. I always tell that story. "Whatever you do, don't do needles." She knows that her father and I were using marijuana when we were younger. There's no problem with that. She tells me about her friends using coke. She said she doesn't use coke. She's got very bad sinuses. She doesn't even use marijuana. I think that physical disability has affected her … it makes her uncomfortable. She hates being around people using marijuana. In fact, she drops friends because they sit round using marijuana all the time. She thinks it's unbelievably boring. I'm not quite sure if she's done coke or not. I've never actually asked her. Only because I just don't think it's important.'

It's fantastic that you're so open with her, I say. 'Yeah, yeah, I know,' Morrison replies. 'It was no big deal. I mean, what's the point? She's going to read about my stuff eventually, when she takes an interest. She has no interest in my life at all. That's what daughters are like. It doesn't worry me. But one day she'll take an interest – probably after I'm dead. She'll take an interest and read David Nichols' *Go-Betweens* book. There's not much that isn't exposed there.'

These matter-of-fact statements are made all the more interesting by the fact that, towards the end of our conversation, Lucinda enters the apartment. We shake hands. She's blond, like her mother. While Morrison is on the phone – which rings several times during our hour together, calls that must be taken, as some of Support Act's beneficiaries can be hard to get hold of – Lucinda asks me, 'Are you doing an interview?' I tell her that we're talking about drugs. 'Oh, that's fantastic. Is it just about musicians? The whole book?' I nod. 'Oh, wow,' she replies. Morrison's call ends. She looks at her daughter and asks, in a vague, motherly tone, 'Does your generation use cocaine?'

'Mum, *everybody* uses cocaine,' says Lucinda.

'Oh, right. Do you use cocaine?'

'No, I don't use cocaine. It's too expensive.' We all laugh.

'Does anyone in your generation use heroin?'

'No one I know.'

'Do they use marijuana?'

'Yeah. Everyone except for me.'

'Do they?' replies Morrison, intrigued. 'I explained about your sinuses. So you would use cocaine if you could afford it?'

'Yes!' says Lucinda, laughing. 'If I could afford it, hell yes. I'd definitely use cocaine over anything else. Like, I'd definitely have cocaine over marijuana. I'd definitely have cocaine over MDMA.'

'What is MDMA?' asks Morrison. 'Like ecstasy?'

'Yeah, ecstasy.'

'Do you like ecstasy?'

'No.'

'Why?'

'Because I'm a grandma,' she replies. We all laugh again. 'One of my best friends is really, really into cocaine.' Having recently returned from a visit to Colombia, and Argentina the year prior, Lucinda has decided that her friend should never go to South America because she'd 'probably die over there. She's highly dependent on people, and on substances.'

There's a pause in the conversation. Then Morrison says, without ceremony, 'All right then. Bye-bye.' Lucinda heads to her room with a smile. This light, motherly grilling illustrates the shrinking gap between the two generations of Morrisons. Lindy couldn't have had that frank a discussion about this subject with her own parents but, with her own daughter, chatting about drugs appears so banal they might as well have been discussing their plans for dinner later that night.

Growing up in Brisbane in the late 1960s and early 1970s, Morrison and her social circle used pot as the drug of choice. She moved out of home and share-housed with 'very many creative people', including several who shared her passion for acting. 'I think it really increased our ability to think laterally, to be creative and silly and childlike,' she says. 'And to be able to do things like play music, and expose our vulnerabilities, and practice our art.'

At the time, Morrison was more interested in acting than playing music, but those interests reversed in 1980, when she joined Forster and McLennan in The Go-Betweens. The drug tastes of their peer group of rock and pop musicians matured from pot to speed. 'Everybody used quite a bit of speed,' she says. 'It was cheap, it was available, it kept you up. That's what people wanted. They wanted to stay up all night, play music …'

Her phone rings with a doorbell tone. She walks away to talk in private; when she returns, she says, 'I've got to save that guy's number – he just offered me a ticket to Neil Young, for god's sake!' She holds up her iPhone 5 like a blunt instrument. 'I just got this. I don't know how to work it. I broke the screen within a week.' I show her how to save a contact, and ask whether speed appealed to her.

'Well, I liked it because you didn't eat, and it kept you thin.' She smiles. 'But the jittery effect wasn't that useful. It wasn't creative like marijuana was. Marijuana made you consider the world. It made you creative. It made you think differently. It gave you an altered state. White powders don't alter your state of mind. And, surely, if you're using drugs, you're wanting to alter your state of mind, so that you can consider the world differently.'

Tastes soon matured once again. 'Everyone who was using speed moved onto heroin,' she says. 'I was thinking about this when you were coming over, the way people used to use it. People didn't have any money; it was a really cheap recreational drug for everyone to use. I mean, it replaced alcohol, of course. People used to get stoned, nod off, listen to music ...' She laughs at the memory. 'They'd get stoned, and ... I don't know. People didn't seem to participate a lot on heroin. There seemed to be a lot of sitting round quietly in rooms.'

Morrison clarifies that The Go-Betweens shouldn't be classified as a band that was using heroin; some members of the band used the drug, not all. I ask whether it was hard to be in a band with individuals who favoured that drug. 'No, it wasn't hard,' she says, before a long pause wherein she appears lost in thought. A distant look settles onto her face as she relives what she saw thirty years prior. 'It wasn't hard,' she repeats. 'It was just ... I find people who use heroin to be manipulative. Unbelievably good at lying. Totally and utterly selfish. Absolutely lacking in empathy. And blacker than you could possibly imagine.'

This is what you learnt? I prompt. 'Yeah,' she replies, face and tone neutral. 'I've had junkies steal from ... I'm sorry. Let me rephrase that. I've had people who use heroin steal from me, who were close to me, because they could. And because they were desperate for a hit. It's not nice. I've watched junk—' She smiles, corrects herself again. 'I've watched people who use heroin manipulate situations so that they can convince people to do things for them, so that they can get more heroin. I've seen people using heroin steal blatantly, from shops, in people's homes, backstage. I've seen them treat other human beings, exploit other human beings in a really mean way, so that they don't have to pay rent, or contribute to anything in a household. So that they can have enough money each week to buy heroin. While the people in the household pay the rent and buy the groceries and hide the butter so that nobody can find it until it's needed, and have absolutely nothing to live on, because they're paying the rent and buying the groceries.' She gives a hollow chuckle. 'I saw terrible things happen. Just terrible.'

And you saw people change, too, I say. 'I saw people change incredibly,' Morrison replies. 'I saw the children in families affected, and become heroin users. I saw that one of those children died, because the people were doing heroin in the house. The two kids who were growing up with their parents doing heroin, then in late adolescence they began to use junk. One of those kids died from a heroin overdose. That's directly attributable to the fact that people were doing heroin in the house as they grew up and it wasn't hidden from them. That's terrible.' Her face is stricken with agony, as if she blames herself for failing to intervene.

'But it sounds like I'm on my moral high ground,' she says, suddenly self-conscious. 'If I climb any higher, I'm going to need to take some blankets and a coat. And I don't want to sound that way. I'm just saying it as I feel it, because I saw so much terrible stuff happen. I just can't talk about it.'

Do you think heroin is romanticised? I ask. 'Everyone was so cavalier about it,' she replies. 'It was so hip to do it. It was de rigueur to be hitting up heroin. People would hit up and start listening to' – she starts chuckling – 'Ornette Coleman, Miles Davis; all the contemporary eighties rock musicians were hitting up and listening to all these jazz artists. As if they had something in common with them! What they had in common with them was that they were using heroin. And I guess that was the justification. Then, heroin became an end in itself. Everybody had to have it to "feel good", to feel warm and without pain.

'Well, then the question is: did everybody have pain? There's no doubt that so many people who are musicians really are on the margins, or on the fringes. But being on the fringes doesn't necessarily mean that you have more mental-health problems than other people, in other occupations. It just means that you can't fit into the mainstream. And not fitting into the mainstream doesn't mean that you've got more mental-health problems, so the buzzword these days is "self-medication". Everyone's "self-medicated". I'm hyperactive; I could say I used marijuana [because] "it slowed me down". And it did, considerably.'

'You'll never experience the rush.' That's what heroin users told Lindy Morrison when she refused to use needles. The tone of Dr Ion Morrison's voice and his prescient medical advice ensured that his daughter's future self would remain blood-disease-free. Others have not been so lucky. Hepatitis C, in particular, has afflicted many within the Australian music industry, particularly those who carelessly shared needles during the 1970s and eighties. Despite it all – despite the terrible things she saw surrounding drug abuse – Morrison continues to push against the attitude that Support Act's beneficiaries aren't worth supporting because of the perception that they've shot their life savings up their arms, or up their noses.

'I've had promoters, journalists and venue owners say that to me,' she says. 'I've had huge public rows with people [who say], "Musicians deserve what they get. Why should we help musicians? They've put themselves in that situation."' One step above sideshow alley.

That pervasive attitude is frustrating. So Morrison does her best to dispel the misconception. 'I've now got testimonials from a number of people, and put up case studies on the Support Act Limited website,' she says. 'None of those are drug-related, to change the perception of the sort of things that can happen to musicians that are not drug-related.' Among the examples: sudden, severe, one-sided deafness and associated ear problems; prostate cancer; organ failure; emergency neurosurgery; lymphoma; grants to support the widows and children of those who worked in the music industry.

One testimonial reads, 'I found Lindy to be a very compassionate and caring person. She goes out of her way to make things possible, and this is done efficiently and with heart.' Another: 'For me the face of Support Act Limited was Lindy Morrison. The emotional and logistic support provided by Lindy was immeasurable.'

Morrison speaks enthusiastically during our interview about the organisation's newly appointed CEO, Joanna Cave. Despite the six hours a week that she is contracted to work for Support Act, it's clear that Morrison's role as national welfare coordinator is rooted in passion and empathy. I wouldn't be surprised if she regularly exceeded that six-hour workload. 'I really believe in the work,' Morrison says. 'I really think that I am the right person for the job. No one could be better. I have a social-work degree. I've lived the life, and I get it. When people contact me, I know what they're going through.'

IAN HAUG

Dozens of metallic boxes containing a great many sounds are scattered all over the floor and desks of Airlock Studios, but so far none of them holds the sounds their owner has in mind. Prior to my arrival, Ian Haug has been searching for an old recording session, to no avail. He's optimistic, though; the search is far from over. Surrounding the clutter of hard-disk drives in the centre of the room is what can only be described as a musician's wonderland. At one end is an impressive mixing board that dwarfs a laptop, where Haug sits pecking out responses to urgent emails.

While he's otherwise occupied, I take in the hefty speakers installed up near the ceiling; the walls covered in music artwork, posters and photos; the shelves stacked with tomes devoted to Zeppelin, Bowie, the Stones and nearly every other classic rock act; Elvis statuettes, old music magazines; and a Nintendo Wii and television situated before comfy armchairs. Nearby, several sharp, silver ARIA awards are perched up high, which

Haug earned years ago as a founding member and guitarist of Powderfinger, a band named after a Neil Young tune. Clearly, this man worships rock music. Airlock appears to be his altar.

Situated in the Samford Valley town of Camp Mountain, twenty kilometres north-west of central Brisbane, the studio is a short walk down the driveway from Haug's home, which overlooks a small body of water complemented by a beached canoe. Out the front of the building is a converted rainwater tank used for guest accommodation: four single beds and a dusty PlayStation 2 fill out its cosy confines, while posters of world maps are presumably hung to encourage the recording artists to dream of faraway lands. 'Everything a band needs,' he says, taking in the snug spot with a smile.

We walk through a space adjacent to the studio's control room, where a piano, racks of guitars and a dismantled drum kit sit. Haug is a man of intimidating stature offset by a kind nature and boyish facial features. He leads me out to a separate building containing a kitchen, and we go inside. Rain beats on the tin roof while he boils the kettle. Through the windows is a calming view of the surrounding bush. It seems like we're the only humans in a wide radius.

'I've met lots of rough people over the years, and I've been friends with quite a few of them; people that are pretty fucked up in various ways,' says the forty-three-year-old. 'There's a lot of those "gentle giant" types out there; they look pretty rough on the exterior, but they're actually smart, sensible people. And they've always said, "Just be careful of those who've got nothing to live for."'

This message was instilled in Haug at a young age. A student of Brisbane Grammar School in the mid-eighties, he would catch up with his state-school friends at the Indooroopilly Shopping Centre each afternoon. The bus exchange was an ideal meeting place for teenagers: McDonald's and a doughnut store were nearby for salty and sugary fixes, while the rooftop car park was a popular locale for the boys to smoke cigarettes and hang out with their girlfriends. A few older characters would circle these schoolkids like vultures, viewing them as a captive market for the wares on offer: needles fitted up with heroin, for five dollars a pop.

'Heaps of my friends at Indooroopilly High got into smack at a very young age, when I was about fourteen,' Haug says. 'It was offered to me, and I was always a little scared to do it. I'm really glad I didn't do it, because I know now that my personality is "all or nothing". I can think of three people immediately that are no longer with us from Indooroopilly High who were introduced through that scenario. Smack was quite big in Brisbane in the eighties.' After rolling a cigarette, he pushes down on a pop-up electric toaster and bends down for a light by pressing its end against the heating element. Sensing my amusement, he stands up and deadpans, 'It's all I have,' miming that he carries the appliance with him everywhere.

Heroin never appealed, but Haug did try speed. 'I don't like needles, for a start, and that would've been shit speed, too,' he says. 'It wasn't crystal, put it that way. Base, I suppose. But I always thought, "No, I'll save [heroin] until when I'm an invalid." So I'm lucky. I know some people that are still working jobs now that have literally used for twenty years and they managed to maintain their use to a certain level. I'm not going to tell them not to do it, but you can certainly tell when they're on the gear. I'd prefer they didn't come around to my house and nod off. It's not really good company.' He smiles. 'But at the same time, as far as I know, none of them have ever ripped me off – touch wood – because it's always been like that. I've never moralised it. It's their choice. They know what they're doing. They're not stupid people.'

Pop culture and his elder brothers attuned the young man's ears to the possibilities of drug experimentation. He read *Fear and Loathing in Las Vegas* and listened to The Beatles, knowing that the Fab Four had indulged in LSD. 'My parents certainly are very straight, and they didn't condone drug use,' he says. 'My brothers were both starting to be doctors at the time, so they didn't take drugs. A few of their friends did, and I was aware of that, but none of them ever offered me anything. So I kind of had to search it out myself.'

The 'bad dudes' at his school dealt weed. The first time he smoked it, the experience was 'pretty mild', with some friends in a band-rehearsal room in the western suburbs of Brisbane. Before the end of high school, he had tried LSD and mushrooms, the latter acquired by hunting around fields in the Sunshine Coast town of Maleny while dodging angry farmers armed with salt-loaded shotguns.

Powderfinger formed in 1989 as a trio, later expanding to a quintet in 1992. Early on, the five members took acid and had 'sort of life-changing experiences together', Haug says. '[They were] mostly good, but I think everyone that's taken acid a few times has that trip when they go, "Okay, that was enough. That was a bit too close. I didn't really enjoy that." I wouldn't say we were ...' He pauses. 'We certainly weren't the Meat Puppets,' he smiles, referring to an American alternative-rock band formed in 1980 that was renowned for its consumption.

One trip sticks out in Haug's mind, during the annual 'Market Day' event organised by Brisbane community radio station 4ZZZ FM. He's not sure whether Powderfinger played early in the day, or even played at all. 'There was some acid going around in the early nineties called "Red Dragons". They were particularly strong; I think they were a lot of people's last trip,' he says. 'I remember being really scared. No one had mobile phones. You couldn't find anyone. It was just dark, and there were dogs everywhere; everyone seemed to have pit bulls that were fighting each other. There was lots of loud music coming from different stages. The aura was a mess.

'And I remember thinking at that stage, "I'm just going to take myself to the hospital and check myself in, because I can't handle this." Some other people from the band had a similar experience that day. One of them climbed a tree and sat there by himself.

'I remember going to sit somewhere and just calmed myself down, and walked across a golf course to go to someone's house, and they looked after me.' Haug is lost in thought while recounting this story, reliving the experience. 'That's a pretty strong memory where I definitely felt vulnerable, and I really had to focus to bring myself back from … I don't know. I've often wondered if I hadn't had willpower then, maybe I would've not come back. There's plenty of people in psych wards around the place who lost that battle.'

While we talk, standing in the kitchen, we lean against an impressive hardwood bench that looks like it was cut from a monster of a tree. On the windowsill are three bottles of beer, with candles sticking out the top and spent wax running down the side. Early in the band's career, playing regular gigs at various Brisbane pubs, the friends made a rule: to never go on stage tanked. 'We could have two beers before we played,' he says. 'I always thought, "What if I have something and think that's the best gig ever? I'm always going to want to do that." So I always abstained until after the show.' This rule came about after some shaky gigs in the band's early days. 'I think we all made that mistake once,' he says. 'And whoever that person was, everyone let that person know. It's not something to be proud of.' It was decided that quality performances were far more important than getting buzzed beforehand.

Altered states of mind while writing weren't particularly helpful to Haug, either. 'At the time, you think you're doing something fantastic, and then quite often you listen back to it afterwards and it's sub-par,' he says. 'But you definitely go in different directions that you wouldn't ordinarily go in. You look at a lot of eighties music, though, and it's obviously very terrible because everyone was high on cocaine and they thought it was great, but it wasn't. Aerosmith made some terrible records. There's a lot of bands that would admit that, I'm sure; they were just high, and they don't remember doing it. Cocaine's not a good creative drug.'

It increases the output but not necessarily the quality, I offer. 'Exactly,' Haug replies. 'Whereas smoking a joint, you definitely hear stuff differently; different vibrations. I mean, some people like trance without being under the influence, but that's the culture, really. I don't know if you've ever been to a rave when you're totally straight, but it's pretty surreal. You can definitely feel the influence.'

Haug didn't come across ecstasy until his late twenties and admits to still being confused by how the drug is used in some situations. 'I've never understood how people can take a pill and then want to go out and have a fight,' he says. 'That just doesn't make sense. But that seems to be what happens now. So it's obviously a bad drug; people aren't doing it for the right reasons. Drugs have existed in all cultures. It's meant to be some kind of spiritual thing; it's not meant to be how fucked up you can get.'

He recalls recently staying overnight at an apartment in Fortitude Valley, which was established as Brisbane's 'special entertainment precinct' in 2005. While sitting on the balcony, minding his own business, he could clearly hear a group of youths on the floor above planning their intake for the hours ahead. 'They were talking so loud that, if I was a cop, they were busted, because they were talking about splitting up whatever drugs they were having,' Haug says. 'One of them said, "Oh, just take a quarter, this is really strong." And the other guy's like, "No, no, fuck it. It's awesome. When it came on, I couldn't walk ..." I thought, "Well, I don't know if you necessarily want that if you're in a club ..."'

This is the sort of reckless consumption that troubles Haug as a father of two children, aged eight and four. He hopes that it'll be ten years before his kids take an interest in drugs, just as the words of Hunter S. Thompson piqued his interest as a young teenager, but he doubts it'll take that long for them to cotton on. 'You want to create a safe environment for your kids,' he says, as a cockatoo screams out among the dripping gum trees. 'I guess there are drugs around everywhere. I'm never going to tell people that they can't do something. Who am I to judge? But I've learnt to say no when I'm offered things. And I still have fun.'

The question of how to navigate this conversation is one that Haug doesn't yet have an answer for. 'My wife and I talk about this,' he says. 'Do you literally let your child do it at home for the first time? Or do you let them do it for the first time in an alley in the Valley? We just don't know. You would never want your kid, or your kid's friends' parents to think you're encouraging it. At the same time, I wouldn't want my kids to be with dangerous people. It's a tricky one.'

This is where the cautionary note, about being wary of those with nothing to live for, rings true. 'Sometimes, being high makes you paranoid, but there's usually a good reason why you don't feel safe in a situation,' he says. 'And I think you've really got to listen to what you feel.'

Haug rolls a second smoke and continues, 'I don't know if necessarily people can be psychic. But I think the opportunity for that is more prevalent when you're under the influence of certain things. And your whole soul and aura – if you believe in that sort of thing – becomes very ...' He pauses, leans down to use the toaster again, then rephrases. 'The protective barriers are down, so you've got to be careful. You've got to be in a safe environment, sometimes with lots of people who are experiencing the same thing. But some people become violent, or do something bad that maybe they wouldn't do ordinarily. Maybe they try to use that as an excuse. I don't think that's right.'

That's the big question mark that hangs over every drug: you don't know how it's going to affect you until you try it. You can research and theorise all you like, but how a substance interacts with your own body may be vastly different from how your best friend deals with it. 'Exactly,' he replies. 'And that's what concerns me about these synthetic [drugs] that are out there at the moment: they're just not tested. The dosage of mushrooms is never really a quantifiable thing, either, but normally people know someone that's had some.'

The American psychologist and psychedelic drug enthusiast Timothy Leary developed the idea of 'set and setting' for responsible drug use, including the enlistment of an experienced 'psychedelic guide' to keep tabs on the newbies. While Haug was aware of these theories as a young man, they weren't always adhered to. 'I've definitely been in scenarios where it's been irresponsible, and there's been no one "straight" who could've driven us to a hospital if someone stabbed himself in the eye with a skewer by accident. People always panic if something goes wrong; someone needs to keep it together. Those scenarios are never fun,' he says with a grim smile.

Nevertheless, Haug believes that he learnt things about himself, and the world around him, while under the influence. 'I think I'm not the only one,' he says. 'People are inquisitive to see if it does open your mind. I guess we'll never know, really, because of that feeling when you think you've got all the answers, but then two seconds later' – he snaps his fingers – 'it's like, "Huh? How did I solve that?" It's as if everything is just within your grasp, but it's kind of not. That's when you need a stenographer following you around, to capture those great ideas.' Similarly, when the band took acid together, Haug says, 'We didn't do anything particularly world-changing; it was more bonding within us.'

This was always one of the main attractions of illicit drug use, as far as Haug was concerned: to enhance shared experiences. 'And there's definitely an element of escapism, whether you like it or not, I reckon. That's part of it – to forget about the mundane. I think the last thing you want to be doing if you take some acid is an Excel spreadsheet,' he says with a laugh.

Sobriety's great, I offer, but sometimes there's a desire to add an extra few percentage points on top. Haug nods. 'I think it's really boring when you're on drugs to talk about drugs, or to talk about how "out of it" you are,' he says. 'I think you can actually have fantastic conversations about stuff uninhibited. So that's definitely part of the appeal – losing some inhibitions. But creatively, when it comes to music, you can enhance things, and hear things differently; when you watch a movie, you see it differently; when you look at art, it definitely makes you see a different dimension.'

Those altered perspectives aren't always productive. Haug says that, after lighting up and listening back to his own recordings, he'll become 'too focused on the sound of the snare, rather than listening to the overall beast. So it can work against you.' These days, he tends to dabble only occasionally. 'Maybe I'll have a reefer by myself if I want to jump on the whipper snipper and listen to some music, you know?' He laughs. 'Or play guitar, but nothing beyond that.' Pot doesn't help him when mixing, either: 'I get really unfocused and distracted, and don't finish the immediate task at hand. It's good to have a final listen, but I can't do it [during the mixing process].'

As he gets older, Haug finds that he feels anxiety the day after drinking alcohol. 'It's just the alcohol coming out of your body,' he says. 'The "drink to blackout" sort of thing is not what I attempt to do, but sometimes, if you're drinking wine in the sun and you've had too many, you get that sensation the next day of, "What happened after …?" It's never a nice feeling, that remorse of, "What did I say to them? Maybe I've offended someone …"'

He also recalls that, while visiting his good friend Grant McLennan of The Go-Betweens – with whom he played in a band named the Far Out Corporation in the late 1990s – they'd sit and drink ten Long Island ice teas while talking about everything under the sun. Everything, that is, except McLennan's occasional heroin use. 'I would go around to his house some days and he'd be pinned,' Haug says. 'But we'd still have a relationship, and I wouldn't even mention it. I just can't see the point. He never offered it to me, 'cause he knew that I didn't use. Maybe he'd had a bad experience with [offering it to] other people.' (McLennan died at home after a sudden heart attack in 2006, aged forty-eight.)

As we near the end of our chat, I bring up his earlier joke about only trying heroin when he was an 'invalid'. Haug replies, 'When I'm ninety, yeah, for sure. I'm sure the medical-grade stuff that's out there will ease my pain then. But, in the meantime, it's just probably a bit of a waste of time for me. And then, when you look at drugs like speed, I think that's borrowed time. You might feel like you're staying awake, getting lots done and having a lot of fun, but you pay for it afterwards. Maybe I'm mature enough to realise that now. I don't think you think about that sort of shit when you're younger.'

As a wide-eyed teenager absorbing the wit and wisdom of an accomplished drug enthusiast such as Hunter S. Thompson,

Ian Haug was attracted to the 'other' world that these substances offered. So, did they live up to his expectations?

'I think they probably did at the time,' he replies, as we walk back into the studio, past a wall that features a timeline of Powderfinger's gold and platinum records, framed and ordered chronologically. 'And then a lot of the bands that I was into; for some reason, people admire [Rolling Stones guitarist] Keith Richards for his constitution. But I realised that you can't do that, unless you're someone like him. That's all. I would hate to be inside his head, actually. I've got no idea how he deals with it. I've realised that going that hardcore's not for me.'

PHIL JAMIESON

On the morning of Saturday 17 February 2007, Phil Jamieson was at a cafe in the southern New South Wales city of Wagga Wagga sharing breakfast with his wife and young daughter. He wasn't in great shape. His home for the past five days had been Odyssey House, a detox centre. After breakfast on Saturday, he was scheduled to check into a rehabilitation clinic named Peppers. This was the last time he'd see his family for a little while, and he was enjoying their time together. His eyes fell upon a nearby copy of *The Daily Telegraph*. 'STAR'S ICE HELL' read the headline in bold type. The adjacent photograph was of a man in his late twenties. It took Jamieson a moment to recognise himself on the front page of the country's biggest-selling newspaper.

'The lead singer of chart-topping rock band Grinspoon has become the first Australian celebrity known to succumb to the drug known as ice,' read the story, which was written by Kathy McCabe and Lillian Saleh. It went on:

Singer Phil Jamieson is undergoing treatment for addiction to crystal methamphetamine as the drug continues to claim thousands of victims from all walks of life. Jamieson was last week admitted to Odyssey House's detox unit at Ingleburn, in Sydney's south-west. The singer/songwriter left the centre yesterday to complete a four- to six-week rehabilitation program at a private clinic. His wife Julie Fitzgerald is expecting their second child in four weeks. The singer for the ARIA award-winning band admitted himself for treatment after an intervention by his wife and family, who had become concerned about his erratic behaviour.

Jamieson didn't react well to the front-page story. 'Is this a joke?' he asked Julie, panicked. 'Has somebody cut out something? Is this somebody being funny?' But he wasn't laughing. The singer rang his manager, Gregg Donovan, who thought that his client was still in detox. 'He didn't know that I could have a phone,' Jamieson says. 'He was like, "Oh yeah, Kathy rang me last night and said the story was coming out." I was freaking out because I didn't want anyone at rehab to know who I was. I wanted to try to remain anonymous. I didn't want any bullshit, because this wasn't like a "celebrity rehab"; it wasn't anything fancy. This is Wagga Wagga – the wrong side of the tracks. Sharing rooms; very, very, *very* cheap. We couldn't afford anything else.'

Upon arriving at Peppers, the rehab clinic, Jamieson quietly asked a nurse, 'Look, I know this is difficult because I'm on the front page, but could you try to keep my job and occupation on the down-low?'

The story had come to *The Daily Telegraph* after a tip-off from a nurse who worked at Odyssey House, following an unedifying exchange between Jamieson and the detox-centre staff. They wanted to give the singer drugs to calm him down, including Subutex, a semi-synthetic opioid used in high dosages to treat heroin addicts. 'I was really adamant that I didn't want to take any more fucking drugs,' Jamieson says. 'I'm like, "I'm trying to get off drugs!" I was being a bit "coming down"-ish. I don't have violent behaviour. But I was like, "Listen, this is who I am!" I was being reasonably boisterous about the whole thing.

'So I did my lucid, "Don't you know who I am?" [act] in my weird, "coming down" way. They didn't believe me. They thought I was having a psychotic episode. Then they did the research. I've got no idea which nurse leaked it, but one of them rang *The Daily Telegraph*, who couldn't reveal their sources. But it made me really angry. I was really upset that it leaked, because I went voluntarily to fix myself up. Julie dropped me off. I wasn't saying "Look at me"; I was trying to do it to save my life, and also my new, unborn child, and my family – all sorts of shit.' He believes the newspaper-tipping nurse got the sack as a result of his or her loose lips. 'The duty of care by Odyssey wasn't overwhelmingly great, in my opinion. I was paying to be there. It was a cheap facility, don't get me wrong; we had no money.' With a remorseful chuckle, he says, 'Honestly, I'd spent all the money that we had.'

Jamieson's road to Odyssey House was marked by nine months of potholes that began to develop after he started using crystal methamphetamine in 2006. He is adamant that the drug deserves to be called by its full, scientific name in each instance, rather than reducing it to the level of street slang. 'It was sold to me as "meth", or "crystal", or "shabu"; it was never really sold to me as "ice",' he says. 'That term never came up, and it wasn't really my thing to call it [by] that term. It just makes light of a very, very serious substance.' While I respect his vehement belief in referring to its full name, for brevity's sake I'll use abbreviated versions throughout this chapter.

We're seated at the living-room table in Jamieson's three-bedroom home in Port Macquarie, northern New South Wales, on a Tuesday morning in February 2013. I met him for the first time the previous afternoon, when he picked me up from my hotel in his four-wheel drive with a six-pack of XXXX Summer Bright Lager in the front seat. In the back, his two blond daughters, Lyla and Evita, were securely strapped into child seats. He stopped in at the Shelley Beach Store and bought some sugary treats: a reward for the pair, who had both finished their homework. After he picked up Jules from her workplace in the Port Macquarie CBD, I was drawn into a heated illustration contest with the girls and ate a delicious curry with the family. The next morning, intricate piano music tinkles from a stereo in the adjacent music room while we speak about a time in Jamieson's life that, while it only occurred six years earlier, might as well have been a lifetime ago.

Since my knowledge of his former drug of choice is limited to its depiction in the American television show *Breaking Bad* – where the protagonist, a high-school chemistry teacher, develops a reputation for cooking the finest crystal blue meth to ever hit the streets of Albuquerque – I ask Jamieson to describe the drug for me. 'It comes in rock form,' he replies. 'I guess that's where it gets the nickname "ice". It's smoked in a glass pipe. It's quite tricky; the technique's not easy. That's why people get really into cleaning your pipe; the whole [ritual]. It could be cheap; it could be expensive. It was very much a cyclic thing.'

You always smoked it? I ask. 'Yeah,' he replies. Never snorted? 'No.'

Then he makes a *phwoar*-like sound of disbelief while shuddering at the thought. 'Unless it's crushed really, really small, it's ... no, I wouldn't snort it. I don't think so. I don't really remember. It's been six years. I remember the smoke, the lungs, the breathing out, that immediate high. The whole rigmarole of finding dealers, "waiting for the man", the money, and all that stuff. I remember that.' He pauses. 'The drug was pretty hard for me to do successfully. I don't know many people who can, with that particular drug.'

'Successfully' strikes me as an odd word in this context, so I challenge Jamieson on it. 'Well, I know that William Burroughs, for example, was a successful heroin addict,' he replies. 'He wrote amazing literature, he didn't die till he was eighty-three, and it wasn't because of an overdose. I'm sure there's a percentage of society who are functioning junkies on heroin. I'm sure there's people who smoke a lot of pot that function in a successful manner. But I don't know many people who function successfully on having a crystal meth habit.'

In 2004, Grinspoon released its fourth album, *Thrills, Kills & Sunday Pills*. A greatest-hits collection, *Best in Show*, followed in 2005. Both were commercially successful. 'We were on a bit of a good run, and I was writing lots of songs,' he says. 'I like writing anything, at any time. It's nice to write music; whether it be good or bad, it's a really fun thing to do. It's what I've been doing since I was thirteen.' The following year, Jamieson was twenty-nine, living in Bondi with his new wife and baby daughter, flush with cash from recent successes. In retrospect, he describes himself as being in a period of 'going from a child to a man, turning thirty. I believe that, in that time of your life, you hit this age where you're no longer a kid anymore; you're turning thirty.'

The singer was also in a band called The Lost Gospel, which released one self-titled album in August 2006. 'We had a high output of good songs, in my opinion,' he says. 'More pop-based than Grinspoon. I really found myself in a snuggle with three great artists: Ryan Adams, The Rolling Stones – I'd never heard *Let it Bleed* – and Wilco. I don't need many more [artists] than that. I was awash with all these great sounds, and some very strong amphetamines as well. I liked a lot of the songs I wrote on the album.

'But I'm not a card-carrying member of saying it was healthy.' He laughs. 'I don't think it was a great idea. But, in some ways, planets aligned for me. I was with a group of really creative people who I adored; incredible musicians that I loved playing with. After ten years of being in Grinspoon, it was something different. The drugs kind of worked alongside that. But then, at the end, they kind of took over. While they existed in a parallel way, working hand in hand – which is weird for me to say – it was okay. I thought some of the output was really good.'

Reviewing photographs of himself taken during that period, Jamieson thinks he looks 'very foreign'. 'I had bleached blond hair, very long, painted nails, I was wearing really wild fashion at the time – ripped clothing, suspenders half-hanging off; "hobo chic", I called it. I fully embodied what I'd become. I was "living the dream".' He chuckles. 'You don't really hang out with crowds on crystal meth. You hang out with, like, one person, or a dealer. It's not very social.' Jamieson lived in Bondi in 2006; throughout September, The Lost Gospel supported rock act The Casanovas on a national tour.

Concert reviews from that tour paint a picture of a band barely keeping it together. 'They played so strongly, even though the lead singer was flailing about the stage in what looked like drug-induced stumbles, yet it all added character,' wrote a FasterLouder critic of the Sydney show. A writer for TheDwarf.com.au saw the band in Geelong on a Thursday night: 'I have never seen anyone so wasted put on such an amazing show. That guy is talented; he was off his chops but mesmerising. Though he did have the help of an incredible band of extremely talented musicians, who kept him going through his increasingly more bizarre antics throughout the set.'

Scoring at home was easy enough, but the unfamiliar locales presented some difficulties. 'Melbourne was pretty easy,' Jamieson says. 'You'd go through one of the members of the band, who would know someone that used to deal, or a brother of a roadie that was a lighting guy that used to know that guy. That guy was *him*. That was reasonably simple.' Hobart was harder: 'You'd just ask at the end of the night at the pub, or even at sound check if you were really hanging out. You'd ask the bar staff if anyone got on. Most of them in Tasmania didn't know what we were talking about. That was a bit of a disaster. In Canberra, we ended up with pure speed, which made everyone really angry.' He cackles at the memory.

Perhaps their desire for crystal was lost in translation, I suggest. 'We were drug addicts,' Jamieson replies. 'We had no idea what we were really talking about. We weren't exactly healthy people. I'm sure it was probably our fault. We weren't the main act; we were scumbags. We'd try to sell t-shirts to score. That's basically how we did it.' If they couldn't score, he'd process the withdrawals by 'hanging out, being unhappy, drinking gin'. The singer points out that the band weren't all using. 'The drummer was clean. So he held everything together. As long as your drummer's a reasonably good machine, you're pretty much fine.'

Phil Jamieson first tried marijuana at age fifteen, growing up in Wauchope, on the New South Wales mid-north coast, nineteen kilometres west of his current home in Port Macquarie. One of his first LSD experiences was the 1994 Big Day Out festival at the Gold Coast Parklands, aged seventeen. 'I took it really early on in the day. It was terrible. [Melbourne alternative-rock act] TISM played, and they had these giant things on their heads. They came into the crowd. I was fuckin' freaking out. I don't like being that out of my head, or that out of control. I like to be in some sort of control, which sounds weird, but LSD and psychedelics ... I don't think it's admiration; I can see people that get a lot out of it, but it's not really for me.'

He moved to Lismore to start university study in 1995, where he became a 'dedicated pothead'. 'It was very social; it wasn't an isolating thing,' Jamieson says. 'Everyone was smoking bongs. It was bongs back then, not joints. It was full-on: wake up, have a cone. So all my friends were doing it, and it was just part of what we did. A bit like having a schooner.' Jamieson and his housemate, Grinspoon guitarist Pat Davern, would often write in this mode. The band's name is a tip of the hat to a well-known pot advocate, Dr Lester Grinspoon, whose book *Marihuana Reconsidered* was published in 1971 and spotted by the pair in a psychedelic-drug encyclopedia. 'It's just a name,' Jamieson says. 'We weren't a fan of his. We never read his books.'

By 2006, the band had enjoyed nearly a decade near the top of the Australian rock scene, following a string of strong singles that garnered national airplay and three platinum-selling albums, beginning with their debut, 1997's *Guide to Better Living*. After the release of the greatest-hits collection, though, Jamieson was spending a lot of time alone, or writing with his Lost Gospel bandmates. This insular, secretive personality was vastly different from the outgoing performer that Julie Fitzgerald first met in 2002, then married in 2005.

Ahead of Jamieson checking into Odyssey House, the married couple sought outside help. 'Julie and I were seeing a relationship counsellor, because obviously I'd been doing everyone's head in, treating everyone like shit because of my insane behaviour,' he says. 'The relationship counsellor was like, "I think you've got a drug problem." I'm like, "No shit!" She goes, "I think you should see a drug counsellor." I'm like, "Well, what am I paying you for?" And then, when the newspaper front page came out, the relationship counsellor texted me saying, "Great to see you got help!"' He cackles at her naivety. 'I was like, "That's not help! That's really not helping!"'

In the weeks leading up to detox, Jamieson made a couple of moves that signalled his desperation: he stole money from his bandmates, and he cashed in one of his guitars in order to score. 'Even when I took the guitar into that Bondi hock shop, they thought I'd stolen it,' he says. 'My appearance was of an addict.' When I ask about the instrument, he stands up, walks into the next room and brings back a red Gibson Les Paul. 'I bought this when we did *Thrills, Kills & Sunday Pills* in Los Angeles, when I'd finally graduated to playing guitar in Grinspoon. I didn't really play guitar on *New Detention* live. But, by the time *Thrills* had rolled around, I'd written a few songs: "Hard Act to Follow", "Better Off Alone". I was playing guitar a lot more. I bought it for $1000 at the Guitar Factory. It's a great guitar; I love it.'

He looks at it proudly. To the hock-shop owners, it was worth $150. 'They thought I'd stolen it,' he repeats. 'I was fuckin' hanging out by this stage. This is maybe a week before I went into detox. When I was in rehab, and the story had come out, I said to Pat, "Can you go down to get this guitar out? The docket's somewhere; it's my guitar." They rushed down there and they got it out for me, for $150. Definitely worth getting out.'

The story behind stealing from his bandmates isn't as dramatic as I had imagined: Jamieson is set up as the director of a company – Grinspoon Incorporated, essentially – and the four band members each have access to a shared account. 'So I was just going down to the local ANZ [bank] in Bondi and getting a $500 advance,' he says. He did this two or three times. 'It took our bookkeeper a couple of months to figure it out. Then she called me and I was like, "Oh, okay."' He pauses. 'Throughout the recording of *Alibis & Other Lies*, I was really sick, in the throes of addiction.'

After rehab, Jamieson called his bandmates individually, to come clean on stealing from Grinspoon Inc. He rang drummer Kris Hopes, who replied that he didn't give a fuck. '"Big deal,"' Jamieson relates. '"Why couldn't our bookkeeper tell us? You'll pay it back. Forget about it." Pat and Joe [Hansen, bass] took it more personally. Pat thought I meant I was stealing cash from his wallet.' This sentence causes me to burst out laughing. Jamieson continues, 'I'm like, "No, I wasn't stealing cash from your wallet. I was siphoning money out of the band's account." They both just wanted me to sort my shit out. So did I, by that stage.' He laughs. 'I was like, "Yeah, I'm going to sort it out. You'll get the money back."'

Owing to the leaked *Daily Telegraph* story between detox and his eventual rehabilitation, Jamieson suddenly became a coveted interview subject among current-affairs television producers. 'There was a hysteria about my "getting better".' He chuckles. 'And about the actual substance. In 2007, people didn't have any idea about methamphetamine. It was "scary". *60 Minutes* and *Australian Story* both wanted to do exposés.' *60 Minutes* offered him money, as did a number of gossip magazines.

The producers of the ABC television program *Enough Rope* contacted Jamieson's manager with an invitation to be interviewed by Andrew Denton, the diminutive, charming host with a reputation for being one of the warmest interlocutors on Australian television. The show's name referred to the adage that a person will 'hang' themselves in conversation if given enough leeway. 'I really enjoyed Denton's stuff and found him very credible,' Jamieson says. 'I said, "That's fine. I think this is a good idea to do this; I think Andrew won't try to be exploitative, won't be sensationalistic. It'll be honest and quite true." I had trust in him. Maybe my ego wanted to be on TV speaking with Andrew Denton, as well.' He smiles. 'That might have been part of it.'

An *Enough Rope* producer conducted preliminary phone interviews with Phil and Julie. 'A nice lady producer,' he remembers. 'Very soft. She interviewed Jules for an hour or two, got all the back story. I think Jules really needed to talk to someone. She'd been put through hell. It was good for her. It was probably really good for both of us, in a way.' By that time, Jamieson had been clean for three or four weeks. During initial discussions with the *Enough Rope* producers, they agreed that the on-set interview with Denton would be filmed around three months after the preliminary interviews – until, that is, they called back and told Jamieson that the interview would actually take place the following week. 'We felt we couldn't back out,' he says. 'So whether it was *A Current Affair* [-esque] trickery on *Enough Rope*'s part, mixing up the dates ... That's the only real swindling I felt went on. Maybe they didn't mean to; maybe it was an honest mistake.'

Originally broadcast in late July 2007, the twenty-five-minute conversation – edited down from around an hour in the studio – saw Denton leading Jamieson on a breezy stroll through his life story, though the druggy sting in its tail was evident in Denton's introduction: 'Ice is now the drug of choice in Australian emergency wards and rehab clinics,' he said. 'Far more destructive than heroin, it can tear your world apart, as Phil Jamieson, the lead singer of one of Australia's biggest bands, Grinspoon, can testify.' Julie was brought into the discussion at key moments. 'I hated the man that Philip had become; so different from what I'd married, and who I'd loved,' she said when asked about her husband's addiction, which also led to an affair and, as a result, her leaving him. The interview concluded with Denton asking Jamieson how he can make up the hurt he caused his wife. 'I can't,' he replied. 'It's impossible. It's done, so I just have to reassess myself, and try to be positive, for our future. Pretty tough, that situation.'

Jamieson has never watched the interview or read the transcript. 'Julie watched it and said it was fine; it was "light-hearted",' he says. 'Weird; it felt pretty intense to me! In the twelve-step program, they have a thing called "shares", where you get up and say, "This is what I feel ..." I think Denton was just a long "share", essentially. Anyway, it must have been good TV – it rated well. I'm glad Twitter wasn't around in those days!' He laughs. 'I don't want to be trending on that shit, really.'

Are you happy you did the interview? I ask. 'Whether I'd done the interview or not, people were going to know I was associated with methamphetamine because of the headlines it attracted,' he replies. 'Basically, every subsequent interview after that was about it. I was in a bit of a lose–lose situation. Once the nurse leaked my story, I wasn't really capable of getting out of that world. I'm not unhappy that I did the interview, no. I don't think it was a negative.'

Two years of sobriety followed Jamieson's rehabilitation. The 2008 Big Day Out tour – headlined by Rage Against the Machine – marked Grinspoon's return to the stage. 'It wasn't easy. I don't think the shows I delivered were particularly great, because I felt really naked up there. Really weird.' He shivers at the memory. 'Singing lyrics like "I got drunk and I got stoned …" [from the song "1000 Miles"] felt foreign to me. And I think the crowd could see that. They weren't our best shows. They were fine singing-wise; I was hitting great notes. But no one comes to see me hit notes. I'm not Ian Kenny!' He laughs, referring to the Birds of Tokyo and Karnivool singer known for his broad vocal range. 'It's just one of those things where I had to work out a balance for how I would continue to enjoy Grinspoon and also move forward. I didn't see Rage once on that tour: that's how important my sobriety was.' Instead, he'd leave straight after his band's set and see a film or visit an art gallery by himself.

Six years after leaving crystal methamphetamine behind, Phil Jamieson seems happy. He's there for his family, who love him. At one point during my two days in Port Macquarie, his eldest daughter, Lyla, played a song for me on her recorder and showed me a journal entry in her schoolbook where she wrote that, when she grows up, she'd like to be a musician. I asked if she liked watching her dad perform. 'Yes,' she replied. 'That's why I want to do that too.' Her dad exercises regularly, though not as often as he'd like. To help him out, I offer to take his fluffy dog, Pablo, for a forty-five-minute walk around the neatly maintained streets in the rain.

The most surreal moment during my time with the Jamiesons occurs when Jules drives Phil and me into the city centre on the Tuesday night for a few drinks at a local pub. I'm sandwiched between Lyla and Evita in the back seat again, as Phil plays 'Regulate' by Warren G and Nate Dogg loud on the stereo. The parents groove and rap along to the lyrics, while their daughters scream '*WHOA!*' on the off-beat. If I could've whispered this scene into the ear of my fifteen-year-old self, as he got boozed and sang along to Grinspoon's debut album *Guide to Better Living* with his high-school friends ten years ago, he wouldn't have believed me for a second.

As the chat winds down, Jamieson tells me that he drank three cups of coffee prior to our interview, because he was up until 2 am and knew that he 'needed to talk eloquently about quite a difficult subject'. I thank him for dosing up, and ask how he manages this aspect of his life now. 'When I did my twenty-four months sober, I realised how easy it is for me to lose it,' he replies. 'Over the eighteen years I've been in the band, I've had ups and downs with substances, and I think it's time to draw a line under what I can do and what I can't do.' (At the end of 2013, the four members of Grinspoon play a final show in Brisbane and announce an indefinite hiatus; the singer is pursuing a solo career.)

Though having lived through a drug addiction has certainly made him a wiser man, Jamieson is cautious about promoting recreational use. 'There's a great element of having fun on illicit substances that I'm not a total advocate for, because I ended up pretty seriously damaged by ...' He pauses, catches himself. 'Well, I'm alive, so not *seriously*. But there are serious connotations to any kind of drug use, I think. It's something I'm looking at very, very carefully now that I'm raising two daughters: what are the skills I've learnt about how I can guide them? It weighs on my mind: where they'll be, and whether I can have any relevance to them.'

HOLLY THROSBY

While holidaying with friends on the New South Wales south coast at the age of twenty-nine, Holly Throsby tried cocaine for the first time. She had studiously avoided all illicit drugs for over half her life because she was afraid of their potential effects. 'Being a musician and never having taken any drugs, and being on tour, people always thought it was a bit weird,' she says. 'People thought it was weird in high school, too.' But there on the coast, enjoying the company and the locale – 'this very nice, mature, safe holiday' is how she describes it – her friends started racking up lines. Throsby was hesitant. She'd always been curious about this particular drug. This time, her curiosity won out.

'I just loved it so much,' she says, accompanied by a self-conscious laugh. 'Like most people do. I just thought it was pretty much the greatest thing I'd ever felt in my life. God, was I just king of the world. And then, unfortunately, after that, I got quite a taste for that particular drug. When I was twenty-nine, and thirty, and maybe thirty-one as well, I did *heaps* of cocaine.'

Define 'heaps', I prompt. How often are we talking about here? 'It depended on the time,' she replies. 'My partner at the time and I had a house guest come and stay with us, and he was just so into drugs. I seem to have lost a few months with him. We just went a little bit crazy, and at that point I had this guy that home delivered, which is the worst thing you can possibly have! And, plus, the guy that was staying with us was happy to finance this, because he was like, "Come on, come on!" and I was always wanting him to buy more. And so there was … *Jones!*'

For some time now, Throsby's chocolate Labrador has been banging her tail against the leg of the high kitchen table where we sit. I had been warned about Jones via email: 'I hope you like Labradors. They like you. That you can be sure of,' Throsby wrote, and the boisterous dog is certainly a presence in her Marrickville home. While we talk, Jones laps water noisily from a bowl in the kitchen and whines at the back door until her owner allows her outside.

'There was a time there where it was *a lot*,' Throsby continues, reflecting on her cocaine usage back then. 'Anytime I was going out, or doing any kind of social activity. And there were some times where, if I just had some left over, come an evening, I would inevitably just do it.' Jones growls, looking up at the dark-haired singer-songwriter. 'And I did start to feel a bit guilty about that, because I was kind of [being] a little bit "teenager" with drugs. [I thought that] I was too old to be acting like a teenager with drugs. There was part of me that thought it was a bit "uncool", but I also really enjoyed it.'

Uncool? I ask. 'Ah, just because … I don't know.' Throsby pauses. 'I mean, I'm not against drugs, but they're not very good for you, and I don't think they're good to be doing a lot. They certainly increase your anxiety. After having a really big night, I started really not enjoying the next day. And that was something that kept creeping up on me more and more, because you always drink heaps more as well, when you go out [on coke]. But it's also one of those things. Cocaine's such a moreish drug, but it's not that great when you do heaps of it. You're always chasing that first line, you know? It's one of those things. And, plus, when you're really high, you can keep drinking and staying out. At the core of myself, I'm actually a really quiet person who enjoys a quiet night in, more than anything else. I kind of went a little bit mental!' She laughs.

In my experience, I've found that the inevitable problem with that drug is that, once you start, there's never enough. 'No, there's never enough, and that's the thing,' Throsby says. 'You always think, "Oh, if there's a bunch of people, we can get two grams," but then if you've got someone who home delivers … everybody goes broke, and nobody gets any sleep.'

There's the financial aspect, too. 'It's incredibly expensive, and it's not worth it,' she replies. 'It's really not worth it. It's one of those things where if someone else is paying for it, it's great. I've certainly spent a decent amount of my own money on it. But I think everybody who does cocaine in any regular way in Sydney, or anywhere in Australia, knows that it's off the charts. There was a couple of New Year's Eves where no one had cocaine, so people were doing ice and stuff, and it's just *yuck*! There's some really horrible drugs out there that you end up doing, 'cause there's nothing left and you just want to snort something.'

Raised in Balmain, in Sydney's inner west, Holly Throsby says she had a late puberty when it comes to drug use. 'I was really scared [of drugs], probably subliminally because there were people in my universe who had problems with them. I was quite frightened by the potential damage. You know when you're little, and it sounds like it's this big, scary, horrible world? I remember finding out that certain people close to me used drugs. I thought that was just so shocking. I was a really pious ten-year-old.'

Throsby attended Hunters Hill High, a lower North Shore public school that she describes as 'full of drugs'. 'When I was in Year 7, everyone was smoking pot, but also there was a lot of ecstasy and acid,' she says. 'The girls that I was hanging out with were pretty out there. I found it really stressful. They were the popular group, and I was the dork of the popular group. They were all hanging out with boys that were older, in Year 8 or Year 9. They were all getting really drunk, and everyone smoked cigarettes; that was quite normal. But doing drugs and drinking, and all that kind of stuff, I just wasn't ready at all for that kind of thing at that age. When I got to Year 8, I started sitting with a different group of people, and stopped hanging out with [the others], because I felt really stressed out by it all. And, also, I just wasn't interested in partaking.'

A formative experience around this time solidified Throsby's fear of illicit drugs. 'I wasn't at all interested in acid or ecstasy; I just thought they seemed really scary,' she says. 'I did want to be "cool" and smoke weed. My boyfriend was always smoking weed, so I wanted to do that too. I had a really bad experience with it when I was in Year 8, when I was thirteen. At that point, I'd only smoked leaf joints, just really shitty stuff. My friend's brother was a dealer, and he got us these hectic buds.' She smiles at herself for using that adjective, while I burst out laughing.

At a party one weekend, everyone was smoking bongs – a method of consumption with which Throsby had no prior experience. 'At this point, I didn't drink alcohol,' she says. 'I was really scared of drinking because I'd seen it make people vomit and get really sick and out of control. I just wasn't that kind of kid. I was quite nervous, so I said, "No, I don't want to drink." I thought maybe marijuana was my "cool" drug that I could be in the gang with.'

She smoked three or four cones of those hectic buds with her friends; half an hour later, the high hit her. 'The whole world just went so weird,' she says. 'It went in these three stages of being, "Okay, I'm okay," [to,] "No I'm not, I'm going to die!" to, "Oh, it's kind of okay …" It just felt like the night went forever. I kept going up to my friends and asking, "How long is this going to last?" I hated it. It was the worst night of my life. Plus, I had to stay at a friend's house, and I didn't really know them, and I couldn't sleep. It was really horrible. I remember the next day, I had a bath, and [the feeling] came back in the bath. It kept coming in the next couple of weeks.' The same thing happened to a friend who smoked a similar amount of pot that night.

As a result of that thoroughly unpleasant experience, Throsby hasn't really touched it in the intervening decades. 'I don't [smoke] at all now,' says the thirty-four-year-old. 'If people are passing it around, I just say, "Nup". I don't even like the smell much. It makes me feel a bit weird. It's a shame; it's the kind of drug that I can imagine when I see the effect on other people, and I wish that it affected me that way, because it looks so nice and relaxing. But not for me.' Even now, Throsby isn't sure how to characterise that first peculiar experience, and the fact that the ill feeling recurred in the weeks that followed. 'The fact that my friend had that reaction, too; we must have just smoked way too much of it, and it must have been really strong,' she says. 'But I just don't know. I was really young. I remember it quite well, but I can't explain it.'

At this point, I make a confession: I've heard a story about Throsby and drugs, which is part of the reason why I approached her for an interview. 'Oh, great,' she replies. 'Yeah, right. I knew that you would have! I thought, "Oh, I bet he's heard something ..."' She laughs. 'What's the story?' I tell her that I've heard she approached Phil Jamieson backstage at Splendour in the Grass in August 2007, asking if he had any cocaine. Her eyes widen; she looks horrified for a moment, then starts laughing. 'How did you know that?' Jamieson told me, I say. '*He did?* Oh, that's hilarious. Yeah, I asked him.'

Throsby recounts that she bounded up to Jamieson – whom she had never met before – with a great idea. Surely, the Grinspoon frontman would know where to score cocaine at one of the country's biggest music festivals! 'The look he gave me, ohh ...' She sighs. 'It was so devastating. Such a dirty look.' His one-word response – '*no*' – was delivered in a tone that indicated she was the world's biggest fool.

Confused about the contemptuous reply that she received, Throsby returned to her friends. 'I thought maybe Phil

Jamieson had some ...' she began. 'Everyone looked at me. "*Dude!* He's the most famously sober person in Australia!" But I didn't have an aerial at the time; I didn't watch much TV. I read the newspaper, but I just totally missed that one.' She laughs.

'I was thinking about telling you that story, but it's *so* embarrassing.' She sighs again, smiling. 'It was my least classy moment.' (Jamieson, during our interview: 'Holly Throsby asked me where she could get some coke, which I thought was really weird, because I was clean.' He finds it funny in retrospect.) 'That was the worst Splendour in the Grass ever,' she continues. 'I ended up taking this horrible ecstasy; it was a bit hectic and intense. Anyway, that moment was really bad, because I was in the height of the phase [where] I did feel like I was doing myself damage.'

Were there any long-term effects from that period? I ask. 'No, I don't think so,' she replies after a short pause. 'Nothing that I can personally detect. I remember the main thing that frightened me is when I read that cocaine is a neurotoxin, in that it depletes your brain cells, because I like to feel vaguely intelligent!' She laughs. 'That's one thing that I would be disappointed by. I mean, I feel just as sharp as I did before. Who knows? I think that it was ... there's always different stages that you go through in your life. I don't regret it at all. I had heaps of fun. I learnt that it's not really where I want to be, I guess, which was useful. I also learnt that I can very easily just do it and not really think about it again for months and months, which is a good feeling.'

To illustrate, she describes a forgotten stash. 'I haven't bought any for so long,' she says. 'The last time I did buy some, which was probably last year sometime, I remember I did a little bit one night, and then it was just sitting in the drawer for months, actually. Which was just incredible; when does that ever happen?' She laughs. 'Nobody does that! It was just sitting there. I forgot about it until, "Oh yeah, that's right ..." The old me, that would never have happened. I'm just not that attracted to it anymore. There's a couple of times recently that I've been out, and I've had one line and been offered more, and I've said "Nup", which is so amazing compared to me a few years ago, who would've just hoovered the whole lot!'

Her use of cocaine didn't hinder her creativity or writing process. 'I tend to write in big clumps,' she says. 'I'm not the kind of writer that sits down with a guitar every day and writes songs. I tend to write for months and months and months, and then, if I'm recording and touring, I tend to stop until that cycle [ends]. Not deliberately; it just sort of happens that way. Sometimes, towards the end of a tour, I might start writing again.' During her extended fascination with cocaine, Throsby was touring most of the time. 'I think that's the thing – it's a great touring drug,' she says. 'Because [touring] is tiring, at the end of the day. But I don't directly relate [cocaine] to creativity at all. I certainly don't remember ever writing songs when I was high.'

It doesn't strike me as a drug that'd allow you to sit by yourself in a room and focus on a task. 'No, it's not,' she says. 'It's really not. On my last record, there's a lot of songs that came out of that period – the whole album, actually, now that I think about it.' She laughs. This admission amuses me, because I was listening closely to her albums ahead of our meeting and didn't detect any overt drug references in her lyrics. 'No, I don't think there is, really,' she replies. 'Maybe there is one, in one song, but it's very incidental.'

I ask whether she used cocaine overseas, where it's much cheaper. 'Yeah, and it's better, too,' she says. 'In New York, it's a really uncool drug to do, because it's so "cheap and nasty" over there. I remember thinking that it was so great that it was so cheap, and actual New Yorkers being like' – she adopts a look of deep offence – 'turning their noses up at it. It's high quality, but the effect of it is so nasty. When people can get high all the time, it doesn't necessarily bring out the best parts of your personality. You always find yourself rambling, and super excited about stuff you're actually not super excited about.'

If you were sober, I begin, you'd look at yourself … 'And think, "What a douchebag!"' She laughs, finishing my thought. 'It's really unattractive, especially when you see people who are really high. I hate thinking about that for myself now. *Ugh*. I mean, it's so fun, and you can have so much fun, when used "correctly". My favourite thing now would be, if you're having a dinner party, everyone might have a couple of lines after dinner, which is the kind of way I was enjoying it towards the end. I think that's a really fun way to use cocaine.' Yet, just as Throsby's taste for the drug has subsided, so too has that of her peer group. 'The people I hang out with are getting older, because everyone's in their early thirties and they've left their twenties behind them.' And much of their cocaine use, too, it seems.

Which isn't to say that Throsby is totally done with the drug; it's just that she doesn't seek it out anymore. 'If someone offered me a line, I'm sure that I'd probably do it.' She pauses.

'But, then again, not always, though. It depends on my feeling. If there was a big, massive, epic party that I was going to, I would think about buying some, but I don't even think I would [buy it]. Something in me just turned itself off it, I guess. Because I haven't had a great time with it the last six months, or even a year. I just lost the feeling of enjoying it. There was a couple of times where it felt a bit too "speedy"; that thing where you need to walk around the block because it feels a bit too intense. And I *hate* that feeling. It's really unpleasant.

'I guess the last time I did it was last New Year's Eve, and, oh my god, that was the most nanna experience on cocaine.' She laughs. 'I had one line and then still went to bed really early. Everyone else was up, but I said, "Yeah, nah, I don't want any more." I just really lost my taste for it. I'm sure that I can and will enjoy it again, but in a very occasional and minor way, I would imagine.'

Throsby's avoidance of alcohol meant that she came to it much later than her peers, at around the legal age of eighteen. 'And I *looooved* it,' she enthuses. 'I thought it was so great. I used to drink way too much. My relationship with alcohol is that I'm quite dependent on it, but in terms of my own health I try not to drink much. As I've gotten older – I'm at the ripe old age of thirty-four – I don't really enjoy getting very drunk anymore. I drink small amounts regularly. I'm quite health-conscious now. I mean, if you read the guidelines for what women are supposed to drink, our "daily recommended drinks", it's so minimal compared to what most people actually drink. So, certainly, over the years, I've whittled down my alcohol intake. I drink light beer heaps when I'm at the pub.

I've become quite measured with it. It's one of the few things that relaxes me, I guess.'

A recent alcohol-related experience has forced Throsby to examine her relationship with that drug more closely. After contracting appendicitis earlier in 2013, she was prescribed Flagyl, an antibiotic that has a strong adverse effect when mixed with alcohol. 'The chemist tells you that you're not allowed to drink even a drop of it,' she says. 'I think it's probably a little bit [of a] scare campaign, but they recommend not even cooking with any alcohol.

'So I was off alcohol completely for two weeks, and just bored out of my brain!' She laughs. 'But I was remarkably productive! I read heaps more; I was up at all hours of the night, just totally awake. I was wondering, "How do I differentiate my day from my night? I can't work it out!"' She mentions reading a couple of reviews for a book named *High Sobriety: My Year Without Booze*, by Scottish-Australian journalist Jill Stark, which examines the author's social reliance on alcohol.

'I thought that book sounded interesting,' she says. 'I was supposed to go to a show that week; a friend of mine from overseas was playing. I was going to take my friend, but he said, "Oh, but you're not drinking!" I could see the nervousness in his eyes. "But that's how we bond! We have a beer together! That's what we do!" I said, "You can still drink!" He was so anxious. It was just really funny. If you go to the pub with someone and you're not drinking, you tend to make other people anxious by your not drinking.'

I've read Jill Stark's book, and enjoyed it very much. One of her central messages is how challenged many Australians are by the concept of not drinking. 'It's *so true* in this country,' Throsby says. 'If you're not pregnant, nobody understands what the hell you're doing if you don't have a beer or glass of wine in your hand. So it is strange how we so heavily celebrate alcohol, but sort of ...' Shun the other drugs? I offer. 'Yeah. It's a funny thing.'

Throsby has some experience with prescription drugs, too, having been prescribed Valium. 'I quite like it,' she says. 'I can be a bit anxious sometimes. I don't take that much of it, but I usually get them in five-milligram tablets. If I take half when I'm really stressed about something, it certainly helps me. Valium's a hard one. I think people certainly can have dependencies to that, and that to me sounds very damaging. And I'm not really scared of that happening to me, because I don't think I have that kind of problem. But I think when used correctly, it is an amazing, amazing relaxant. I've taken beta blockers, too,' she says.

I'm intrigued, and ask her to tell me more. 'They're a prescription drug, but they're not a brain thing. They're a physical thing, for your heart. They just slow your heart rate down, so you can't have symptoms of panic or anxiety. So people that take them for medical reasons have generally had heart attacks or something. They might be on them every day for the rest of their life, so their heart rate is never going to get above a certain level. But performers, public speakers and lawyers take them; I've used them for performances.' At all shows, or just occasionally? 'Sometimes I go through bouts of having stage fright, so I use them [then],' she replies. 'But they're incredibly effective. My god, I'd recommend them to any musician having stage-fright problems.'

This reminds me of my conversation with Wally de Backer, who has struggled enormously with nerves before going on stage. I mentioned beta blockers to him as a possible solution, but he had never heard of them. 'Oh, tell Wally they're amazing,' she says. 'They really are. They're an amazing safeguard. Even if you just have them, it makes you feel better about it, because they work quite quickly – within ten minutes or so.' She pauses. 'I usually get a problem with my voice when I'm singing, where it sounds "nervous", whereas other people have problems with their hands, shaking when they're playing piano or guitar. It fixes all that kind of stuff. They're quite amazing.'

Throsby began using beta blockers a couple of years ago, when she felt nervous before a couple of 'really big shows'. With Seeker Lover Keeper? I ask, referring to her indie-pop collaboration with Sally Seltmann and Sarah Blasko. 'No, more like when we did that Crowded House show at the Opera House,' she says. *They Will Have Their Way* was a series of tribute shows in late 2011 wherein Throsby covered that band's songs alongside singers such as Paul Dempsey, Clare Bowditch and Lior. 'I've played at the Opera House a couple of times. I just found that venue so daunting. I think the main thing for me is, when I'm doing my own shows, I can really do my own thing. My shows are really small, and even if I'm playing at a big show in support of someone else, it's still *my* show. But doing that kind of thing, where it's a big production and everyone's depending on you, I find that makes me so much more nervous, that I couldn't really let anyone down, or something.' She laughs. 'I remember using them for that, and it was just amazing. It was quite great.'

Talk turns to her feelings towards how illicit drug use is viewed in Australian society. 'For some people, drugs can overtake their life; it *is* your life, and it runs your life,' she says. 'That's a really sad story for anyone. The general view is that people will get sucked into this "black hole of drugs". But the people I know who've had really bad problems, I swear you could just see it in their eyes that they were going to, you know? A lot of highly functioning people readily enjoy drugs and it doesn't dictate who they are, or how they need to live. But I'm not really sure.'

Jones begins whining at the back door once again, wanting to escape the rain outside, and Throsby gets up to let her in. 'My feelings about it when I was growing up were based on my personal experience. I guess there is this societal [message of] "don't smoke, don't drink, don't take drugs". I mean, that is the message that we're given, but I'm not sure if I really listen to those messages that strongly. I've never actually really considered the illegality of it that much. I would never really put myself in a position of "high risk", in terms of getting caught or something. I never even really thought about that, though. Which I found interesting, because I'm sure you're supposed to be scared about that, but I didn't even consider it because ...' She pauses. 'I'm not sure why.' She smiles. 'For some reason, it never occurred to me as a deterrent.'

As she leads me from the kitchen towards the front door, we pause in her lounge room, wherein an assortment of pots and pans are gathering water that leaks from several spots in the roof. It's not an ideal situation, especially considering that one of the leaks descends directly down a light fitting. I caution her that it's probably not a good idea to turn on that light switch for a while. While bidding me farewell with a smile, Jones panting at her side, Throsby says, 'If I get electrocuted and die today, I expect a dedication!'

SPENCER P. JONES

Spencer Patrick Jones is remembering a Wayne Kramer song called 'Junkie Romance', from the MC5 guitarist's 1995 solo album *The Hard Stuff*. In the first line, Kramer sings of an aspiring rock star who wants to look like Johnny Rotten of the Sex Pistols, and wants to act like 'Keef' Richards of the Rolling Stones. In the chorus, the singer points out the harsh truth: that when it comes to junkie romance, nothing comes for free.

From behind a pair of black sunglasses, Jones fixes me with a cutting look and says, 'That song says it all. For sure it's true, because I personally know a lot of guys that had no fucking reason to be going anywhere near heroin, but they thought it would somehow make them some kind of idea of what they think a rock star was. *Hey! Hello! Reality check!* Why don't you wait until you've got a million dollars like Keith Richards and indulge in it, rather than just being another arsehole that's going to be dead in six months, and who's not going to sell anywhere near as many records as the Stones' first single did?'

The story behind Jones' own heroin use, observed in fits and starts since 1990, when he was thirty-four, is one that takes quite some time to tell. It helps that the narrator has an excellent eye for decades-old details; it hinders that he's prone to wild digression that regularly takes us away from the primary reason we're talking. I meet with the singer, songwriter and guitarist near Moreland train station in February 2013. It's an innocuous inner-city Melbourne locale that will take on a more sinister character later in our conversation. We walk together down Moreland Road, the suburb's bustling main strip, and stop in at a coffee shop owned by a couple of his friends. I get the impression that the fifty-seven-year-old Jones has a lot of friends. He's a gregarious guy, equally at home telling his stories and listening to other people's.

When we first shook hands, I took in his entirely black outfit and thinning, backward-combed, black hair. A moment later, I registered the absence of his signature cowboy hat, a regular fixture atop Jones' head since the 1980s, when he joined the 'cowpunk' band The Johnnys. It stayed throughout his tenure as guitarist in Sydney rock act Beasts of Bourbon, his solo career, and while he played in bands fronted by well-known figures such as Paul Kelly and The Saints' Chris Bailey, as well as an exhaustive list of his own projects, mostly recently the Nothing Butts, with two members of The Drones.

I'd been aware of his reputation as an influential axeman for many years, but it was only a few days prior to our meeting that I saw Jones on stage with the Beasts of Bourbon for the first time, at the All Tomorrow's Parties festival outside of

Melbourne. It was a great gig, and I tell him as much, singling out the light show for particular praise. We hop a tram and head south for five minutes, while he dives into a series of intricate stories about the travails of that particular lighting technician.

We alight in Brunswick and breeze into the Retreat Hotel, where Jones knows the owner. Before long, the guitarist is chatting him up about booking a solo gig in the near future. I order lunch – beer-battered fish and chips – from the kitchen across the room while marvelling at his hustle: a working musician in action, making his own luck. Outside, the beer garden is almost empty on this afternoon, but the PA is pumping. We find a table within a tin shed, which shields some of the noise. I drink a Coke; Jones drinks nothing at first, but smokes a dozen match-lit cigarettes throughout our four-hour conversation, which is occasionally punctuated by his expert ears pricking up when a favoured melody – 'This is one of my favourite Dylan songs: "The Man in Me"!' – seeps into the enclosed space.

Born in 1956 in the town of Te Awamutu, on New Zealand's north island, Jones grew up admiring punk bands such as the Ramones and the Stooges but was particularly fond of Lou Reed. After leaving high school, he played in a three-piece band that covered Velvet Underground songs such as 'Sweet Jane' and 'White Light/White Heat'. 'I didn't know a lot of the terminology that I was singing about,' he says. 'I was singing his lyrics, but I didn't know I was actually singing about getting a blow job or whacking up speed. I'm just reading these lyrics without any idea what the fuck it's about.' Jones bought a copy of William Burroughs' *Junky* around this time, which opened his eyes to those themes.

Jones worked at a Fisher & Paykel home-appliance factory and started buying pot off a biker he met there. One day, the biker offered him something new: black hash, with white streaks through it. He was told that it was opiated hash, 'all the way from Afghanistan'. The teenager had heard of opium, but he didn't know that heroin was a refined form of it. 'The white fucking powder in the hashish was smack, and I'm smoking this stuff at sixteen years old. The idea of even the word "heroin" terrified me! I just thought I was smoking marijuana, but it seemed to put me to sleep every time I had it. No one said, "Oh, by the way, you're smoking heroin." I would've been shocked. I thought, "Opiated hash? That means it's extra good!"'

Jones was nineteen when he moved to Australia. 'I was a good kid!' he recalls. 'Wide-eyed and willing. My whole plan had been to go to the UK, to join a decent rock and roll band.' The latter dream was realised soon enough, and he'd eventually get to the UK, but as a touring musician, never as a resident. Upon crossing the Tasman, he took the temperature of the Melbourne rock scene and started playing in a few bands, including The Cuban Heels with Steve Connolly, who'd later collaborate with Paul Kelly. One Sunday, he was invited to join The Johnnys, a band in need of a second guitarist. It helped that they had a contract with Mushroom Records in hand. A broken relationship meant that Jones had no reason to stay in Melbourne.

What follows is a perfect example of the freakish memory recall that this man possesses: 'The following Saturday was Easter weekend, 1983. I arrived in Sydney and got picked up from Central Station by Roger in this Super Snipe, a fantastic V8 English car. First port of call from there was the Dolphin

Hotel in Crown Street, Surry Hills. At the Dolphin, we had the five-dollar lunch, which was steak and chips, or fish and chips, but with really good garnishing. It was pretty cheap for back then ...'

Within three months, the Beasts of Bourbon had formed, and Jones would alternate between rehearsal, recording and touring with the two groups for several years. He claims that, in 1986, The Johnnys played more shows than any other band in Australia – some three hundred and twenty gigs in total, beating The Radiators' number by seventeen. Naturally, this touring regimen demanded frequent travel. 'Our entire sustenance was beer and speed,' he says. 'Occasionally, it'd be coke, but that was not something anyone could ever really afford.' Jones says he's never been too fond of the ephemeral bang-for-buck that cocaine offers: 'Why don't you just get a wire brush and shove it up your nose, then set fire to three $100 notes? There's the effect!'

Jones was only comfortable snorting speed; he would witness other bands injecting and think to himself that this act was 'quite tough; quite bad-arse'. A dressing room in Perth before a Beasts of Bourbon show was the site of his first spike: a bandmate offered him some speed in a loaded syringe. 'Oh. I haven't really done that before. Can you do it for me?' a drunk Jones replied. After procuring a belt and tying off, his friend showed him how to find a vein. 'There's one there, feel that?' he asked the guitarist. Jones felt it. In went the needle. *Whack.* The effects were immortalised on vinyl: the flipside of the Beasts' 'Psycho' single was recorded live that night. 'So it's on record!' Jones laughs. 'You can hear the guy in the corner, playing faster than everyone else.'

While playing gigs in Western Australia in 1986, The Johnnys visited the home of the tour promoter, who had booked Lou Reed for a show that night. 'I don't know if you guys would be interested, but I've got a little bit of something else,' said the promoter. 'What's that?' they replied. 'Smack.' At first, they all shook their heads, but one band member reconsidered, saying he'd give it a go. Jones changed his mind, too. 'I thought I'd try anything once,' he says. 'I figured, "Well, this guy knows what he's doing." We said, "We don't really use it, so don't give us too much."'

One member chose to shoot it; a couple of others snorted. Jones followed the promoter's lead and 'chased the dragon': 'I put it on a foil, heated it from underneath, got a Bic ballpoint with the nib and the ink taken out, and when it starts to smoke ...' He demonstrates inhaling sharply while pinching his fingers together, holding an imaginary Bic. 'You suck the smoke off it. It was like smoking really strong weed, and being unable to get up off the couch.'

Afterwards, they all went to the Lou Reed gig wearing sunglasses. 'I thought, "This is the correct music to go and see while under the influence of this stuff."' He smirks. 'The whole show was hilarious, because the guy who whacked it up was throwing up every two minutes. Me and the promoter were kind of okay; we were really fuckin' high. The guys who snorted it sat down; I don't know if they were asleep or not, because everyone was wearing sunnies.'

That first taste of heroin was a one-off that wouldn't be revisited for several years. The Beasts of Bourbon played a string of shows in Europe in 1989; Jones remembers it as 'one of those weird situations where you go away as kids and return as men', owing to the necessity of having to overcome language barriers and learn key phrases just to get through the day. That trip also sparked his creativity. 'I started to entertain the idea that, "Hey, maybe I could really be a songwriter! Maybe that Paul Kelly guy's just been faking it, plundering all these other sources and getting away with it!"'

Constant touring with both the Beasts and The Johnnys started to take its toll on the guitarist, however. 'Physically, I was up for it, but mentally I was quite burnt out. The speed and booze didn't help. The beer became Stolichnaya. There was a time there where I'd wake up in the morning, reach under the bed ...' – he mimes raising an unfinished bottle of vodka, necking it, exhaling and shaking out his shoulders, before exclaiming, 'Okay, let's get up and do something!'

Jones supplemented his alcoholism with speed and cocaine. That year got worse: his father died, his brother died of AIDS, and upon return from Europe he discovered that his wife had left him for a coke dealer. 'My head wasn't in a good place,' he says, before detailing a couple more instances of 'chasing the dragon' with some musician friends before selling the house he'd recently bought and heading south. 'It was a little bit weird being in Sydney, knowing that I couldn't trust anyone,' he says. 'All these so-called fucking friends of mine – none of them had told me about my wife while I was in Europe.'

In 1990, he moved in with his former bandmate Steve Connolly – then a guitarist in Paul Kelly's band – who wore a 'Ned Kelly beard' and had a heroin habit. Jones started using with his new housemate. He recalls a gay couple who home delivered: deals-on-wheels, as it were. 'The perfect set-up!' says Jones. 'You'd call a guy's mobile number, they'd come around and you'd hand over the $50 to get a little balloon off them. You didn't have to go anywhere; these two blokes were driving around Melbourne with three of those little plastic containers you got inside a Kinder Surprise – you know, the chocolate egg? These guys would have these plastic things packed with maybe twenty deals. They'd have a bunch of them lying around the car, looking innocent.'

The ease of access offered by deals-on-wheels meant that Jones had soon put the leftover cash from the sale of his house – around $20,000 – up his arm. 'When I realised I'd gone through twenty grand, I was quite shocked,' he says in a typically understated manner. The gay dealers got busted. 'There was an accessibility problem for me,' he notes, which coincided with meeting another woman.

'When she turned up in my life, she really picked me up, and got me off that shit.' Jones pauses, weighing the consequence of his next action, then decides to roll up his sleeve to reveal a bold tattoo that covers his right inner elbow. It reads 'Mary-Ellen'. 'That was partly to cover up a bit of a mark in there,' he says. 'But that means a lot to me, that tattoo. Every time I thought about [using], I'd take a look, and at that point her name alone stopped me from doing anything stupid.'

He was off heroin for seven years with Mary-Ellen. Another European tour with the Beasts put paid to that streak, though: he'd tag along on scoring missions to train stations. 'I don't know why,' he says. 'It's a junkie thing: just go to a train station and look for people who are scratching or nodding off' – in search of *narcotica*, a word that transcended language barriers. 'I was back on it in 1998,' he says. 'I had enough to go every day while on tour. Then you fly back to Australia and you've got a runny nose, and you're scratching, and sweating on a cold day.'

The tour went well, which meant that Jones had money; around this time, he also started playing in the Coloured Girls, Paul Kelly's band. 'If I'd come home broke, I would've just ridden it out. I've always done cold turkey. I just don't have [the drug]. I don't go to the doctor' – here he adopts a nasal voice; his impression of a junkie – '"Please give me some naltrexone" or whatever. I did do Suboxone one time: you go to the chemist and they come out with this bit of paper with some white powder on it, which you have to take orally, in front of them. But I stopped doing that because it made me look more pinned than I did when I was on heroin. I was clean, and really happy to be clean, but all these people were saying, "Spencer, dude, don't go out looking like that!" I knew that I was clean, and I'd tell them, but they wouldn't believe me. "Oh yeah, you're clean, sure. Take a look at yourself in the mirror." I've never done methadone; that's opening up the door to another problem. Methadone erodes your teeth, your bones. It's the worst shit ever.'

He left Mary-Ellen and had a child with another woman. This time, Jones lasted nearly three years without a taste, before that relationship ended and he again turned to drugs: heroin, cocaine, pot, alcohol. His band leader wasn't too impressed by the self-abuse that his friend was putting himself through. 'Paul got really angry with me, around 2000,' Jones says. 'He could tell that I was back on the gear. He actually took me aside and said, "Look, dude, do you want help with this? I can get you into a rehab place." I said, "No, I can handle it, man. I'm okay. I haven't got a habit. I don't let the team down on stage. I turn up. Just let me sort out my private life. Don't worry!'"

Here Jones pauses, then laughs in hindsight. 'Anyway, I should have listened to him! But he was really supportive. I was still in the band until halfway through 2003, you know? Paul is not hypocritical,' he says, referring to Kelly's own heroin use. 'He was definitely there for me. I'd played with him on and off for eight or nine years. So I think, in a lot of ways, it'd run its course. Or maybe he was starting to perceive me as a serial fuck-up. Maybe I might've been a liability if I was in his band for much longer. In the mid-nineties, when I first started playing with him, we had a little bit of a drug-buddy thing going for a couple of months. And then he just stopped it. He said, "What you and me are doing, it's time to stop it." And I did. We both did. But we were working a lot then. I don't think a lot of work would have got done if we hadn't done something about our personal choices.'

But then Jones fell back into that familiar pattern of using – only, this time, there was an element of self-awareness that had previously eluded the now middle-aged musician. 'That was another thing I had to stop doing: running to dope whenever something went wrong. It's like: stand up; step up; be a man. Don't fuckin' be like …' – he readopts that ugly, nasal tone – '"My life is shit, pass the syringe." I had to get out of that mindset and be like, "This has happened, now what can I do to go into damage control *without* turning to drugs?"'

How did you solve that? I ask. 'I found that honesty is the best policy.' He pauses, staring down at the half-full tequila and orange juice that he's been nursing for over an hour. 'It's almost like it's an easy way out. The truth about me is that

I pretty much collapsed under pressure. Each time there'd been some significant stage of my life where things have really turned to shit, I let 'em turn to even *more* shit by doing that. That's where I could go and hide, and lick my wounds, basically. Which was stupid, but I know that now. I didn't know that at the time. It's very easy to use drugs as your ...' He searches for the right words.

Coping mechanism? I offer. 'Yeah. But it's really hard to stay sober, and be honest, and face up to yourself. I've been fortunate that I channel a lot of that out through music, and through writing my lyrics. I'm able to do that. Sometimes, a lot of those songs are very, very personal, in order to get the story across.' He looks up at me from behind his sunglasses, seemingly ready to offer up one of his biggest secrets. 'But if you want to know the real personal songs, the "drug songs" that are actually about me, it's probably where I'm singing about a [different] gender. I'll cover my tracks by talking about a woman who has all these problems. Which might be me, talking about myself.' He smiles, then changes tack. 'Or they might be red herrings, so that people don't read too much into those lyrics.'

Jones is such a fascinating storyteller that I barely notice four hours have passed since we entered the Retreat Hotel. While he stalks over to some strangers to borrow a light, I stretch my back and crack my neck, both of which are aching after slouching forward for the duration. He re-enters the tin shed and crows, 'The Wolf! Here we go! *Exactly* what we're talking about.' He sings along to 'Spoonful', a fifty-three-year-old Howlin' Wolf track, and resumes sitting before me.

'I think there's such a misconception about people that use heroin, that they're all villainous,' he says, blowing a plume of smoke over his left shoulder. 'It can be anyone's affliction. But if you're predisposed to dishonesty and criminal behaviour, and you suddenly become a heroin addict, then you're *really* going to start doing bad things. I went to a Catholic boarding school, you know? It was all fire and brimstone stuff. The idea of taking heroin was such a bad one to me. It had been born out of that. It wasn't in me to be the kind of person who'd be involved in criminal activity like theft or burglaries. I'd always been able to at least be honest about it. When I think about it, all the damage has been done to *me*. I've done it to me. I've put two record collections up my arm. They were my records, not anybody else's.

'My advice would be to not treat people with the affliction of addiction as "junkie scum", because everyone is different. Every single case is different. Not everyone's a criminal. Many, many people have character flaws, not just junkies. I've got nothing good to say about that drug, really. I think it's fucked. It's really ...' He catches himself, and amends the agency of his sentence. '*I* have ruined my own career because of my weakness for it.'

I'm a little taken aback by this remark; drugs or not, he's still written, played guitar and sang on some excellent Australian rock albums. 'I look okay, but all my teeth are gone,' he replies. 'Physically, it's damaged me quite a bit. I don't feel a lot of vitality that I used to have. I've always been kind of fit, but now, I've been sitting on one tequila, with a lot of orange juice in it, and that's kind of how I am now.' He looks down at his glass. 'I drink a bit of beer, but my liver's damaged. Not necessarily because of alcohol. I've got a kind of hepatitis C. Fortunately, it's a very mild form; it's not the worst type. If I were to be reaching under the bed for a bottle of Stoli, the hep C would probably take me out within six months.'

As our conversation winds down, I ask for Jones' closing thoughts. 'I'm gettin' on,' he says. 'I'm getting old and I want to get on with it, without any obstacles.' Heroin has been a big obstacle, one that's endured for over two decades, on and off. 'It wasn't a problem that I resolved; it has been a recurring problem for most of my adult life, even though I was into my thirties when I started. I was such a strong kid. I was determined that I was never going to end up with a problem like this. But how wrong was I?' He reflects on his younger self. 'I was also one of these guys throwing rocks. "Ah, look at those junkie scum …" And then suddenly I *was* one. It didn't take much, that transition from being a good kid to being "junkie scum".'

For Spencer P. Jones now, it's a matter of getting through today without using, then tomorrow, then the day after. 'Pretty soon, the days turn into weeks, into months, into years. And then when someone says "When was the last time you used?", I can proudly go "Two and a half years ago", or "Three years ago". The trick is to not get tempted five years down the track. If you're going to straighten out, stay straight.'

We exit the Retreat Hotel and stand on the footpath of Sydney Road, sizing each other up again. Talk turns to lighter matters. I'm a big fan of his 2012 record with the Nothing Butts, a quartet that features former Beasts of Bourbon drummer James Baker behind the kit, as well as Gareth Liddiard and Fiona Kitschin of Melbourne rock band The Drones. I'm curious to know how Jones rates Liddiard among all the guitarists he has ever played with.

He looks away, into the passing traffic, and thinks about this question for quite some time – perhaps longer than for any of the drug-focused questions I threw him in the hours preceding. 'You know, he's probably the best,' he says. This answer pleases me greatly. Earlier, he'd told me that his last two records – *Sobering Thoughts* with The Escape Committee, and the Nothing Butts' self-titled – contain 'the whole story. All of it. It's all there. Totally black and white. The truth about me is in – or between – those lines.'

After he bids me farewell while running for a tram, I insert my earbuds and replay the Nothing Butts record for perhaps the fiftieth time, paying special attention to the fourth verse of 'Conditions Apply', the album's shortest and poppiest song: 'Selection or protection, injection, infection / It's all a downhill slide till the day that you die / Like all fallen angels, redemption is nigh / But you're never gonna fly 'cause conditions apply'.

JAKE STONE

From the front window of a bar named Different Drummer, I watch Jake Stone cross Glebe Point Road and unlock his car. Moments ago, I had asked him not to drive home, as we had spent the last couple of hours drinking beer and whisky together. 'No, I'm good, I'll walk,' he assured me with a smile, before we parted ways. I believed him then, but do my eyes now deceive me?

I send a text message – 'Thought you said you wouldn't drink drive …' – while he sits thirty metres away in a small purple car.

'Damn you caught me haha I'm literally just going around the corner,' he replies. 'Ill be alright i swear. x.' Moments later, I get another message from the thirty-three-year-old singer of Sydney indie-pop band Bluejuice: 'Come on man, i can't be bothered picking up the car ;).'

'You naughty bastard,' I type. 'Please be extra safe.'

'Will do,' reads the response. I look up again, but the car is already gone.

Soon after we sat down in the smoking section, our first beers in hand, Stone – a thin, bearded man with curly, black hair who wears a dark-green jacket and a habitually cheeky smile – told me that he was stoned. I asked whether this was because he knew that he was coming to talk to a journalist about drug use. 'It wasn't a thought-out process,' he replied, lighting a cigarette. 'It was more like, "Hey, there's a bunch of sweet weed. We're doing a session; I'm going to get high. Oh, look at that, that's a strange coincidence! Well, I suppose that would have happened anyway."' He laughed, then said, 'If there was a Venn diagram of me smoking and doing this interview, there's quite a lot of crossover with "always stoned".'

Earlier that afternoon, Stone and a few friends had been tracking music for a television program. 'It's essentially animated squirrels making stupid jokes,' he says. 'It's great for stoners!' His role in that band is to come up with musical concepts on keyboards, and a bit of production. 'It's just fun to play when you're a bit high,' he says. 'It gives you access to the music in a very basic way that can be quite creative, and stops you from being bored [while] sitting in a studio for four or five hours. It adds to the sense of fun, creativity and ridiculousness in the studio that can bring a project to life.'

Weed allows Stone to imagine things in great detail, and concentrate for extended periods of time on tedious tasks. 'Say we've written a drum part, and I want to fill out a tom part behind it,' he says. 'With weed, I might layer three different types of toms with pan settings on them, and time it in. If I was straight, I might not take that time to do all that weird shit. I just enjoy working like that when I'm a bit high. It's hard to sit at the computer and do tiny, little edits all the time.'

It's not always worth it, though. 'It can negatively affect the content, too. You can completely get off track with the mix. [You can] get high and then mix the bass way loud because you think it needs to be really bassy; you listen back the next day, and it's just mud.'

Stone describes these positive interactions between psychoactive drugs and the creative process as a 'key in the lock' feel. 'They click into a certain place, in those kinds of people's brains,' he says of musicians. 'But I do think that it's different when you're engaging that creative part of your brain. For me, it does have a profound influence on some of the things that might come out.' He pauses, wondering whether to continue. 'This is going to sound so stupid … Your experience is so extreme when you're on drugs that when you're making music, harking back to that experience gives the music an urgency – a "pop" quality – that sometimes really cuts through.' He cites the example of a popular Australian dance act. 'Sometimes, they make really druggy club songs. I don't think they could have made those songs if they weren't out clubbing, taking shit, going, "My god, that bassline feels amazing!"'

'We're always reflecting this unseen experience back into the music,' he says. 'And the music is getting more and more muscular in that direction every time it happens. Then, suddenly, we associate "cool" with the sound of those experiences. It's got a bit of a pop-culture edge, too, the experience of taking drugs. It always has in pop music. It's a cliché to say it, but the nastiness, the meanness of those feelings when you're really fucking high – that really has attitude when you express it in music. Drugs multiply and subtly shift your perceptions in a way that allows you to reframe reality in a catchy, sometimes delightful kind of way for people. And people will latch onto it, because it's either humorous, or it has visual style, and that's all part of music, too. It pushes strange ideas into the fore.'

Jake Stone has been 'recreationally involved' with drugs since his early adolescence. He attended Fort Street, a public high school in the inner-west Sydney suburb of Petersham, where he befriended fellow musicians and 'random geeks'. At age twelve, he packed a film canister full of weed – acquired from a friend's dad, without his knowledge – and took it on a school camp, where he'd sniff the contents in the belief that he was experiencing its effects. 'I was just being a douchey little kid,' he says. 'I was trying to be *bad*, you know? "I've got this weed and I'm getting high, yeah!"'

A formative drug experience took place on a school excursion in Year 10, which followed Stone's first successful stage performance. In a play named *Ernie's Incredible Hallucinations*, Stone played the titular role. When his drama teacher treated the group to seeing *Radiance* at the Belvoir St Theatre, he decided that his life should imitate art. After buying some LSD from a classmate, Stone took the tab, then turned to his nerdiest friend and said, '"Look, I'm going to need a bit of help, because I'm going to be on acid in about two hours." And he was like, "What?" He just didn't even know what I was talking about. I was like, "Oh god, this is going to be terrible! The only person who can look after me really has no concept of what I'm talking about!"'

While walking up Elizabeth Street with the drama class, a shop full of hippie designs proved impossible to resist. Stone became separated from the group and was standing in the store, fascinated by the crystals, when his confused teacher rediscovered the tripper. During *Radiance*, the Belvoir's mudflat set was flooded using a real-water effect. 'I was just tripping balls in that theatre,' he says. 'I remember thinking it was wonderful.'

Another memorable teenage experience involved a member of Stone's family, who took his younger relative to see Helmet and the Beastie Boys at the Hordern Pavilion. Beforehand, the group – all five or six years Stone's senior – smoked cones. 'I was ratshit,' Stone recalls. 'I wanted to see Helmet because I was a metalhead, and I loved them. But the whole of Helmet's set, I hid under a parked car because I was so paranoid about getting caught by the cops.' His relative eventually discovered him. Bemused, he asked Stone why he was hiding. The best response that he could muster was, 'I don't know, man. I'm pretty high. I don't know what to do.' After being guided to see the headline act, Stone says the show was 'great, but I didn't really understand. The Beastie Boys kept coming off and going on; they'd do the hip-hop stuff and then the [live] band set. I was like, "Is this two different bands? What the fuck?"'

Ecstasy and speed use became commonplace when Stone moved to Bathurst to study media production at Charles Sturt University in 1998. He discovered dance music for the first time – a genre he describes as 'a bit of a gateway drug' – and fell in with a crowd that threw regular parties and booked DJs. 'Dance parties were an opportunity to take drugs,' he says. 'But they were also a good introduction to the form, content and style of house music, breaks, and drum 'n' bass, which were all popular at the time.' That environment – and Stone's altered state – expanded his musical vocabulary. 'It does broaden your palate,' he says. 'You might not stand in a club for four hours dancing if you were completely straight, but you might if you were on ecstasy. And you might fall in love with that music because of the positive association with the experience that you had. It's a bonding technique.'

Pills were distributed through uni contacts, and easy enough to acquire, but speed and pot necessitated risky drives out to the suburbs of west Bathurst, where two families controlled the local drug trade. 'You end up wandering through this zombieland, junkie town,' Stone says of those drug runs. 'It was some fucked-up shit.'

His use of amphetamine coincided with a spike in his depression. The spectre of mental illness had lingered at the fringes of his psyche throughout his adolescence, but at university those silhouettes were drawn into sharp focus. It was a combination of his 'self-indulgent, lazy' nature and the lifestyle he had embraced. 'Speed is really toxic to your system,' he says. 'It's not easy to have a productive life if you're doing that a lot. Some of my friends were using it intravenously. I felt like that was a bit too far.' Winter would worsen the depression. 'When you're a student, you're always very poor, so you're not eating great,' he says. 'Generally, your health is poor. And speed is just not a great drug to do all the time; my comedowns are very severe. I'd be very depressed and unproductive for a week, and that wasn't ideal.'

It was at age nineteen that Jake Stone was first prescribed the antidepressant Zoloft. 'I never stayed on it at that stage,' he says. 'I'd do it for a packet or two, and then not really think that I needed it anymore, and that maybe it didn't make much of a difference anyway. I'm a bit obsessive; I'm a bit inclined towards depression, in patches, so I didn't really sort that out properly for years and years.' His mother was always concerned about her son's mental health; he'd get into a lot of trouble after being caught smoking pot, but even outside of those experiences Stone readily acknowledges that he was a 'moody prick' throughout his teens. At the same time, though, he was also a 'full-on attention seeker'.

These two distinct sides to Stone's personality have become more pronounced over time. It wasn't until he voluntarily admitted himself to a psychiatric hospital in early 2012, however, that the true nature of his mood disorder became clear. After the breakdown of a four-year relationship midway through 2011, he realised that he was unable to cope on his own. The handful of different antidepressants he'd been prescribed over the years didn't seem to balance his mood with much consistency; the positives in his life still tended to be overwhelmed by negativity.

Months after the break-up, Stone spent a week and a half in St John of God hospital in Ashfield, in inner-west Sydney. 'I felt like I needed to go and get assessed,' he says, 'and get some kind of prescription that was ongoing, manageable and reasonable. My mood was too low from the events that had occurred. I couldn't seem to get back on the horse and figure out what I was supposed to do, so I thought it would be good to go and sort the medication stuff out.' He was prescribed the antidepressant Cymbalta, which he has found to be 'a reasonable middle ground', and sodium valproate, a lithium substitute taken in very small doses. 'They prescribe that for manic depressives, schizophrenics; those kinds of personalities,' he says. 'And it works for me, as a person who I think has a slight mood disorder. I probably shouldn't smoke weed with it, but I do sometimes.' He grins. 'But that's just crazy old me.'

Between the aborted attempts of a nineteen-year-old university student prescribed Zoloft and the happily medicated thirty-three-year-old who sits beside me in the smoking section at Different Drummer, there was over a decade wherein the wiry musician and performer seems to have been self-medicating his depression with illicit drugs. When I put this to him, Stone replies with a shrug. 'I don't know,' he says. 'That's what [the doctors] said, but I just don't know whether that's true. I think I liked drugs as well, so I'd have used them recreationally regardless. I think my early use of drugs influenced my ongoing mood issues. I was already a fairly sensitive person emotionally, and probably given to self-indulgence; the side effects of using drugs possibly concentrated, or intensified, those potential disorders.'

We talk further about depression and anxiety, two conditions that often overlap. 'You really do get people offside when you have those mood disorders,' he says, after borrowing a light from a young group nearby. 'It makes it hard for you to get ahead, and hard for you to be at rest and have a normal life. Sometimes, it does pay off creatively – I won't lie. But after this long with it …' He pauses. 'The end of that relationship was a huge turning point for me, and not necessarily in a completely positive way. I really had to support the outcomes of that with some kind of medication, because it seemed like it was a difficult thing to move past. It still is.'

As a casual fan of Bluejuice's music – bright, energetic, keyboard-led indie pop featuring two vocalists, in Stone and Stavros Yiannoukas – since their breakout single in 2007, I'm a little taken aback by his statement that undercurrents of mental illness run through their most popular songs. '"Vitriol", "Broken Leg", "Act Yr Age", "Head of the Hawk": all those songs are essentially about depression, I suppose, and emotional calamity – which is something you could say I was probably addicted to, as well, because I got into the habit of feeling like that,' he says. 'So it's been a huge part of the band, but the thing that made me think I needed to change was when my girlfriend left me, and I was like, "Well, I'm an adult now. It's not ideal to be always drawing on these feelings." I just seem to write when I'm in those moods, quite a lot.'

He pauses, then changes gears entirely. 'I was reading a story on Edvard Munch,' he says, referring to the Norwegian painter best known for his 1893 work *The Scream*. 'I love his stuff; it's actually sort of ugly visually, but the content is really interesting. The way that he represents women; there's just a full-on, strong story and feeling in all of those paintings. I get the impression, from what I was reading, that he spent the majority of his life suffering from anxiety and depression. He said, "Without anxiety and illness, I am a ship without a rudder. My art is grounded in reflections over being different from others. My sufferings are part of my self and my art."

'Now, I'm not saying I'm fucking Edvard Munch. I mean, he had a really fucked-up life. But I'm just saying I know how the guy feels, in terms of having generated songs out of that feeling in the past. I do associate with that. And, as a kid, I probably thought that was cool. I thought it was cool to be some "crazy guy". Now, I'm just some crazy guy. I don't think it's cool anymore.'

Do you have bipolar disorder? I ask. 'That's what they said; that I was "type two manic depressive",' he replies. 'Hypermania. Which is not delusions of grandeur or dislocative, crazy, "I think I'm Jesus" moments. More just pitched differences in mood that are really rapid and heightened. I sometimes tend towards depression. I have mania; I find that I have periods where I go out and spend a bit of money, and be impulsive. And I certainly get high moods; often, I'll write in those moods.'

Bluejuice's biggest hit to date, the 2009 single 'Broken Leg', is a sunny pop song with a dark theme. 'It's about having a fatal flaw that lames you,' Stone says. 'You're limping around, trying to keep up with everything. But it's defined as well. I always felt quite different in some ways, so I thought, "Fuck you, this is the kind of difference that I have" – which is childish, actually. But that's the feeling of that song. It's this terror that all of your relationships will end, and nothing will work; "you don't even want to talk to me anymore". All your personal relationships are filled with this chaos, and this pejorative clashing of things. It's due to this one thing. You're just stuck; it's this thing that you've got to wear around. It's your "scarlet letter".'

The thing about a broken leg, though, is that you can see the evidence, I say. You can observe that someone is injured, whereas mental illness is often hidden, and can manifest in bizarre or abnormal behaviour. 'I guess I was trying to explain to people how it felt,' he replies. 'And I also had a broken leg at the time.' He laughs, then says, 'Hey, do you want to get a chicken burger? I'm kind of hungry.'

We walk a few doors down to a store gloriously named Chickens Plus. We're the only customers. I watch Stone's eyes light up as he gazes at the brightly lit menu. He orders a burger with chilli; I settle on chips and gravy. A Jennifer Lopez music video, 'Love Don't Cost a Thing', plays loudly from a flat-screen television positioned at chest height, in line with the bar at which we sit and stare out onto Glebe Point Road. 'Speaking of drugs: this shit is a drug,' he says, gesturing up at the menu while we wait for our food. 'Chicken burgers, done right, I can get very addicted to. I get very hooked on things. I'm obsessed with chicken burgers. I have to eat them. I don't want to, but if there's a new one that I haven't tried and I see it on a menu, I'll definitely get it.' Stone demolishes his burger within minutes of its arrival. I pick at my chips, impressed by his effort. 'Yeah, it is nice,' he says. Also, you are high, I offer. 'I was so hungry,' he says, grinning contentedly.

For years, Stone's music career with Bluejuice ran in parallel to his work as a music journalist, writing for Sydney street press. I ask whether he ever mixed pleasure with business. 'Sure. Absolutely,' he replies. 'The first two years, I was working at *Revolver* and *The Brag*. I'd turn up, start work, maybe do one interview or start a project – a story, review, whatever I had to do that day – and go outside, smoke a scoob. And then I'd go back into my little cubicle and just smash out a few thousand words. It was just easier for that kind of shit.'

Transcribing? I ask, referring to the tedious act of listening back to recorded interviews and typing out the questions and answers. 'Fuck yeah!' he says. 'Abso–fuckin'–lutely. That's the shit, right there. Probably ninety-five per cent of the time, it would be that. And then there was, like, six thousand words of news a week. I'd just write a bunch of stupid shit. It was fun.' When we meet in mid-2013, Stone is working for Triple J, filling midweek 1 am to 6 am shifts with his bandmate Yiannoukas. 'Even though it's not journalism, it fills the same hole in my mind. It's nice to be able to talk about music on the air and play new stuff.' He put music journalism aside once the band started doing reasonably well, but says he isn't particularly opposed to returning to it.

I ask whether Stone's drug use had any impact on his bandmates. 'It made me really moody,' he says. Was there ever any sort of intervention? 'Yeah,' he replies. 'Well, it wasn't just me. Bands have a dynamic. We went to a psychologist.' We? I ask. 'The band. Like Metallica – but on a much lower scale,' he says, referring to the revealing 2004 documentary *Some Kind of Monster*, which saw the American metal quartet engage the services of a 'performance-enhancing coach'. 'There were three fairly big personalities in the band,' Stone says of Bluejuice. 'There was a lot of friction, but we were always united towards our cause at the end of the day. Along the way, you start working out that you're directors of a business that's worth a bit of money. You're all band members; you're all making some decisions, and you've got a lot of opportunities.'

The band only went to two sessions with the shrink. Was it worthwhile? I ask. 'We did the Myers-Briggs personality test,' Stone says. 'They're 1960s personality tests that tell whether you're extroverted or introverted, and to what relative degree. It was revealing, because it showed where the balance of personalities were in the band. She gave us practical ideas about how to better communicate [among ourselves]. We still had heaps of fights. We probably had more.'

We return to Different Drummer, where Stone's friend behind the bar pours us each a Japanese whisky named Yamakazi. As we find seats at the back of the venue, I ask whether he's ever been caught by the police with drugs on him. 'Strangely, no,' he says. 'Not for marijuana, not for any other drugs; not for anything, really. I don't know why I've managed to [avoid] it. I'm pretty habitual about the way that I go about doing things; where I choose to do it, and how. But I also drive stoned a fair bit. I mean, I drove here. I've certainly driven drunk and done all of those things. I don't think it's a good thing ...'

Interrupting, I ask whether he's intending to drive home after this. He doesn't answer immediately, so I tell him that I'd feel responsible if he did. 'I live one street that way,' he says dismissively, pointing out the front door. Why did you drive? I ask. 'I was coming from Redfern,' he says, then responds to my concerns directly. 'I could live with that. I probably will leave the car there, to be honest.'

I would prefer you did, Jake Stone, I say. I am your conscience. 'All right, good.' He laughs. 'Thank you. Although the thing is, I'm not wildly ... I'm in that state ...' He wrestles with this decision. 'I would just be going around ... But, yes, that's bad. That's morally bad. I don't want to kill a kid or anything. I would feel terrible.'

Picking up the conversational thread, I ask where money fits into this discussion. 'In my life, I've probably spent a lot of money on drugs, but not so consistently and with such intense regularity that ...' He pauses, rephrases. 'I can pay my rent. I can afford to eat. I'm not living on the street. I have clothes. I have a laptop. I live a life. I think it's more the overall depressive effect it's had on my life. It's probably lowered my horizons a little in some ways, and that's what I worry about.' The musician wonders whether he'd have been more successful, more intelligent if he hadn't been so fascinated by these things. 'But maybe not. Maybe I'm just as dumb as I naturally am. You waste a lot of time with drugs.'

This hints at regret. But is it a waste? I ask. You seem to have got something out of them, at least occasionally.

'I guess in some ways in my life, it's clouded my ability to function and do things like "decent people",' he says. 'It's clouded my relationships in a negative way – along with me being a cockhead. I'm a cockhead, but it's also exaggerated some elements of that, too. So it makes it harder for me to be totally "on it", or be an awesome person all the time. I think that's [the case], certainly.'

When mentally well, Jake Stone says, he always wants to smoke pot. If he's not well, then he doesn't smoke at all. 'I would say I'm a bit addicted to it,' he says. The conventional wisdom is that you can't get addicted to cannabis, I offer. 'I don't think that's true,' he replies. 'I mean, I think weed's been around for so long; the strength and quality of it has really changed since people used it more recreationally in the sixties and seventies. Now, it's grown hydroponically, with lots of chemicals, into a really powerful drug. If you're smoking hydro with lots of shit in it, you definitely get hooked on the feeling of it, and then when you come off it you experience noticeable withdrawals. I mean, if that isn't addiction, I don't know what the fuck is!'

Following our interview, Stone plans to meet his pot dealer. 'That's indication enough that I'm losing that battle,' he says. 'But it's all right.' I wonder aloud whether he always tends to see it as a battle. 'Sometimes,' he says. 'Sometimes I see it as a battle when I'm feeling like I'm lagging behind my ex – which I am – and when I'm not keeping pace with professional lives of people around me; when I'm not growing or changing as a person, being lazy or whatever. Then, yeah, I see it as a negative.'

Besides the obvious effects on his respiratory system, Stone finds that his mood is 'pretty decent' when he's smoking. Anxiety is less prevalent. It's when he stops, he says, that he notices the side effects. 'I feel a bit semi-brain-damaged from the length of time I've smoked weed. My reaction times are a little slower. I'm definitely a little blunted. A little *faded*.' He smiles, emphasising a word most often used by heavy-smoking American rappers.

'I don't know whether I'm trying to justify it morally or not,' he says, after I return to the table with a pair of beers. 'It sets you back, I think. It's partially a self-indulgence, and also a good way to change [your] brain chemistry, which should probably be left as is. But, in a way, once you do it habitually, that's what's happening already. You have to decide whether it's part of your lifestyle or isn't. You'd hope that the relationships, interactions and professional life that you have, and the rest of your potential, is left untouched. But I'm not sure it is.

'It's just adults coping with being adults by self-medicating with alcohol and drugs. It's all over the place. It's not just musicians. It's fuckin' every adult, basically. Some of my friends can afford to take cocaine; the ones who can't ...' He raises his beer. 'People do [cocaine], but they just don't do it every night of the week. But a lot of people drink every night of the week, and I think that's really worth taking note of, because that's the most pervasive drug use that goes on. We're drinking all the time. I wasn't really that connected to that as a kid, so I always find that much more noticeable and semi-insidious, because nobody's really thinking about it.'

The habitual use of any drug is probably ill-advised, Stone says, because it has a negative effect on your biochemistry. But one-offs, or using on special occasions? He doesn't see how that could ever be bad. 'You're just going to have an interesting time,' he says. 'That's the whole point.' He pauses. 'I think that, philosophically, it's a bit strange to need to be in a dislocated place, emotionally, to enjoy yourself. Being sober is a drag sometimes. You can be too sober for too long. If you're trapped in your own brain, it's not always all that much fun.'

People use drugs recreationally for all sorts of reasons, I offer, but usually as either an escape or a way to enhance normal life. 'Well, I think of it as an escape,' Stone replies. 'I wanted to get drunk [tonight] because I wanted to be chill about stuff. I'm not saying it's good; I don't really think it is. To be honest, it's a pervasive lack of discipline. I can only really speak for myself. I rely on smoking pot probably too much, but, at the same time, however you get through your adult life is however you get through your adult life. Provided you're ticking the boxes that you want to tick for yourself, while not impacting your earning, your living conditions, the lives of your friends and family, your own life – I mean, I have no issue with it. I wouldn't want to legislate [against] it, because I have no issue with it.

'I think California's done a great thing by making pot legal [in 1996]. It just means that people who want to smoke it can go and get it, and the people who don't, can't. Who gives a shit? Some people are probably going to have pronounced mental illness as a result, but it's going to happen, I guess. People are definitely doing drugs; I don't really have an issue with legalising certain things.'

Suddenly, Stone has had enough. He's only swallowed a few sips of our last beer, which he hands back to me to finish before I catch a plane back to Brisbane. 'I'm going to go home,' he says. 'I'm kind of drunk and tired. That might be a good idea. I have to work in another five hours; I think I probably should hit the sack. Is that crazy?' You're sane, I reply, as long as you don't drive home. 'No, I'm good, I'm good. I'll walk. That's cool.' We embrace and farewell. I relocate to the front window of Different Drummer with two near-full beers in hand. I certainly don't need them, but they cost $8.50 apiece, so I feel obliged. I'm pulling out my iPad to type a few notes when, across the road, I notice Stone unlocking his car.

'Let me know when you're home, buddy,' I text to him ten minutes later, while Sydney flashes past from the back seat of a taxi. 'My conscience is killing me.'

'Im home, all good! X,' he writes back immediately.

'Sleep tight ;),' I reply.

It's a bullshit response. I certainly wouldn't abide this sort of behaviour among my friends or family. But Stone is a stranger, a willing interview subject for a book I'm writing. I cannot control him. Nor should I want to. On the flight home, a little tipsy, I keep tripping over the thought of how these substances and chemicals impair our decision-making abilities. Drugs can be fun. They can offer an escape from normality. They can assist the creative process. They can relax the mind so that sobriety is easier to deal with. But rarely, it seems, are great life decisions made while intoxicated or high.

Afterthoughts

In keeping with my desire to avoid anything resembling a
scientific approach to a topic that's so often bogged down by
stuffiness and statistics, I didn't work from a prepared list of
questions for these interviews, instead preferring to set my
recorder down between me and my subjects and tease out
their responses organically. However, I did have some general
lines of enquiry in mind.

Among them: how were drugs framed for you while
growing up? When did they become attractive to you? Were
you concerned by their illegality? Which substances appealed
to you? Which substances were repellent? Did you find that
they helped your creativity or hindered it? What's your sense
of how Australian society views the use of illicit drugs? Do
you have strong feelings about decriminalisation? And so on,
until we exhausted the subject.

In an era of entertainment journalism where fifteen-minute
phone interviews are the norm, it was always my intention to

speak to each of my subjects face to face. It was clear to me from the beginning that drug use was a topic that demanded serious discussion, and that it would be remiss of me not to make the effort to meet my interviewees in person. I wasn't requesting these interviews in order to harvest only the most interesting quotes to generate headline-grabbing 'clickbait' articles for online publishers; instead, I wanted to discuss in detail each individual's life through the lens of their illicit drug use.

As you might imagine, this was a confronting request for these public figures to receive, given that the only time we tend to hear about celebrity drug use is through sensationalist headlines that inevitably seek to demonise and dehumanise anyone who voluntarily confesses or gets caught. I approached a long list of musicians. I experienced many rejections. Handily, years of pitching stories as a freelance journalist had toughened my skin. I took none of these rejections personally, because I knew that, ultimately, it was up to the individual whether they wanted to share their story.

The shortest interview was forty-five minutes (Tina Arena); the longest, four hours (Spencer P. Jones). Most clocked in between sixty and ninety minutes. What I found during these hours of conversations about one topic with fourteen distinctive musicians was that there is no simple story when it comes to drugs. Some people are early bloomers and try substances in their teens; others, such as myself, actively avoid the matter until their mid-twenties or even later. Some choose to abstain completely. At the heart of each conversation was a simple question: why do you think people use drugs? Where applicable, this question sometimes morphed into: why do you use drugs?

There is no correct answer to either form of the question, of course. That was the point. Individuals are drawn to substances for a wide variety of reasons, just as some choose to avoid them. Though some of my interviewees' experiences with drugs were publicly known, in some cases I had no idea about how a conversation would play out until we were face to face. It's for this reason that I believe the abstainers have just as much to add to this conversation as those who have experienced addiction. Both groups have an equal stake, because even if an individual chooses to avoid drugs, they won't have to look far to find those who choose to use – especially in the music business, where heightened emotional states are as common as the booze stocked in backstage riders.

I designed *Talking Smack* as a collection of stories starring public figures who were willing to discuss matters that are almost always kept private. Drug use is a society-wide issue, yet it's usually only the same handful of stakeholders who are willing to speak up about their experiences. Most of the time, it's those on the critical side of the argument who speak loudest: police, politicians, public-health officials and the media. It's easy to generalise and demonise those who use illicit drugs – Western societies have been doing this for decades now – yet, by tarring all of these people with the same brush, we tend to miss the diverse and nuanced reasons why people choose to use.

Plainly, the illegality of drugs isn't a significant deterrent. Prohibition hasn't worked, because humans are clever when it comes to obtaining what they want. I think about this every time I log onto Silk Road, the anonymous online marketplace that caters to the tastes and needs of drug users throughout the world – myself included. This entire ecosystem is built on human nature and ingenuity: technology, trust, commerce, faith and, ultimately, desire. The users get what they want in the mail; the vendors get paid in return. All completely illegal, of course, yet evidently where there's a will, there's a way.

Something that Paul Kelly said in our interview has stuck with me, as my attitude towards drugs continues to evolve: if you don't respect them, they won't respect you. These are powerful psychoactive substances we're talking about, after all. They can affect our perception of the world around us, as well as our moods, egos and how we interact with our peers. They can boost our creativity and our ability to articulate our thoughts, or they can seriously impair both of those outlets.

In the upcoming final pages, you will find a comic named *War On Drugs*, which was written and illustrated by my brother, Stuart McMillen. It was originally published on his website, stuartmcmillen.com, in October 2012. Reading it still brings me to tears, because it is a story so beautifully told. I'm honoured to include his work alongside mine.

Not a single word of this book was written while I was under the influence of anything stronger than caffeine. I believe in barriers between work and recreation. I believe that the decision to use drugs should not be made lightly, or spontaneously. I believe in forethought when it comes to set and setting. I believe in measuring doses. I believe in researching the effects of psychoactive drugs long before you put them inside your body. I believe in using drugs to enhance experiences shared with friends and loved ones. I believe in buying from reputable vendors who sell quality products. I believe in the use of safe-drug-testing kits. I believe in moderation.

Above all, I believe that drug use is a subject that demands honesty, respect, empathy and compassion. This is a topic that has been confined to the shadows and fringes out of fear, shame and embarrassment for too long.

I thank you for taking the time to consider the range of views presented in this book, and I encourage you to continue thinking, reading and – most importantly – talking about this subject with those closest to you. As far as I'm concerned, the more honest conversations about drugs that take place, the better.

Andrew McMillen, Brisbane

Acknowledgements

My sincerest thanks to the following individuals.

My fourteen interviewees, who let me into their homes and their lives to be a part of this book. *Talking Smack* would not exist without your contributions. I am eternally grateful that you all said yes. Special thanks to Phil Jamieson, who was the first to agree, and helped immensely during the early stages of this project.

My parents, Paul and Debra McMillen, for their unconditional support and love. You guys did a great job of raising me. Special thanks to your excellent music collection, which shaped me in ways I still can't fathom.

My brother, Stuart McMillen, for his advice and great music taste, and for allowing me to reprint his comic *War On Drugs* here in my first book. What a talent.

My publisher, Alexandra Payne, for sending a three-line email in August 2012 that asked whether I'd be interested in writing a book. I'm glad you asked me and I'm glad that I said yes. A true pleasure.

My mentors, Nick Crocker and Richard Guilliatt, for helping every step of the way. Two finer gentlemen I might never meet.

My editor, Kevin O'Brien, for casting his expert eyes across these pages and shaping *Talking Smack* into its strongest form.

Josh Durham for the fantastic book cover.

My friends and family, for conversation, support, borrowed cars, beds in other cities and your open minds. This book continued to grow long after I signed the contract, and a lot of that can be attributed to the viewpoints, substances and food for thought that I shared with you all along the way.

My loving and patient partner, Rachael Hall, who completes me. I proposed to her during the writing of this book, in front of her fantastic parents, Phil and Roslyn. I'm so happy she said yes.

17 June 1971 - US President Richard Nixon declares a 'war on drugs', naming drug abuse as "public enemy number one in the United States."

Criticism of the policy comes early from a source close to home...

...Nixon's former election advisor Milton Friedman.

Living outside the law, Mafia groups used violence to get their way...

...leading to a jump in crimes such as assault, burglary and homicide.

With alcohol now illegal, quality control laws were replaced with a total ban on production...

...causing drinkers to turn to producers of dubious quality...

...and move from weaker, bulkier drinks such as beer and wine...

...to concentrated hard liquor, which was far more profitable for bootleggers to smuggle.

The American prohibition experiment ended in 1933.

As producing, selling and drinking alcohol returned aboveground...

...the violent crimes resulting from Prohibition began to drop to pre-1920s levels...

PROHIBITION ENDS AT LAST!

...and the black market crime syndicates withered in the face of legitimate bottlers resuming business.

The demand for drugs would not be stopped by the laws.

Drugs would become a 'forbidden fruit', increasing their lure to impressionable youth.

With lucrative profits to be made from recreational drugs, criminal organisations would enter as sellers in a black market.

People wanting to obtain drugs would be forced to associate with criminals with little concern for their safety or well-being...

.....and users may resort to crime as a way of financing their now-expensive habits.

Knowing their power over drug purchasers, dealers would play by their own rules regarding price, quality and marketing tactics.

Producers would be incentivised to grow stronger, more potent versions of certain drugs...

...or would be incentivised to produce hard drugs over soft drugs.

Branded as criminals, drug addicts would be reluctant to come forward and seek help.

Drug users affected by prohibition would resent the laws and be less likely to respect the other laws of society.

The sums at stake would increase the possibility of police officers and government officials becoming corrupt.

More and more citizens would be arrested and imprisoned for crimes which did not exist before.

More and more jails would be needed to house those imprisoned for crimes which did not exist before.

More and more police resources would be diverted from solving other crimes.

Violent crime rates would rise among drug users in American cities...

...and would also rise in the countries which produce and smuggle the drugs into America.

A multitude of miseries...

...reverberating through society...

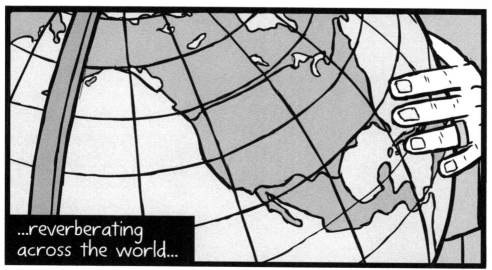

...reverberating across the world...

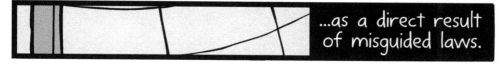

...as a direct result of misguided laws.

There are uncanny parallels between Prohibition and the 'war on drugs'.

The gangs.

WANTED

TARGET

The violence.

The police busts always promising to 'turn the tide...

...and the sure-fire operation of drug markets undeterred by the busts.

Prohibition laws cultivate a drug culture of amplified danger and risk...

...with the tragedies of drug abuse used as 'evidence' for even tougher laws.

But how much harm is caused purely by the laws themselves?

Rather than acknowledging the drawbacks of their laws...

...authorities instead embrace the uncertainty caused by prohibition...

...and weave it into their arguments for why people should not take drugs.

"Drugs are sold by gangs of criminals...

...who probably mixed it up in their dirty basement."

"You don't know exactly what you're getting when you **buy** drugs...

...and you don't know how much you're taking when you **use** drugs."

All are perfectly valid reasons not to buy drugs today...

...all were perfectly valid reasons not to buy **alcohol** during Prohibition.

All are problems caused by the laws, not the chemicals.

Forty years into the 'war on drugs', most of us have not known a time when drugs were legal...

...and so we find it hard to disentangle...

...the problems that surround drugs...

...from the drugs themselves.

www.stuartmcmillen.com